Hearts & Hazards
WRITING
THE
GAY COZY MYSTERY

QUEER CLUES & COZY MOODS

Dive into the world of cozy mystery writing with a twist—murder and romance through the lens of LGBTQ+ characters—guided by the hand of a seasoned author who's made her living in both mainstream and self-publishing for more than thirty years.

Packed with analysis, writing exercises, checklists, tips, and tools, *Hearts & Hazards: Writing the Gay Cozy Mystery* offers more than just the ABCs of Character, Plot, Setting, Theme, and Dialogue. It delves deeper, exploring the nuances that will elevate your book from good to unforgettable, infusing your mysteries with the richness of LGBTQ+ life and love, all while ensuring your tales are wrapped in the warmth, wit, and intrigue cozy mystery readers adore.

With a rare blend of industry insights, tailored advice, and practical strategies informed by an author who's actually "been there, done that," *Hearts & Hazards: Writing the Gay Cozy Mystery* addresses the unique challenges and opportunities of weaving LGBTQ+ themes into the cozy mystery genre, providing a roadmap to not only craft your story but also connect with an audience eager for representation.

To Christina Boys. For taking a chance on the unknown.

Hearts & Hazards
WRITING
THE
GAY COZY MYSTERY

JOSH LANYON

Hearts & Hazards: Writing the Gay Cozy Mystery
April 2024
Copyright © 2024 by Josh Lanyon
Edited by Jennifer Jacobson
Formatting by Debbie McGowan

Print ISBN: 978-8-32449-2
Published in the United States of America

JustJoshin Publishing, Inc.
3053 Rancho Vista Blvd.
Suite 116
Palmdale, CA 93551
www.joshlanyon.com

CONTENTS

Good advice is always certain to be ignored, but that's no reason not to give it.

– Agatha Christie

INTRODUCTION

WHY COZY MYSTERIES?

N O, I AM NOT ASKING *YOU*, THE PROSPECTIVE WRITER, WHY YOU WANT to write a gay cozy mystery. You know your reasons. You might actually sincerely love the genre. Or, as happens far too often in contemporary publishing, you might have very little interest in the genre, but you're hoping to get traction somewhere—anywhere—with your writing career, and you think there might be a little bit of room for you amidst the flower boxes and cobbled streets of the cozy mystery subgenre.

Your odds of success are higher when you're motivated by genuine love versus calculation, but either way, you can succeed if you know what you're doing. And part of knowing what you're doing means understanding *why* readers love this genre so much.

In the same way that certain literary authors look down their noses at authors of genre fiction, some mystery authors look down their noses at the cozies. Please don't do that. Please don't look down on or attempt to write for an audience you don't understand.

From a psychological standpoint, cozy mysteries cater to the human desire for order, safety, and connection. They offer a comforting escape into a world where chaos is safely contained within the confines of a charming setting, and big-J Justice reliably restores balance by the story's end. Relatable amateur sleuths provide readers with a vicarious sense of empowerment and cleverness, solving puzzles and crimes through wit and intuition rather than violence or extensive professional training. The genre satisfies our innate curiosity and love for puzzles while fostering a sense of belonging and community through its recurring characters and settings.

Cozy mysteries thus serve as a gentle, reassuring balm for the mind, blending entertainment with a subtle reaffirmation of moral order and human resilience. In short, in our unpredictable, often alarming modern world, cozy mysteries offer diversion and reassurance.

I think we all need a bit of that now and then.

NOW, FROM A PRACTICAL STANDPOINT, *YOUR* STANDPOINT, WHY COZY MYSTERIES?

A reality check: If you are just in it for the money, cozy mysteries are not the number one category of the Mystery Thriller Suspense category. However, they are relatively quick and easy to write. Let's explore that idea a little further:

Simpler Settings and Smaller Cast: Cozy mysteries often take place in small, close-knit communities or confined settings, which can simplify world-building efforts compared to the sprawling urban landscapes or intricate political plots found in many thrillers and procedurals. The cast of characters is usually more limited, making it easier to develop and manage relationships and interactions.

Less Technical Detail: While police procedurals and many thrillers require a deep understanding of law enforcement procedures, forensic science, and legal intricacies, cozy mysteries often focus more on puzzle-solving through observation, common sense, and interpersonal skills. This can reduce the amount of technical research needed.

Gentler Tone: The tone of cozy mysteries is generally lighter, focusing on the puzzle and community dynamics rather than the graphic details of the crime itself. This can make the writing process less emotionally taxing and potentially faster, as the narrative doesn't delve into the darker aspects of human nature as deeply as thrillers or procedurals often do.

Formulaic Structure: Cozy mysteries follow a more predictable structure, with a murder in a seemingly idyllic setting, an amateur sleuth personally invested in the investigation, a series of clues leading to a reveal, and resolution that restores order. This formula can provide a clear roadmap for plotting the story, making the writing process more straightforward.

Focused Conflict: The central conflict in cozy mysteries is often the crime itself and the puzzle it presents, whereas thrillers and procedurals might weave together multiple complex plotlines involving political intrigue, psychological depth, or high-stakes action. The more focused scope of conflict in cozies can simplify the plot and character dynamics.

All that said, it's crucial to remember that writing a compelling, engaging cozy mystery that stands out in the market still demands creativity, meticulous plotting, and the ability to create relatable characters and a charming setting. The "easiness" is relative and more about the type of challenges the author faces rather than the overall difficulty of the task. Every genre has its own complexities and nuances that writers must navigate to craft a story that resonates with readers.

OTHER CONSIDERATIONS IN CHOOSING TO WRITE IN THE COZY MYSTERY SUBGENRE

1. The Cozy Subgenre Continues to Grow in Popularity: It's a bit amusing to recall the big publishing houses almost universally dropping or drastically cutting back their cozy mystery lines back in the early 2000s. Oops! No one ever expects the Spanish Inquisition AKA ebook publishing and, its accelerant, self- or indie publishing. In fact, in recent years, cozies have seen an even greater resurgence in popularity, partly due to readers looking for escape and comfort in their reading material. This trend has led to a broader acceptance and interest in the genre, creating more opportunities for new authors.

2. An Engaged and Loyal Readership: Cozy mystery fans consume titles at a rate more typical of romance fans than mystery readers. The cozy audience is known for their loyalty and eagerness to follow series and authors over *long* periods. This engaged readership can offer a stable platform for authors to build their careers, with opportunities for cross-promotion and community building.

3. Digital and Self-Publishing Success: While this highly adaptable genre continues to do very well in traditional print, it has *thrived* in digital and self-publishing arenas. Ebooks and audiobooks have opened new avenues for distribution and reader engagement, making it easier for new authors to enter the market and find their audience.

4. Structured Parameters Provide a Blueprint: We've largely covered this. Cozy mysteries have certain expectations (like the absence of graphic violence or explicit content), which provide clear parameters for crafting stories and characters—while leaving ample room for creativity within these bounds. Authors can craft intricate plots, develop rich characters, and weave in humor or romance, all while delivering satisfying mysteries that adhere to the cozy formula. Once you master that formula, the rest is easy.

These factors combine to make cozy mysteries a vibrant and promising field for both new and established writers. Whether you're drawn to crafting puzzles, developing quirky characters, or exploring unique settings, the cozy mystery market offers a welcoming and rewarding space for creative expression.

BUT IS THERE REALLY A MARKET FOR GAY COZY MYSTERIES?

This is one of those awkward questions that has to be addressed.

The demand for particular stories with particular characters is always both activist-driven and reader-driven, which means that a perceived demand does not always translate into the expected financial rewards for publishing houses or writers. That doesn't mean the books shouldn't be written, published, and promoted, but it does mean the writing, publishing, and promotion has to be approached with a realistic attitude.

The publishing industry is gradually becoming more inclusive, and the success of books featuring diverse protagonists reflects a changing landscape. Reader appetite for diversity is influencing market trends, pushing publishers to broaden their catalogs with more representative works. While challenges remain, the trajectory points toward a more inclusive future in publishing.

Still, our question taps into a nuanced aspect of the publishing industry, and it's a valid point of curiosity for any writer or industry observer. The distinction between "activist-driven" and "market-driven" demand is not always clear-cut, as these forces can overlap and influence each other in complex ways.

Activism can play a significant role in highlighting the lack of diversity in literature and the need for more inclusive representation.

This can lead to a heightened awareness among readers, publishers, and writers alike. Activist-driven initiatives may pressure publishers to diversify their lists. While this might start as an effort to address underrepresentation, it can also unveil untapped market potentials that were overlooked. At the same time, books featuring diverse characters and stories often receive strong support from communities and organizations advocating for representation. This can boost visibility and sales through word of mouth, social media campaigns, and community events.

Meanwhile, the market-driven demand for these books means a genuine interest and desire for these stories already exists. In particular, there is reader interest in stories that reflect a broader range of experiences and perspectives. When books featuring characters with disabilities, characters who are non-white, characters who identify as LGBTQ+ achieve commercial success, it encourages publishers to invest more in similar titles. The market for books is global, and audiences are diverse. Catering to a wider range of readers can open up new revenue streams and expand the market—something of which publishers are well aware.

With the gay cozy mystery, we have an intersection of activism and market demand.

Activist-driven efforts can reveal market demands that were previously underappreciated or ignored by the industry. Once publishers recognize that diverse books can be commercially successful, market-driven mechanisms take over, with the initial activist push leading to a broader, sustained demand.

That's no small thing, and it's not just a hopeful theory. Readers seek quality storytelling and authentic representation. Books that meet these criteria, regardless of what lies behind the initial push for their publication, can succeed on their own merits, indicating that the demand is not solely activist-driven but supported by genuine reader interest.

At this point, it's challenging to quantify how much of the demand for gay cozies is activist-driven versus market-driven, and I'm not even sure if it matters. It's clear that both forces contribute to the current landscape. The success of diverse books in the wider market suggests that the demand is not solely driven by activism but by a genuine appetite from readers for stories that reflect a wider array of experiences. Moreover, the publishing industry's response, including the increased publication and promotion of such books, indicates recognition of their commercial viability.

When I first suggested writing a gay cozy mystery series, I received a fair bit of pushback from both the M/M and gay mystery writing communities. The prevailing idea seemed to be that there was no demand for M/M mystery that did not contain erotic content nor for gay mystery that did not contain sexuality, violence, or, at the very least, political activism. But the Secrets and Scrabble series is now one of my highest selling series (low six figures with no single title earning less than five figures).

There is not as great a demand for cozy mysteries featuring gay protagonists as there is demand for cozy mysteries featuring straight female protagonists. That's the reality. But that reality doesn't mean that you can't be successful writing what you love and what is important to you.

Ultimately, it boils down to the best advice I can give, which is write what you would love to read.

Which brings us to another question—one that's unique to our particular time and space in the illustrious history of publishing...

WHY WRITE THE BOOKS YOURSELF? WHY NOT HIRE A GHOSTWRITER OR EVEN USE AI?

I'm assuming if you've bought a book on writing, you already know the answer to that, but some of us may be feeling overwhelmed by the advent of AI or the flood of newcomers eager to take part in a gig economy, or simply at how much publishing has changed in the past years. Everywhere we look, we see "writers" flooding the lists, taking shortcuts in writing—if they're writing at all—filling every molecule of airspace with the unrelenting white noise of promo-spam, faking, cheating, gaming every and all systems, and seemingly being successful at it (although everything is relative and appearances can be deceiving).

Guess what? There are practical, as well as ethical and emotional, reasons for writing your own books.

Have you ever heard of something called the Pareto Principle?

The Pareto Principle, also widely known as the 80/20 rule, is a fascinating concept that applies across various domains, from economics to personal productivity. The principle is named after Vilfredo Pareto, an Italian economist who, in 1906, observed that 80 percent of Italy's land was owned by 20 percent of the population. Pareto developed a mathematical formula to describe this unequal distribution of wealth, and that principle has since been applied to a wide range of fields beyond economics.

At its core, the Pareto Principle suggests that roughly 80 percent of the effects come from 20 percent of the causes. (This ratio is not fixed at exactly 80/20 and can vary, but you get the idea.) The key insight is that there is often an imbalance between inputs and outputs, effort and reward, or causes and results.

In other words: Life is not fair.

Do you see where I'm going with this?

There are all kinds of ways to apply this principle, but for our purposes, it suggests that roughly 80 percent of the genre's success—measured in sales, recognition, or influence—could be attributed to 20 percent of its authors.

This reflects a common pattern where a relatively small number of authors generate the majority of sales and engagement within a specific market segment. These authors often have a strong brand, a dedicated readership, and a significant backlist of titles that keep readers engaged over time.

(In fairness, it likely highlights the importance of not only the quality of writing but also consistent output, effective marketing, and building a loyal reader base in order to become part of that impactful 20 percent.)

You've seen this play out time and time again in publishing. Even if every author were to try the exact same tactics—putting all their books in KDP, hiring promotional companies, hiring ghostwriters, using AI, you name it—the success ratio will not change from what it is at any given moment in time. Roughly 20 percent of authors will *still* get 80 percent of the pie.

How can that be so?

It's actually not all that mysterious.

Inherent Talent and Skill Disparity: In any field, there's a natural variation in talent, skill, and dedication. Some authors will always stand out due to their exceptional storytelling abilities, unique voice, or genre innovation. This disparity means that even with equal opportunities, outcomes will differ significantly based on individual capabilities and the appeal of their work to readers.

Quality and Resonance of Work: The success of a book often hinges on its quality (in terms of writing, storytelling, and editing) and its resonance with the audience. High-quality work that strikes a chord with readers will naturally rise to the top, attracting more attention, reviews, and word-of-mouth recommendations. This aspect of quality and resonance cannot be uniformly distributed, leading to some authors consistently performing better than others.

Brand and Platform Building: Authors who invest time in building their brand and engaging with their audience often see better long-term success. This involves activities beyond writing, such as social media engagement, public appearances, and email newsletters. The effectiveness of these efforts varies widely among authors, contributing to the differences in their success levels.

Market Saturation and Visibility: Even if all books were made free or placed in Kindle Unlimited, visibility would remain a challenge. With thousands of books published every day, standing out requires more than just availability. Marketing efforts, cover design, and strategic pricing play crucial roles in capturing reader interest. Authors who master these aspects tend to stay ahead.

Reader Preferences and Trends: Reader tastes and market trends are always in flux. Authors who can anticipate or even set these trends have a better chance of staying at the top. However, adaptability and foresight are not uniformly distributed across all writers, leading to some being more successful than others.

Luck and Timing: Finally, success in publishing can sometimes come down to being in the right place at the right time. While not a strategy, luck can play a significant role in an author's breakthrough. This element of randomness further supports the idea that not everyone can achieve equal levels of success. It's not a happy thought, but it's the reality.

Again: Approximately 80 percent of the genre's success—measured in sales, recognition, or influence—will be attributed to 20 percent of its authors. There isn't any changing that.

What does potentially change is *who falls within that 20 percent*.

The idea that success can be emulated by following the exact same steps as someone else, in particular, someone selling a how-to-get-rich-quick course, is nonsensical.

Unless you just arrived in publishing five minutes ago, you've seen this truth play out over and over again.

You need a home-court advantage, and in the current publishing paradigm, the biggest advantage—frankly the most cost-effective *and* with the greatest long-term benefits—is actually learning how to write well.

YOU NEED TO WRITE BOOKS THAT PEOPLE *REALLY* WANT TO READ—AND YOU NEED TO WRITE THEM *BETTER* THAN EVERYBODY ELSE.

Writing your own book allows you to infuse your unique voice and perspective into every page. This authenticity is something readers can sense and connect with on a deeper level. It's the difference between a story that feels lived-in and one that merely exists. Your personal touch can turn a good story into an unforgettable experience for the reader.

There's an unparalleled sense of fulfillment and pride in creating something from scratch. By writing your own book, you maintain complete creative control over every aspect of the story, from plot development to character arcs. This control ensures that the final product is exactly what you envisioned, providing a sense of accomplishment that's hard to achieve through other means.

Writing is a craft, and like any craft, it requires practice to improve. Are you here for the long term or are you just hoping to make a quick buck?

If you're here for the duration, you need to become the best possible writer you can be.

By tackling the challenges of writing a book head-on, you'll hone your skills in storytelling, character development, and language use.

This ongoing process of learning and mastering your craft is not only rewarding but also critical for long-term success in the literary world.

When you write your own book, you're not just creating a product; you're inviting readers into your world. This direct connection between author and reader fosters a loyal fan base and can lead to meaningful interactions. Readers tend to gravitate toward authors who share themselves through their work, which can be a powerful tool for building your brand and audience.

Writing your own book ensures that you're putting out original content that you can stand behind. In an era where authenticity is highly valued, being genuine and ethical in your creative process sets you apart. This integrity not only enhances your reputation but also contributes to the richness and diversity of literature.

Now, let me say that I have nothing against ghostwriters. Having a subordinate secret coauthor could be very useful—if that coauthor is genuinely good. And AI... AI can be a very useful tool for all kinds of things. But at the time of writing this book, AI fiction is pretty horrendous. The only threat it poses to writers of fiction are human writers who are also kind of horrendous. Will AI get better? Yep. Of course. But I guess I'm never going to understand choosing to become a writer if you don't actually enjoy writing.

Believe me, there are easier ways to earn a living.

Anyway, while hiring a ghostwriter or using AI might seem like shortcuts to publication, writing your own book is more beneficial in the long run. As you develop your voice and build your portfolio, you're more likely to attract attention from agents, publishers, and readers. The investment of your time and effort can lead to greater financial rewards, recognition, and opportunities for career growth.

Remember—and this is as true of writing today as it ever was—writing your own book is about more than just telling a story; it's about expressing your identity, engaging with your craft, and building a lasting legacy in the literary world. The journey might be challenging, but the rewards—both personal and professional—are immense and deeply fulfilling.

Happy writing!

1

WHAT IS A COZY MYSTERY?

WHEN WE SAY SOMETHING IS *COZY*, WHAT DO WE MEAN?

THE TERM "COZY" CONJURES UP FEELINGS OF WARMTH, COMFORT, and relaxation. It's often associated with childhood memories, environments, activities, or objects that make us feel safe, content, and sheltered. Coziness is subjective and can vary greatly from person to person, but there are several key elements that commonly contribute to something being considered "cozy":

Warmth: Both physical warmth, like being wrapped in a soft blanket on a cold day, and emotional warmth, such as the feeling of being surrounded by loved ones, are essential to coziness.

Comfort: Comfort is key to something being cozy. This can mean physical comfort, like sitting in a plush, comfortable chair, or emotional comfort, provided by a sense of familiarity and security.

Peacefulness: A cozy setting or situation is often quiet and tranquil, offering a respite from the hustle and bustle of daily life. It's a space where one can relax and unwind without interruption.

Simplicity: Coziness is often found in simplicity and the absence of clutter or chaos. Simple pleasures, such as reading a book by the fire or sipping a warm cup of tea, epitomize coziness.

Sensory Pleasure: Cozy things appeal to our senses in a gentle, soothing way. Soft textures, warm colors, pleasant scents, and soothing sounds all contribute to a cozy atmosphere.

Intimacy: Small, intimate spaces or gatherings can feel cozier than large, open areas or crowds. Coziness often involves close connections with others or personal time spent in solitude.

Nostalgia: Items or activities that evoke fond memories can also be cozy, as they bring a sense of comfort and happiness from the past into the present.

Overall, coziness is about creating a personal haven of contentment and security, where the stresses of the outside world seem far away. It's a universal desire for warmth and comfort, manifesting in countless ways across different cultures and individual preferences.

NOW, WHAT *EXACTLY* IS A COZY MYSTERY?

In literature, particularly in cozy mysteries, "cozy" also refers to a genre characterized by crime stories set in close-knit communities, where violence and sex are downplayed or treated with a light touch, and the focus is on the puzzle-solving aspect of the mystery. These stories prioritize the sense of community, the charm of the setting, and the intelligence and intuitiveness of an amateur sleuth, all wrapped up in a comforting, often whimsically detailed narrative.

(Remember that when we're discussing writing cozy mysteries, we're almost always talking about writing a series. In **A SERIES OF UNFORTUNATE EVENTS**, we'll discuss the elements of successful series writing.)

The roots of the cozy mystery genre can be traced back to the Golden Age of detective fiction, primarily that period between the two World Wars. Authors such as Agatha Christie, Dorothy L. Sayers, Margery Allingham, and Ngaio Marsh were instrumental in shaping the genre. Their works, characterized by elaborate puzzles that emphasized "whodunit and how" over graphic violence or police procedural details, laid the groundwork for what would eventually become cozy mysteries.

Agatha Christie's Miss Marple series, in particular, is often cited as a prototype for the cozy mystery. Miss Marple, an amateur sleuth solving crimes in her village, embodies many characteristics of cozy protagonists: she's intelligent, perceptive, a spymaster-grade expert at eliciting valuable intel through gossip and idle chatter, and always operates in a small-community setting, even when in a luxe hotel in the heart of London or a Caribbean resort.

Here's something to think about: As of this writing, sales in the "traditional" mystery genre are in decline, while the boom in contemporary cozy continues unabated.

While the Golden Age set the stage, the cozy mystery as a distinct genre began to take shape more clearly in the latter half of the 20th century. It was during this time that the genre started to be recognized for its unique characteristics: amateur sleuths, minimal violence and sex, and settings in small communities where everyone knows each other.

The 1960s and 1970s saw a rise in mystery novels that focused on character and puzzle over hard-boiled detective work, further paving the way for the cozy mystery genre. However, it wasn't until the 1980s and 1990s that cozy mysteries began to be marketed and recognized as a distinct subgenre. Publishers started to capitalize on the growing market for mysteries that eschewed graphic content for a gentler, more character-driven narrative.

Today, the cozy mystery genre has expanded to include a wide variety of themes and settings, from culinary cozies to paranormal, hobby-based (knitting, gardening, etc.), and even pet detective series. This diversification reflects the genre's adaptability and its appeal to readers seeking both comfort and intrigue in their reading material.

The rise of digital publishing and self-publishing has further contributed to the growth and diversification of the genre, allowing more authors to contribute their unique takes and reach audiences directly.

The separation of cozy mysteries from traditional mysteries underscores a shift in some readers' preferences toward stories that emphasize community, puzzle-solving, and relatable protagonists over the grittier, more procedural aspects of crime solving and puzzles that exist more as mathematical equations than organic revelations of character.

The cozy mystery genre offers readers an escape into a world where justice is served in a manner that's both satisfying and comforting, a niche that continues to grow and evolve with changing reader tastes.

Tracking the genre's evolution from the Golden Age of detective fiction to today's diverse offerings provides insight into not only the genre's history but also its enduring appeal. Cozy mysteries have carved out a significant place in the mystery genre by offering something unique and beloved by a dedicated readership.

SUBTLE AND NOT-SO-SUBTLE DIFFERENCES BETWEEN COZY AND TRADITIONAL MYSTERIES

If you're familiar with my work, you know that I write both traditional gay mystery (the Adrien English Mysteries, Holmes & Moriarity, etc.) and M/M or gay cozy mysteries (such as Secrets and Scrabble) as well as mainstream cozies. It might be helpful to examine some of the small but significant differences in these two subgenres.

Cozy Mysteries

Setting: Cozy mysteries often take place in small towns or close-knit communities. The setting itself is usually as important as the characters and plot, providing a charming, often idyllic backdrop to the story.

Protagonist: The sleuth in a cozy mystery is typically an amateur detective, never a professional law enforcement officer or private investigator. Rarely even a retired law enforcement officer or private investigator. This character is often well-integrated into the community, with a profession or hobby that lends itself well to stumbling upon mysteries (e.g., a baker, librarian, or bookstore owner).

Tone and Content: Cozy mysteries are light on violence and sex. Any murder occurs off-page, and the tone is generally light, focusing on puzzle-solving and community. The language and content are clean, making them suitable for a broad audience. There is no obscenity and the crimes rarely have to do with darker subjects such as rape, hate crimes, organized crime, child abuse, etc.

Themes: These stories often incorporate themes related to community, friendship, and sometimes romance. They can also revolve around specific hobbies or interests, such as cooking, gardening, or book collecting, which can attract readers with similar interests (although the mania for such gimmicky "hooks" is—thankfully—fading).

Romantic Subplot: There is frequently—not always—a romantic interest. Angst is kept at a minimum and there is NO on-page erotic content.

Traditional Mysteries

Setting: While traditional mysteries can also use small towns, they frequently employ a wider variety of settings, including urban environments, foreign locales, or historical settings. The setting serves the plot more than creating a sense of community.

Protagonist: The detective in traditional mysteries is often a professional—either a police officer, a private investigator, or a forensic expert—often retired—with a particular skill set for solving crimes. Iconic examples include Sherlock Holmes, Hercule Poirot, and (arguably) Miss Marple (the latter of whom blurs the lines as she's an amateur but operates within what might be considered traditional mystery framework in that the motives and crimes, however delicately described, can be pretty darned brutal—child murders and murderers, for example).

Tone and Content: Traditional mysteries may include more explicit descriptions of violence or adult themes, though this varies widely by author. There is much more latitude regarding the types of crimes and how they are ultimately resolved—or even if they *are* resolved. The focus is often more on the intellectual challenge of solving the crime than on the personal lives of the characters or the community, though that can vary in a series.

Themes: The themes can be darker, exploring the complexities of human nature, justice, and morality. The puzzle of the mystery is central, with less emphasis on the personal growth of the detective or the societal norms of the setting.

Overlap and Exceptions

Traditional mysteries can often feel quite cozy in many aspects, but if they contain erotic content, graphic on-page violence, obscenity, profanity, dark themes, are set in a metropolis with tons of stranger-suspects, or are solved by a paid professional, they are not cozy mysteries. This is why the Holmes & Moriarity stories, despite many cozy elements, are not technically cozies while the Secrets and Scrabble series is.

Some readers and reviewers—probably *most*, really—don't actually know the difference and might mis-categorize a work based on their interpretation of these elements. That's okay. YOU know the difference. Don't mislabel your book. Help readers choose the type of mystery that best suits their preferences, and you'll save yourself a bad review or two.

THE NECESSARY ELEMENTS OF THE *GAY* COZY MYSTERY

A Small, Close-Knit Community: The setting is still a small town or a tightly knit community where everyone knows each other, providing a contrast to the crime that disrupts the peace. While this community should reflect diversity, it must also reflect the communities of cozy mysteries with a varied cast of regulars and eccentrics. A lot of the humor in cozies comes from kooky characters.

An LGBTQ+ Protagonist: Just an ordinary guy or gal who happens to solve mysteries in their spare time—oh, and identifies as a member of the LGBTQ+ community. This amateur detective may or may not have a personal stake in the investigation, but they will always possess keen observation skills and a strong sense of justice. They're typically well-liked, relatable, and have a network of friends and acquaintances who help gather information. Note: Your protagonist cannot be in the closet. Their sexual orientation cannot be one of the mysteries or great conflicts in your series. The protagonist's sexual orientation will never be the primary focus of *any* aspect of a cozy mystery series.

Minimal Violence and Sex: No change from mainstream cozy here. This is a challenging one for authors migrating from M/M romance. Cozy mysteries focus more on solving the puzzle than on graphic depictions of violence or sex. Any crime scenes are usually described with restraint, and the crime itself happens off-page. There is ZERO erotic content. That does not mean there is no romance.

A Puzzle to Solve: No change here either. At the heart of every cozy mystery is a puzzle or mystery that is intriguing and engages the reader to solve it alongside the protagonist. The plot often involves red herrings and twists to keep readers guessing. In the cozy mystery, classic clues take the role that forensics now holds in the modern mystery.

Characters Over Plot: While the mystery is central, the characters, their relationships, and their development are equally important. Readers often return to a series more for the characters and the community than for the individual mysteries. After all, there are only so many possible explanations for murder within a locked room.

A Unique Hobby or Occupation: As tired as I am of the "hook" in cozy mysteries, the most interesting thing about your protagonist cannot be his or her sexual orientation. Give them a unique hobby or occupation that plays a central role in the story, providing a thematic backdrop, clues, and motives related to the mystery.

Humor: Lighthearted humor is a staple of cozy mysteries, often arising from entertaining dialogue, quirky characters, or situations, which helps to balance the tension of the mystery and endear the characters to the reader. Since everyone knows gay people are particularly witty— I'M KIDDING. But you catch my drift.

Justice Prevails: This does not change. Cozy mysteries generally conclude with the mystery solved, the perpetrator caught, and order restored, reinforcing a sense of right and wrong.

A Strong Sense of Community: Beyond the small-town setting, cozy mysteries often emphasize themes of friendship, community, and belonging, with the protagonist relying on a network of friends and acquaintances to solve the mystery. Stressing this aspect of *respected and vital member of the community at large* is perhaps even more important in the gay cozy mystery.

Clean and Comforting Atmosphere: This can be a challenge for M/M mystery writers in particular. Despite the heartwarming romantic relationship your protagonist enjoys with their eventual significant other, there are no kinks or naughty bits in a gay cozy mystery. Regardless of the presence of a crime, cozy mysteries maintain a warm, comforting atmosphere, making them the perfect "cozy" read. The charm of the setting, the engaging characters, and the satisfaction of a mystery solved all contribute to that feeling of *crisp and clean and no caffeine.* Okay, you have caffeine. You can even have a drink or two. But your protagonist cannot be a struggling alcoholic or a recovering sex addict. Not that there's anything wrong with that. But it's a different kind of book.

A Strong and Healthy Romantic Relationship: Yes. Your protagonist needs to find true love (eventually). It can take however long it needs to, but in order to demonstrate that your LGBTQ+ protagonist is not just a trope, they need to have emotionally intimate relationships with other LGBTQ+ characters. We will never see them doing the, er, wild thang on page, but we need to know that they are emotionally developed, psychologically sound people capable of forging lasting connections with other adults.

These elements combine to create the gay cozy mystery's distinctive charm, offering readers both representation and an engaging puzzle to solve within a comforting, familiar world.

What additional elements can you add that make your cozy relevant to today's audience and less cartoony?

Diverse and Inclusive Cast: We've already touched on this. Just remember: tokenism is not diversity. At the same time, you cannot have a village comprised only of gay people. Incorporating a diverse range of characters in terms of sexuality, gender, ethnicity, and background can add depth to your story and resonate with a broader audience. This diversity can be reflected in the personalities, motivations, and relationships within the community.

Cultural and Artistic Elements: Weaving cultural or artistic elements into the plot can serve as both a thematic backdrop and a mechanism for clues. Artifacts, paintings, or performances can be central to the mystery, offering unique settings and motives.

Complex Motivations: Just because the covers are cartoony, doesn't mean the characters in a cozy mystery have to be. While the motivations in some mysteries can be straightforward, adding layers to your characters' emotional drivers—such as personal, historical, or emotional reasons—can make your mystery more engaging and less predictable.

Historical or Thematic Depth: Incorporating historical references or exploring specific themes (such as justice, redemption, or community) can add another layer of interest and give your stories a more profound message or question to ponder.

Romantic Subplots: Your protagonist's romantic escapades aren't the only subplots of interest to your readers. Once a reader becomes invested in your cozy little world, they care about what happens to *all* the people who live there. And, as in real life, there should be changes within that world. Characters will marry, divorce…fall in love, fall out of love…get suspected of murdering their ex… Normal life stuff.

Technology and Modern Elements: Unless you're writing a historical cozy, technological advancements such as cell phones and streaming and even AI should have arrived in your village. Reflecting modern technology and contemporary issues can make your story more relatable and intriguing, especially if you find clever ways to incorporate them into the mystery or investigation. Not including technological advancements of the last century tends to stop readers cold.

Character Arcs and Growth: See above. Developing your characters over the course of the mystery and across your series—showing personal growth, revelations, or changes in relationships—can make your stories more compelling and satisfying. Your world will feel more real to the reader if there is movement within its borders.

Atmospheric Details: Cozy mysteries thrive on atmosphere, so detailed descriptions of settings, meals, décor, and clothing can help create a vivid, immersive world that readers love to keep visiting.

Ethical Dilemmas and Moral Questions: Introducing ethical dilemmas or moral questions—especially ones that resonate with contemporary social issues—can add depth to the narrative, challenging both your characters and your readers. That said, if you're thinking of tackling some heavy issues like capital punishment, euthanasia, racism…these need to be handled delicately, subtly.

Inclusion of Pets or Mascots: Animals or pets can add charm, humor, and warmth to your stories. They can also play roles in the plot, such as providing clues or helping to break down the barriers between characters.

These additional elements not only enrich the storytelling but also allow you to explore a wider range of narrative possibilities and connect with readers on multiple levels. Crafting your cozy mysteries with these aspects in mind can enhance the uniqueness and appeal of your work.

THE HARD AND FAST RULES OF WRITING THE COZY MYSTERY – GAY OR OTHERWISE

Remember, you can write anything you want. But if you're going to try to market your work to cozy mystery readers, then you must adhere to genre expectations. If you submit a sonnet to a haiku contest, you're not transcending genre, you're being a dumbass.

So, yes. These are rules, not guidelines.

1. Never Kill a Cat. No pets or small children may die during the course of your story. In fact, I'd be very careful about killing off *any* animals or humans under college-age.

2. The Age of Consent. Your killer should be college-age or older. Your killer cannot be your protagonist's love interest. Or an immediate family member. Your sleuth may not be the killer. The killer will also not be a serial killer or a hired assassin. And, while on this grim topic, parents may not kill their adult children. Adult children may not kill their parents. Under no circumstances kill off your protagonist's love interest. In fact, dispatch any and all beloved series characters with caution. We're not going for Greek tragedy here.

3. Close Your Eyes, Baby. Minimal violence. You can kill off your victims however you like, but no on-screen violence, no graphic or grisly descriptions of violence or death. The cozy mystery reader is not looking for a trip to the morgue or a peek at the autopsy table.

4. In Fact, No Graphic Anything. Explicit scenes, whether they're violent or sexual, are off the table. Cozy mysteries shy away from graphic descriptions, maintaining a clean and gentle narrative that focuses on puzzles and people and their relationships rather than on shock value. There is a minimal amount of obscenity and swearing. Language is kept clean. Any necessary rough talk is often implied rather than explicit, keeping in line with the genre's overall genteel approach. Should profanity occur, it ought to be for a damned good reason.

5. *Murder is Not Funny*. But seriously. Even though humor is a large element of these books, and even though murder drives the plot, the dead—even the unlikable dead—are treated with a certain amount of respect. They are not merely plot devices but catalysts for unraveling mysteries that often lead to deeper understandings or resolutions within the community.

5. *True North*. Your protagonist's moral compass is in working order. Your sleuth does not agonize unduly over right and wrong. We all have our moments of weakness, but you're writing about a good-hearted human trying to do the right thing, with no inclination toward promiscuity or morally dubious activities. Their personal life shouldn't overshadow the mystery but can provide a refreshing subplot. It's okay to make your protagonist human. Humans jump at footsteps in the night, have drinks with friends, get parking tickets, forget to pay a bill, have trouble quitting smoking, or maybe are afraid to fall in love again. Your protagonist can—*should*—be flawed, but don't turn them into a vigilante or someone struggling with anger issues.

6. *Be Nice. Play Fair*. The crime can be as complicated as you can manage, however you must play fair with the reader. That means the actual murderer must come from within the "community," and be known to both the protagonist and the reader early on—*even if we have not actually met them yet on-page.* The knowledge that the villain is hiding within this closed circle adds to the tension and keeps your readers guessing.

7. *Justice Prevails:* Unlike in real life, in cozy mysteries, bad people do get their comeuppance. These books typically have a positive resolution, with the mystery solved, the perpetrator caught, and order restored to the community. This reinforces the idea that no matter the chaos, normalcy (and safety) can be restored—which is something cozy readers look for in their fiction.

These rules collectively ensure that cozy mysteries remain a distinct and beloved genre, offering escapism, satisfaction, and a sense of justice, all wrapped up in a community-focused, amiable narrative. But as with any creative endeavor, there's always room for innovation and bending the rules to fit your unique story.

2

THE STAR OF YOUR SHOW - PROTAGONIST

SOMETIMES IT'S HELPFUL TO REFRESH OURSELVES ON THE BASICS.
A protagonist is essentially the main character in a story, the one around whom the plot revolves. They are typically the character readers are meant to root for, often facing obstacles they must overcome throughout the narrative. This character's actions, decisions, and development are central to driving the story forward and engaging the audience.

The cozy mystery protagonist is a little unique in fiction because the rules and restraints of the genre itself are also imposed upon the creation of these particular characters.

Does that mean you have less freedom in developing your cozy mystery protagonist than you would in developing the main character of a traditional mystery?

Yes. It does.

Logically, it must.

It would hardly make sense to create a charming cozy world peopled with delightful, quirky characters and then choose for our guide an embittered, struggling, alcoholic ex-cop.

I'm not saying that couldn't be a brilliant dichotomy for a traditional (and possibly very funny) mystery, but it's not going to fly in the cozy subgenre.

The typical cozy mystery protagonist is a single, white, Christian (unless she's a witch—no, seriously) heterosexual female in her early thirties. Frequently, she is opening a new chapter in her life. This new chapter is both exciting and daunting.

Now, having said that, there are many, *many* successful exceptions to this rule. And you're about to write one! Don't be afraid to make your protagonist younger, older, non-Caucasian, non-Christian (non-wiccan), dealing with physical challenges, LGBTQ+ and/or male. The human shell should not be the point. It's what's *inside* that shell that counts.

Let's consider the character of the standard cozy mystery protagonist. What qualities do these women and men have in common?

Relatability and Aspiration: Cozy mystery protagonists often embody a blend of relatability and aspiration. They're typically portrayed as everyday people with whom readers can easily identify, but they also possess qualities or lead lives that readers might aspire to—be it owning a quaint bookstore, running a delightful bakery, or something as simple as having a close-knit circle of friends. This balance makes them both accessible and appealing. Very often they are someone starting off on a new adventure, a new chapter in their life. Challenges lie ahead, but they are eager to face them. They embrace the adventure of life, and thrive.

Moral Clarity: These characters navigate their milieux with a strong sense of right and wrong, providing a clear moral compass in a complex world. They do not agonize over the big rights and wrongs. Whatever the obstacles, they will try to do the right thing. When they make mistakes, they will try to fix them. This clarity can be comforting to readers, offering a straightforward view of justice that often seems lacking in real life.

Good Citizens: Cozy mysteries are deeply rooted in the sense of community, and protagonists play key roles within their social circles. They care about their community and their neighbors. This emphasis on relationships and belonging speaks to a universal human desire for connection. Readers may be drawn to the protagonist's integral role in their community, seeing them as a pillar of support and camaraderie.

Competence and Cleverness: Even though they're amateur sleuths, these protagonists display a remarkable level of competence and cleverness in solving mysteries. Their ability to connect dots, notice details, and think outside the box can be deeply satisfying for readers, who enjoy the intellectual stimulation of piecing together clues alongside the protagonist. These characters are innovative problem-solvers. Professional detectives have training and resources at their disposal. In contrast, amateur sleuths must mostly rely on their wit, intuition, and the help of their community. This can lead to more creative and unconventional problem-solving strategies, making for potentially more interesting and unpredictable stories.

Courage: The world of a cozy mystery, with its picturesque settings and delightful denizens, offers a perfect escape from the complexities and anxieties of real life. However, this safe little world is regularly threatened by the presence of those who commit crimes and wield violent death. While any normal person would avoid getting involved in any crime, let alone homicide, the cozy protagonist, our guide through this world, doesn't hesitate to come to the aid of their friends or neighbors. Okay, maybe they hesitate. They're not suicidal, after all. But they are willing to risk life, limb, and even the occasional arrest in order to restore balance and harmony to the universe.

Growth and Resilience: Despite the effervescent surface, many cozy protagonists do—certainly *should*—display resilience and therefore experience personal growth in the face of many challenges. This journey can make these characters more compelling and adds a layer of depth to their character, even when that journey is so subtle as to seem almost invisible.

A Sense of Humor: Honestly, this one's a bit optional. Every cozy protagonist need not be a stand-up-comedian-in-waiting. A cozy mystery doesn't have to be humorous so much as *good-humored*. If comedy is not your strength, that's okay. But your main character has to be a pleasant person who can laugh at themselves and not take everything too seriously. By the way, the comedic elements in the cozy are *never* bitingly satirical or mean-spirited.

An Everyman/Everywoman: How ironic, right? But yes, in theory there's an element of the "everyman" hero in cozy protagonists. They're not detectives by profession nor do they have any special powers, yet they manage to solve mysteries—so *many* mysteries!—through observation, intelligence, and the help of their community. This democratization of the detective role suggests that anyone can make a difference, which is an appealing and empowering concept.

Stability and Predictability: Cozy mystery protagonists do not "go off the deep end." They are not going to run amok and shoot up the joint or go on a bender or run off to Vegas with their romantic interest and wake up the next morning with a hangover. That is not to say your protag can't have quirks and foibles—I should hope they do—but they are not going to suddenly "behave out of character." Stability is not dramatic, but it's what the cozy reader wants. There's comfort in the familiarity of these protagonists. They come to feel like old friends, and the predictability of their moral and behavioral codes offers a sense of balance and harmony in an ever-changing world.

In essence, the appeal of the cozy mystery protagonist lies in their ability to offer escapism, moral clarity, and a sense of community and belonging, all while engaging the reader's intellect and emotions in a comforting, yet stimulating, narrative environment. It's a delicate balance that, when achieved, resonates deeply with readers, regardless of the prose's sophistication.

However, your job is a little more complicated than creating a safe and predictable cipher. Unlike in other mystery subgenres, the cozy protagonist cannot merely be interesting, they have to be *likable*, which means you need to consider how you can make your main character even more appealing to readers.

Let's review the traits we humans typically admire in others—and unconsciously look for in fictional characters, in order to relate to them:

Empathy: The ability to understand and share the feelings of another is incredibly endearing. Empathetic individuals are seen as caring and compassionate, making them naturally likable.

Humor: A good sense of humor is irresistible. People who can laugh, especially at themselves, and bring lightness to conversations tend to be very appealing.

Integrity: Honesty and a strong moral principle attract respect and admiration. Individuals who stand by their values and are truthful are seen as trustworthy and reliable—even when we don't agree with them.

Kindness: Acts of kindness, gentleness with those who need help, are a real clue to character. Kind individuals are often well-liked because they make others feel seen, valued, and respected.

Confidence: Confidence, not to be confused with arrogance, draws people in. Confident individuals are comfortable in their own skin, which makes others feel comfortable around them as well.

A Genuine Interest in Others: When people are genuinely interested in their fellow humans, it shows. People who listen actively, paying attention to others' thoughts and feelings, are incredibly likable. This trait makes people feel heard and important.

Optimism: A positive outlook on life is contagious. Optimistic people, who see the best in situations and others, tend to uplift those around them, making them highly likable.

Reliability: Being dependable and consistent in one's actions and behaviors builds trust. People are drawn to those they can count on.

Open-mindedness: The willingness to consider different ideas and perspectives without immediate judgment is a highly attractive trait. It shows a level of respect and curiosity for others' experiences and views.

Passion: Individuals who are passionate about their interests or beliefs are often very engaging. Their enthusiasm can be infectious, making them interesting and likable, even when we find their passion for a particular subject baffling.

Resilience: The ability to bounce back from setbacks and maintain a positive attitude is admirable. Resilient people inspire those around them with their strength and perseverance.

Generosity: Sharing time, resources, or knowledge without expecting anything in return is a trait that naturally draws people. Generous individuals are often appreciated and admired for their willingness to help others.

Courage: We admire those who stand up for what they believe in or are the first to take action in a crisis. We admire those who aren't afraid to try new things or challenge themselves to go farther and do more.

These traits, among others, contribute significantly to a person's likability, which means incorporating a few of these qualities into your characters can make them more relatable and endearing to readers, fostering a deeper connection with the narrative.

This is not to say that your characters have to embody *every* quality we admire in others. How tedious would that be? Beware of turning your protagonist into a Mary Sue or Gary Stu.

If you're not familiar with the term, which originated in fanfiction, a "Mary Sue" refers to a specific type of character who is overly idealized and lacks realistic or meaningful flaws. They read uncomfortably close to author wish fulfillment. Mary and Gary embody the sort of perfection that makes them not only unrelatable to readers but also undermines the narrative's integrity.

When you're creating your characters, watch for the following giveaways:

Everything Everywhere All at Once: Mary Sue characters are often depicted as exceptionally beautiful, smart, *and* talented, excelling in nearly every area without plausible limitations or weaknesses. Their lack of flaws makes it hard for readers to relate to them or see them as believable characters.

Lack of Character Development: Because Gary Stus are already perfect, they don't undergo significant personal growth or development throughout the story. They have no character arc. They end where they began: impressively dull. This stagnation can make for a boring narrative since character development is a crucial element of engaging storytelling.

The World According to Mary Sue: Because Mary Sue characters must *always* be right, the world around them often warps to accommodate their worldview. Other cast members frequently have to act out of character so that Mary Sue can be right, no matter how unlikely her theories or their behaviors might be. The very plot may go off the rails, the stories losing internal logic and coherence, so that Mary Sue can shine.

Bulletproof Vest: If a character can easily overcome any obstacle thanks to their unparalleled skills or virtues, it removes the sense of risk and reduces tension in the narrative. This can make the story predictable and rob it of emotional impact.

Mic Hog: An author in love with their Mary Sue or Gary Stu is an author shortchanging the plot and greater story. Inevitably, too much airtime will be spent on preparing these tiresome characters for their never-ending closeup. The Mary Sue or Gary Stu inevitably sucks all the oxygen from the room, drawing attention away from other characters and plotlines, monopolizing the narrative. The end result is a story that lacks depth and complexity, and a supporting cast of cardboard characters who only function as an admiring chorus for the protagonist.

Creating complex, flawed characters is key to avoiding the Mary Sue trap. Characters should have strengths and weaknesses, make mistakes, and grow from them. This growth is called a character arc.

Let's elucidate.

A character arc is essentially the journey a character goes through during the story, showing how they change, grow, or learn from their experiences. It's the transformation or inner journey of a character over the course of your tale, marked by their struggles, triumphs, and failures. This can involve a shift in their beliefs, understanding, or character traits, often leading to a change in their behavior or perspective by the end of the story. The character arc is a crucial element in creating depth and relatability in characters, making them more engaging for your readers.

You must have some kind of character arc in each and every book and in the series overall.

I know! That can be challenging. But that's your job.

Maybe your main character starts out convinced he's never going to fall in love again or doesn't have what it takes to make the failing bookstore a success. Maybe she's never lived alone or knows nothing about art but now owns an art gallery. For sure, they've never had to catch a killer before.

Your protagonist begins their journey unprepared but hopeful. The journey ends in success, *even if that success was not what the protagonist originally aimed or hoped for.* Story is all about the journey. The journey *is* the story. And what is a journey but a series of challenges/conflicts along the way?

Realistic characters who face genuine struggles and evolve over time are essential for crafting compelling and satisfying stories. In your cozy mysteries, embracing the imperfections and growth of your characters can add depth and authenticity, making your stories more engaging and memorable.

How do you make your characters seem more realistic? You give them flaws. You give them quirks and tics. You give them traits that their enemies will criticize them for but their friends find endearing.

However, a word of caution: your character's "flaw" cannot be something like, for example, he's on the spectrum but otherwise gorgeous, brilliant, and utterly delightful. Autism Spectrum Disorder is not a character flaw, although I have seen more than one Gary Stu/Mary Sue character theoretically made more human by virtue of a developmental disorder. No. Your protagonist needs some legit character flaws.

Maybe they're prone to gossip, or a bit of a smartass when stressed, or a little superstitious or a lot overimaginative. Maybe they're occasionally clumsy or absent-minded, shy or self-conscious. Maybe they're a total slob or a fashionista. Maybe they're prone to procrastination. Maybe they have a couple of fears or phobias—not to the point of incapacitation. An agoraphobe is probably not going to make an effective sleuth, but a fear of spiders or a fear of heights can be fun and useful in a plot. Or they could suffer from allergies. It needn't be life-threatening. You don't want your readers to live in fear for your shellfish-allergic protag living in a quaint fishing village. Maybe they have an allergy to cats or dust or pollen or lies—something that could have comic value when they're trying to eavesdrop or hiding from a bad guy.

Your protag could have a legendary sweet tooth or be a fitness fanatic. They could be too impulsive or obsessive (not like stalker obsessive but maybe they really love Nancy Drew or BTS or they collect baseball cards or china thimbles.) Maybe they have a tendency to overcommit. Or maybe they're a little bit of a micromanager or a perfectionist.

Basically, you're trying to make your protagonist human. Humans have both strengths and weaknesses, as do well-written characters.

At the same time, don't go overboard. Don't turn your main character into a collection of tics and twitches. They have to seem real and relatable to the reader. *They have to be someone the reader wants to be around.*

And maybe avoid saddling your protagonist with these universally loathed traits: dishonesty, arrogance, manipulativeness, selfishness, cruelty, intolerance, irresponsibility, envy, or cowardice. That stuff isn't going to warm anyone's heart. You don't want the reader confused about who they're supposed to root for.

Because there's a very good chance that your gay cozy mystery is going to feature a male sleuth, it's going to be helpful to consider psychological differences between men and women. Remember, the cozy mystery is a *commercial* fiction subgenre. That commercial aspect is probably one of the reasons you want to write these. So, listen up. *Male characters need to* read *male.*

Does that mean your gay male protagonist is going to have some stereotypical male traits? OF COURSE. Just as your female cozy protagonist has to conform in a number of ways to our societal expectations, so, naturally, does your male protagonist. If you've got a problem with societal—and genre—expectations, you're writing in the wrong space.

While these differences are cultural trends rather than biological traits, and individuals vary widely, here are a few very broad considerations for creating your male (straight and gay) protagonists (while keeping in mind the wide spectrum of human experience):

Emotional Expression and Processing: Women are often socialized to be more open with their emotions and may be more likely to analyze and talk about their feelings. A female protagonist might thus be more introspective or more inclined to seek emotional support from friends or community. A male protagonist, on the other hand, might be portrayed as more reserved or might struggle more with expressing vulnerability, although breaking these stereotypes can add complexity to your characters.

Empathy and Intuition: Studies suggest women generally score higher on measures of empathy and emotional intelligence, which could translate into a female protagonist being particularly skilled at reading people and situations, a valuable trait for solving mysteries. A male protagonist could also possess high emotional intelligence, but his insights might be portrayed differently, perhaps with a focus on strategic thinking or a knack for noticing patterns.

Risk-Taking and Caution: Men are often thought to be more prone to taking risks—to this day, there is huge societal pressure for males to be brave, adventurous, *anything* but "chicken," which makes a male protagonist more likely to dive headfirst into dangerous situations. A female protagonist might approach these situations with more caution, though she could be just as determined and resourceful in pursuing leads.

Problem-Solving Styles: While it should go without saying that both men and women are capable of complex problem-solving, they might approach challenges differently. A female protagonist might be more collaborative, seeking input from others and piecing together clues from community interactions. A male protagonist might be more inclined to rely on direct action or logical deduction. Again, these are not hard and fast rules.

Social Dynamics and Relationships: The way your protagonist interacts with others can also reflect psychological differences. A female protagonist might place a greater emphasis on forming a network of allies and leveraging social connections, while a male protagonist might focus on establishing authority or expertise in certain areas. And, let's be clear, *your supporting characters will react and respond differently to a male or female protagonist.*

Conflict Resolution: Women are often socialized to prioritize harmony and may employ negotiation and compromise to resolve conflicts. A male protagonist might be more direct or confrontational, though both approaches have their place in the nuanced world of cozy mysteries.

Again, these are generalizations. The most engaging characters often defy stereotypes and bring a unique mix of traits to the table. The psychological differences mentioned can serve as a starting point, but the richness of your character will come from how you blend these elements with their individual personalities, backgrounds, and experiences. This approach not only makes your characters more relatable but also opens up a wider range of narrative possibilities.

We have to be realistic. Cozy mysteries are primarily written by women and gay men for women and gay men. And there are a lot more women than gay men both writing and reading cozy mysteries. What does that mean in practical terms?

It means you can probably sell more books if your protagonist is a white heterosexual female as described above. You have to consider what is important to you.

Then you have to consider what is important to your target audience.

Writing characters from backgrounds, orientations, or experiences different from your own—writing a character with disabilities, for example—requires a thoughtful, respectful approach. Here are some important aspects to keep in mind to ensure your LGBTQ+ characters are portrayed authentically and sensitively:

Research and Understanding: Before you begin, invest time in researching the experiences of LGBTQ+ individuals. This includes understanding the cultural, social, and personal nuances of being LGBTQ+. Reading books, watching documentaries, and listening to personal accounts can provide valuable insights.

Avoid Stereotypes: Stereotypes can be code, sure. But they are oversimplified and often inaccurate representations that can be harmful. Make sure your characters are fully realized individuals with their own personalities, desires, and struggles, not just caricatures based on their sexual orientation.

Diverse Representations: Just like any group, the LGBTQ+ community is diverse in terms of personalities, experiences, and life goals. Ensure that your portrayal reflects this diversity. Not all gay characters should fit the same mold, nor can their storylines revolve solely around their sexuality. What rings true for one gay reader will not be ring true for every gay reader. You have to accept that and move on.

Consult Sensitivity Readers: Sensitivity readers are individuals from the community you're writing about who can review your work for accuracy, representation, and potential issues. Their feedback can be invaluable in ensuring that your portrayal is respectful and authentic.

Humanize Your Characters: Your characters should be multifaceted and human. Their sexual orientation is just one aspect of who they are. *The most interesting thing about your gay protagonist cannot be the fact that he or she is gay.* Focus on developing their character arcs, challenges, successes, and relationships like you would for any other character.

Understand the Issues: Be aware of the social and political issues that affect the LGBTQ+ community. This doesn't mean every LGBTQ+ character needs to face these issues directly, but an awareness can add depth to your writing and help avoid inadvertently perpetuating harmful narratives. However, given that you are writing a cozy mystery, this has to be handled subtly. Your book must be an entertaining cozy mystery with a gay protagonist *not* a political manifesto. There are no politics in the cozy mystery—beyond the fact that you are writing a cozy mystery with an LGBTQ+ protagonist.

Use Appropriate Language: Language evolves, and terms that were once acceptable may now be outdated or offensive. Make sure to use the current and respectful language when referring to LGBTQ+ characters or themes in your writing.

Show Respect for the Experience: Even with thorough research, there's an aspect of lived experience that you won't fully grasp as an outsider. Acknowledge this in your approach, aiming to write with empathy and respect rather than claiming authority on the subject.

Avoid Tokenism: Including a gay character or person of color or a character with disabilities solely to tick a diversity box can be counterproductive. You don't want the reader to feel as though you were trying to get one of every flavor. The population of your small town or village has to feel organic. Cast every character with consideration for their purpose in the story beyond the brand of diversity they represent. Every character must contribute to the narrative in meaningful ways. They cannot be window dressing.

Embrace Complexity and Conflict: Like any character, LGBTQ+ characters should have complex personalities and face conflicts and challenges. However, this is a cozy mystery, so avoid falling into the trap of portraying their sexuality as the source of all their problems or their identity as a burden. The protagonists of cozy mysteries score low on angst and high on self-esteem.

Be Open to Criticism: After publication, be open to feedback from gay readers and the LGBTQ+ community. If you've made mistakes, listen to the consensus of criticism and use it as a learning experience for future writing.

At the same time, one person's opinion is just one person's opinion. I don't care if you're the best writer out there; your work will not be universally loved. That is not a reflection on your work nor on the readers who don't care for your work. Yes, it hurts when people are unkind. Yes, some reviews are unfair. Shake it off.

Look for a *consensus* in order to get a real idea of the validity of your work.

And never forget: the bottom line, i.e., *your sales*, are indeed the bottom line.

Writing diverse characters responsibly is a continuous learning process. It's about showing respect, doing your due diligence in research, and striving for authenticity in your portrayal. Your role as a writer is not only to entertain but to reflect the diversity of the world authentically and sensitively, contributing to a richer, more inclusive storytelling landscape *within the framework of the cozy mystery subgenre.*

YOU ARE WHAT YOU DO

While people of all sexual orientations can be found in every field and occupation, gay men have historically had a significant presence in fashion design, arts and entertainment, hairdressing and cosmetology, interior design, culinary arts, fashion retail and merchandising, event planning and management, social services and mental health, and hospitality and travel. Professional services (fields such as law, medicine, and finance) have seen increasing representation and visibility of gay men, reflecting broader societal changes toward inclusion and diversity.

People, regardless of their sexual orientation, pursue careers based on their interests, skills, and passions, and can excel in any field they choose. The most important thing is to remember that whatever profession you give your protagonist, it must work within the confines of the cozy mystery universe.

That means, whatever your protagonist does, there has to be some reason/excuse for their constant proximity to, and subsequent involvement in, homicide investigations.

Jessica Fletcher Syndrome is one of the most frequently criticized aspects of the cozy mystery subgenre. How can this retired-schoolteacher-now-prolific-mystery-novelist get involved in more than 264 murders? Regardless of where she lives or travels?!

(Granted, it would be equally ridiculous for a private eye, but for some reason, cozies take the greatest amount of heat for being unrealistic.)

The point is, whatever your protagonist ends up doing to earn his or her daily bread, it needs to be something with regular exposure to a large cast of regular *and* revolving characters.

Cozy mysteries often feature protagonists with occupations that naturally immerse them in community life or allow them to stumble upon mysteries in their daily routines.

Here's a list of the most common occupations for cozy mystery protagonists:

Bookstore Owner: Offers a perfect setting for mystery enthusiasts, providing a backdrop for discussions about mystery novels that mirror the protagonist's own investigations. Probably the most overused of occupations, especially considering the struggles of the independent bookstore owner these days.

Librarian: Similar to bookstore owners, librarians are seen as knowledgeable and resourceful, often stumbling upon mysteries through historical documents or library patrons.

Baker or Chef: Food-themed cozy mysteries are incredibly popular, with protagonists using their culinary skills to solve crimes, sometimes with recipes included in the books.

Bed and Breakfast Owner: This setting brings a rotating cast of characters into the protagonist's orbit, making it a fertile ground for mysteries.

Antique Dealer: Allows for mysteries involving historical objects, provenance, and the occasional treasure map.

Gardener or Florist: These protagonists often find themselves involved in mysteries that have a connection to plants, herbs, or poisons.

Craftsperson: Whether they're knitters, quilters, or potters, craftspeople in cozy mysteries often use their specific skills and community connections to solve crimes.

Journalist or Writer: Their investigative skills and curiosity naturally position them as sleuths, using their research for a story or book to solve mysteries.

Teacher or Professor: Offers opportunities for campus-related mysteries or the use of academic knowledge to solve crimes.

Amateur Historian: Fascinated with the past, these protagonists often uncover long-buried secrets or historical crimes that have modern-day implications.

Witch, Vampire, or Other Supernatural Being: The witch or vampire is a relatively recent newcomer to the cozy mystery protagonist pantheon (although Dean James' gay American vampire sleuth Simon Kirby-Jones first appeared in 2002) and the paranormal cozy is a relatively new sub-subgenre. Witches, in particular, are having a moment in cozies. Though they often have magical powers and special training, they too are amateurs when it comes to sleuthing. The witch's effort to navigate between the magical and human realms is often a source of humor. The supernatural elements of these books add an extra layer of fantasy, making the mundane more exciting—and the books have a lot of cross-genre potential.

Sleuths with paranormal abilities used to fall into what we called a "high concept" book.

Essentially, "high concept" refers to a book proposal with a unique, intriguing premise that can be easily summed up in a sentence or two. It's the kind of idea that grabs attention immediately, often because it offers a fresh twist on a familiar theme, promises an unusual setting, or introduces a compelling challenge that hooks the reader's curiosity right off the bat. In short, it's something that makes someone go, "Wow, I've got to read that!"

In the cozy mystery subgenre, a high concept involved an unconventional sleuth or setting, a clever twist on classic mystery elements, or an unexpected theme. For example, a cozy mystery was considered high concept if it featured: an unusual sleuth, a unique setting or profession, innovative twist on a classic element, and/or incorporation of unconventional themes or hobbies.

The point of high concept in cozy mysteries wasn't—isn't—just about being quirky or unique for the sake of it (although, too often, that's what it boiled down to). It's about finding an engaging, novel hook that can sustain interest over the course of a book or series, offering readers not just a puzzle to solve but a distinctive world or perspective to explore. The problem was everyone writing a cozy began, consciously or unconsciously, trying for high concept, which devolved into some truly preposterous premises.

That was an inevitable development in such a competitive market. After all, how many mysteries featuring bookstore sellers can readers consume before they begin to long for the occasional sleuthing step dancer or stevedore?

My point is, if your writing is better than most, you don't need to twist yourself into a knot trying to come up with a gimmick. Your protag's job is ideally one of the more realistic elements in a cozy mystery because their occupation not only defines their role in their community but also provides them with unique skills and knowledge bases that (can) help them solve mysteries. Ice fisherman is an unusual occupation, but is it really practical or useful in the larger context of your series?

There are no new ideas. There are only interesting variations and your unique voice and style.

But I digress.

Less common possible occupations (though most are still used a lot) for your protagonist include: vintage clothing shop owner, member of the clergy, true crime podcaster or blogger, influencer, professional magician, museum curator or docent, herbalist or apothecary, restoration expert, cartographer or map store owner, tour guide, pet groomer, pet walker or veterinarian, wedding planner, bartender, brewmaster or winemaker, archivist, astronomer or planetarium director, film editor, folk singer, puppeteer or clown (JUST CHECKING YOU'RE STILL AWAKE), theater set designer, sound engineer, street artist or street musician, rare book conservator, dance instructor, ethnomusicologist… I mean, if none of these give you any idea for what your protagonist could do for a living, I give up.

Does your protagonist's job have to be something absolutely unique? NO.

Can your protagonist be a retired cop, retired FBI agent, retired PI? NO.

Is it possible I could be wrong? YES.

WRITING MAIN CHARACTERS
WITH CHRONIC ILLNESS OR DISABILITY

If characters of color and the LGBTQ+ community are underrepresented in cozy mystery fiction, characters living with chronic illness or disability are even *more* invisible.

Can you create a cozy mystery series centered around a main character living with chronic illness or disability?

Yes. With a couple of caveats:

1. Just as the most important or interesting thing about your protagonist cannot be their religious affiliation or ethnic or sexual identity, the most important or interesting thing about your gay protagonist cannot be their illness or disability.

2. The main character's illness or disability cannot keep them from taking the lead role in actively sleuthing and solving crimes.

What will not fly in a cozy mystery novel could very well be something that will work beautifully in a traditional crime or mystery novel. I'm not saying—I will never say—you can't write what you want to write. I *am* saying choose your genre carefully and label your books accurately.

If you can't deal with that, you're not going to succeed in publishing. Period.

Now, far from harming your chances of commercial success, writing a cozy mystery protagonist with a chronic illness or disability could actually contribute to its distinctiveness and appeal in today's market.

1. Unique Perspective and Fresh Narratives

Innovative Storytelling: A protagonist with a chronic illness or disability can offer fresh perspectives and innovative storytelling opportunities. Their unique experiences and approaches to solving mysteries can set your series apart from more traditional entries in the genre.

2. Expanding Audience Reach

Untapped Audiences: There's a growing demand for diverse and inclusive representation in literature, including characters with disabilities or chronic illnesses. By catering to this demand, you can tap into audiences looking for stories that reflect their own experiences or offer new insights.

Cross-Genre Appeal: The inclusion of these elements can also attract readers from outside the cozy mystery genre, including those interested in disability advocacy, readers seeking inspirational narratives, and those who appreciate nuanced character development.

3. Building a Loyal Readership

Emotional Connection: Characters who face and overcome everyday challenges can foster a strong emotional connection with readers. This connection can build a loyal readership that is invested in following their journey across multiple books.

Community Engagement: Writing about characters with chronic illnesses or disabilities can engender engagement from communities related to those conditions, who may become champions of your work.

4. Critical Acclaim and Recognition

Critical Acclaim: There's potential for critical acclaim for works that thoughtfully and accurately represent experiences of disability and chronic illness. This acclaim can translate into broader recognition, awards, and increased sales.

Recognition: Books that contribute positively to conversations around disability and inclusion can have a significant social impact, enhancing their visibility and marketability.

5. Marketing and Promotion Opportunities

Niche Marketing: Your series can be marketed directly to communities and organizations that support individuals with chronic illnesses or disabilities, in addition to traditional mystery and cozy mystery readers.

Social Media and Community Building: Platforms such as X (Twitter), Instagram, and disability-focused blogs and forums can be invaluable for building a community around your series, offering direct lines to readers who are actively seeking stories like yours.

Challenges and Considerations in Writing these Characters

If you're going to write a character living with chronic illness or disability, it's important not to just drop your protagonist into a wheelchair and call it a day. You're going to have to navigate the challenges of accurate representation and balancing your themes carefully—while not overwhelming your lighthearted mystery novel.

Ensuring accurate and respectful representation is crucial. Missteps can lead to criticism and alienate readers. Engaging sensitivity readers and doing thorough research can mitigate these risks. At the same time, balancing the cozy mystery elements with the realities of living with a chronic illness or disability requires considerable skill and subtlety, ensuring that one aspect doesn't overshadow the other.

A cozy mystery series featuring a main character with a chronic illness or disability has the *potential* not only to succeed commercially but also to make a meaningful impact on its readers. By offering fresh narratives, reaching untapped audiences, and building a loyal readership, such a series can carve out a unique and cherished place in the cozy mystery landscape.

But this is my opinion and largely theoretical, grounded in broader trends and observations within the publishing industry and reader communities. I don't have specific data on the commercial success of cozy mysteries featuring main characters with chronic illnesses or disabilities.

What I do know for sure is that writing these characters will require the following:

1. Research and Authenticity

In-depth Research: It's crucial to research the specific chronic illness or disability you're writing about to understand its complexities, symptoms, and the ways it affects daily life. This includes medical aspects, personal experiences, and societal implications.

Authentic Representation: Strive for authenticity in how the illness or disability is portrayed, avoiding stereotypes or oversimplifications. Consider the diversity of experiences within any condition; no two people's experiences are exactly alike.

2. Character Depth Beyond Disability

Whole Characters: Ensure the character is fully fleshed out beyond their illness or disability. Their condition is part of who they are but not their entire identity. Focus on their personality, desires, fears, and dreams.

Avoid the "Inspirational" Cliché: Be wary of framing characters with disabilities solely as sources of inspiration, a trope known as "inspiration porn." While resilience can be a part of their story, it should not define their entire narrative.

3. Impact on Daily Life and Relationships

Realistic Challenges: Reflect the realistic challenges and accommodations someone with a chronic illness or disability might face in their daily life, including interactions with the environment, accessibility issues, and societal attitudes.

Relationship Dynamics: Explore how the character's condition affects their relationships with others, including any support systems, and how it informs their interactions and emotional connections.

4. Agency and Empowerment

Active Protagonists: Characters with chronic illnesses or disabilities should be portrayed as active protagonists of their own stories, making decisions, experiencing growth, and driving the plot, rather than being passive figures.

Empowerment: Highlight their agency, skills, and contributions, showing that they are capable and multifaceted individuals. Their journey can include overcoming obstacles but also many other achievements unrelated to their condition.

5. Sensitivity and Respect

Sensitivity Readers: Engaging sensitivity readers who have personal experience with the condition you're writing about can provide invaluable insights and help avoid unintentional harm or misrepresentation.

Respectful Language: Use language that respects the dignity of individuals with disabilities, preferring person-first language ("person with a disability") or identity-first language, depending on individual preference (as seen in some communities, such as the deaf community).

6. Incorporating the Illness or Disability into the Plot

Integral to the Story: While the character's condition should not be their only defining feature, it can play a significant role in the plot. Consider how it influences their motivations, the obstacles they face, and their problem-solving approaches.

Avoid Magical Cures: Be cautious of narratives that unrealistically "cure" the character's condition, which can undermine the authenticity of their experience and the reality of living with chronic conditions or disabilities.

7. Diverse Perspectives and Voices

Multiple Representations: Recognize that there is no single narrative for any illness or disability. Including diverse representations can help showcase a wider range of experiences and counteract stereotypes.

8. Positive Representation

Empathy and Understanding: Aim to foster empathy and understanding through your portrayal, contributing positively to societal perceptions of chronic illness and disability.

By approaching characters with chronic illness or disability with care, research, and respect, you can create rich, nuanced portrayals that resonate with readers, contribute to representation, and enrich your storytelling.

Always keep in mind that the tone of the cozy mystery novel is light and frequently humorous, which means your protagonist must be an active and engaging—sometimes genuinely funny—guide.

Regardless of the challenges and obstacles they've faced in getting to the place where your story begins, a well-written cozy protagonist will have a relatable personality and a distinct voice. A voice that readers recognize as that of a friend.

Ideally, readers come to love that voice and that character—and look forward to sharing each and every one of their adventures.

EXERCISE:
CHARTING A COZY MYSTERY CHARACTER ARC

Here's a step-by-step exercise to chart out a character arc in a cozy mystery, designed to help you explore and develop your protagonist's journey in detail.

Step 1: Define the Ordinary World

Description: Start by describing your protagonist's normal life before the mystery begins. What is their profession? What are their hobbies? Who are the people in their life?

Exercise: Write a short paragraph detailing a day in the life of your protagonist before the story starts. Figure out their journey to recognizing or accepting their sexual identity. (This is for *your* benefit. It probably won't play a role in the story.)

Step 2: Identify the Call to Adventure

Description: Determine the event that draws your protagonist into the mystery. This should disrupt their ordinary world in some significant way.

Exercise: Create a scenario where your protagonist encounters the mystery for the first time. What are their initial thoughts or feelings about it?

Step 3: Outline Trials and Tribulations

Description: Think about the obstacles, challenges, and conflicts your protagonist will face while solving the mystery. Include both external conflicts (with suspects or situations) and internal conflicts (doubts, fears).

Exercise: List at least three significant challenges your protagonist will encounter and how they plan to overcome them.

Step 4: Growth and Discovery

Description: Consider how your protagonist will grow or what they will discover about themselves or the world around them as they solve the mystery.

Exercise: Write a pivotal scene where your protagonist learns something crucial about themselves or makes a significant discovery related to the mystery.

Step 5: Climax

Description: Plan the climax of the mystery where your protagonist confronts the culprit or solves the central mystery.

Exercise: Sketch out the climax scene, focusing on how your protagonist uses their wits, skills, or newfound knowledge to resolve the situation. This should be exciting, but not violent.

Step 6: Resolution

Description: Imagine how your protagonist's world looks after the mystery is solved. How have they changed? What does their new "ordinary" look like?

Exercise: Write a closing scene that shows your protagonist's life after the mystery has been solved, highlighting any changes in their character or situation.

Step 7: Reflection

Description: Reflect on the character arc and the journey your protagonist has undergone.

Exercise: Answer the following questions:

- What was the most significant change in your protagonist's character?
- How did the challenges faced during the mystery contribute to this change?
- Is there anything your protagonist has lost or given up by the end of the story? What have they gained?

This exercise will help you develop a nuanced and compelling character arc for your cozy mystery's protagonist, grounding their transformation in the unique challenges and discoveries of the story.

EXERCISE:
THE CHARACTER INTERVIEW

Objective: *This exercise aims to help writers explore their character's psyche, background, and motivations through an in-depth interview process.*

Instructions:

Create a Set of Interview Questions: Start with basic questions about the character's background, including their upbringing, education, and key life events. Then, delve deeper with questions about their fears, dreams, secrets, and regrets. Include questions that explore their relationships with other characters, their moral compass, and how they react under stress.

Conduct the Interview: Write out your character's responses as if you're conducting a real interview. Try to answer in *their voice*, capturing their personality and how they might actually speak. This process can reveal new insights about your character and how they view the world.

Reflect on Their Answers and Potential Actions: After the interview, think about how their background and personality traits would influence their actions in your story. Consider how they would react to the main plot points and challenges they face.

For gaining psychological insights into your main character, crafting questions that probe deeply into their psyche, motivations, and fears can be incredibly revealing. Here are some time-honored character questions that can help you uncover the complex layers of your character's mind and heart:

1.   What is your character's most treasured memory, and why does it hold such significance?

     This question can reveal what your character values most and why, providing insights into their emotional world.

2. What is your character's greatest fear, and has it changed over time?

    Understanding their fears can reveal vulnerabilities and how past experiences shape their present actions and reactions.

3. What regret does your character live with, and how has it influenced their choices?

    Regrets can be a powerful motivator or inhibitor, affecting decisions and relationships.

4. In moments of self-doubt, what thoughts are most likely to plague your character?

    This question delves into insecurities and internal conflicts, showing how they might impact the character's self-esteem and actions.

5. What lie does your character tell themselves, and why?

    Identifying a self-deception can unveil deep-seated beliefs and the discrepancies between their perceived and true selves.

6. How does your character justify their flaws or mistakes to themselves?

    This can reveal your character's capacity for self-reflection, denial, or growth.

7. What does your character most dislike about themselves, and how do they cope with or hide it?

    This question uncovers insecurities and how they affect the character's interactions with others and their self-image.

8. What situation or event would push your character out of their comfort zone, and how would they react?

    Responses to stress or fear can highlight resilience, adaptability, and hidden strengths or weaknesses.

9. How does your character feel about being alone?

    Their comfort or discomfort with solitude can indicate deeper feelings about independence, loneliness, and self-reliance.

10. What does your character believe is their purpose or mission in life? Has this belief been challenged?

    This explores the character's motivations, ambitions, and the potential for existential crises or moments of clarity.

11. How does your character react to betrayal or disappointment?

    This can show the character's capacity for forgiveness, resilience, and how they navigate trust issues.

12. What kind of legacy does your character wish to leave behind?

    This question probes into the character's long-term goals and values, and what they hope to achieve or be remembered for.

These questions encourage deep th nking about your character's psychological makeup, driving forces, and how their mind works. But I'd throw in a few more basic questions: Does your character believe in God? What makes your character most happy? What song does your character love the most right now? What is your character's earliest childhood memory? Is your character a good driver? Was your character popular in high school? When and with whom was the first time your character fell in love? What is the funniest movie your character ever saw? Does your character get along with his parents? Is your character an only child or does your character have siblings— and what is his relationship to them? Does your character make friends easily? Does your character believe that everything works out for the best?

Remember, we're writing cozy mysteries, so we don't want to get too dark here. A history of abuse or molestation, or violent experiences are powerful backgrounds for different stories and different characters.

Every book cannot be everything to every reader.

By understanding characters' backgrounds, personalities, and daily lives, authors can create more nuanced and engaging narratives that resonate with readers.

EXERCISE:
THE DAY-IN-THE-LIFE

Objective: This exercise is designed to help authors understand their characters' daily lives and routines, revealing their habits, quirks, and how they interact with their world. Understanding your character's normal routine will show you how to really shake things up once the trouble starts.

Instructions:

Choose a Day: Select a typical day in your character's life before the main events of your story take place. It could be a workday, a day off, or a day with a special significance to them.

Detail Their Routine: Write a narrative or a detailed outline describing their entire day, from the moment they wake up to when they go to bed. Include mundane details such as what they eat for breakfast, how they commute, and how they interact with people throughout the day.

Incorporate Internal Thoughts: As you describe their day, include their internal monologue. What do they think about as they go about their routine? How do they feel about the people they encounter? This insight can add depth to their character.

Identify Character Traits: Use this story to highlight your character's traits, such as their kindness shown by small acts of helping others, their meticulous nature revealed through their habits, or their social awkwardness in interactions.

This exercise encourages you to think deeply about how your character interacts with the world when they are not solving crimes or facing possibly dangerous challenges. By visualizing them going through an ordinary day, you can hopefully see how to make them more real and relatable.

- 3 -

HOME SWEET HOME – SETTING

*The quality of **niceness** is not strained; It droppeth as the gentle rain from heaven*

Upon the place beneath. It is twice blest: It blesseth him that gives and him that takes.

S O YEAH, I'M CRIBBING FROM SHAKESPEARE.
     When we talk about setting in the cozy mystery, we're really talking about world building. In a funny way, the world of the cozy mystery protagonist is just as elaborate as that of any fantasy novel.

But before we get into world-building, let's cogitate about the quality of *niceness*. Because it is central to the cozy mystery.

"Nice" is one of those wonderfully flexible words that can mean different things to different folks, but at its core, it describes something positive, agreeable, or pleasant. When we talk about something being "nice," we're often referring to qualities that evoke feelings of warmth, comfort, or satisfaction.

Niceness can be defined in various contexts: It can refer to the quality of something. Saying something is made of "nice material" suggests it's of high quality or particularly well-made. In some cases, "nice" can imply a level of refinement or subtlety. A nice dress might not just be beautiful but also elegant and tastefully chosen. And, though less common, "nice" can be used to describe actions that are morally commendable or virtuous, suggesting a sense of righteousness or goodness.

I know you know.

But at its most basic, nice means exactly what you think it does, something pleasant or agreeable. It describes something that is pleasing to the senses or the mind. A nice day might be sunny and warm, while a nice meal might be tasty and satisfying. If we're speaking about a person who is nice, we're often reflecting on their kindness, friendliness, and consideration for others. A nice person is someone who treats others well, shows empathy, and is generally pleasant to be around.

Niceness is a trite word for the elements that make civilized society possible.

Cozy mysteries are about nice people in nice places trying to deal with the ultimate in not-niceness: murder.

Some people scorn the idea of niceness. These people probably do not read, and certainly should not try to write, cozy mysteries.

The skepticism or scorn toward the idea of niceness often stems from a variety of perceptions and experiences. Here are a few reasons why some people might view niceness with a critical eye:

Perceived Inauthenticity: Some people equate niceness with a lack of authenticity, suspecting that nice gestures or polite behavior are performed out of obligation or a desire to manipulate, rather than from genuine kindness.

Association with Weakness: Niceness is sometimes mistakenly seen as a sign of weakness or lack of assertiveness. In cultures that highly value competitiveness and strength, being nice might be viewed as a lack of ambition or resolve.

Fear of Exploitation: There's a concern that being nice makes one vulnerable to being taken advantage of. This perspective is particularly prevalent in environments where trust is low, and there's a high emphasis on self-protection.

Overemphasis on Niceness: When people prioritize being nice over being honest or direct, it can lead to situations where important issues are glossed over or not addressed. This can create frustration among those who value transparency and straightforwardness.

Cynicism: In a world where people are often exposed to negative news and experiences, some develop a cynical view toward acts of kindness, questioning the motives behind them or dismissing them as naïve.

Cultural Differences: What is considered nice behavior in one culture might not be viewed the same way in another. This can lead to misunderstandings or a devaluation of niceness as people navigate different cultural norms.

I know. It's a lot of analysis for something you're pretty sure you already understand. But it is relevant because if you're writing a gay cozy mystery, there's a high probability you're going to be writing a gay male protagonist, which means your protagonist is going to be the dreaded Nice Guy.

The term "nice guy" has become a pejorative for men who claim to be nice but feel entitled to romantic or sexual attention because of their niceness. This has led some to be wary of those who overtly emphasize their own niceness. It also, historically, refers to guys who are decent but dull as ditchwater. Nice guys usually don't get the girls (or boys). Bad Boys are typically romantic leads.

Is there anything more damning than to be dismissed as "nice enough"?

Despite these perspectives, it's important to recognize that genuine kindness and consideration for others are valued across many cultures and communities. The key distinction often lies in the authenticity of one's actions and the balance between being nice and maintaining other important values, such as honesty and integrity.

Now, back to world-building.

Your nice guys (and gals) live in nice places.

The ideal setting for a cozy mystery plays a crucial role in setting the tone and atmosphere of the story.

While the "ideal" can vary depending on the story's specific needs and the author's vision, certain elements are commonly found in successful cozy mystery settings that contribute to the genre's charm and appeal. Some of this is liable to feel repetitive because we've already talked a lot about community and place, but here are some of the things that you'll want to take into account when deciding where to set your cozy mystery:

Small Town or Close-Knit Community: Part of why you want to set your story in a close-knit community where everyone knows each other is because it allows the amateur sleuth to use personal relationships to gather clues. It also heightens the tension when the suspect is someone well-known to the protagonist and the community. We just don't expect people we know, and *especially* people we like, to commit murder.

Quaint and Picturesque: The setting often has a quaint, picturesque quality that gives readers a kind of staycation vibe. Think charming villages, coastal towns, or idyllic countryside locations. The beauty and tranquility of the setting contrast with the crime, adding an element of armchair travel as well as depth to the story.

Unique or Niche Setting: A setting that revolves around a particular hobby, occupation, or interest can add flavor to a cozy mystery. For example, a bookstore, bakery, winery, or antique shop not only provides a backdrop for the story but also weaves in thematic elements related to the setting. But so does setting your story in Chinatown or on an archeological site or in a theme park.

Isolated or Contained: Settings that isolate the characters, such as a manor house during a storm, a cruise ship, or an island resort, can ramp up the suspense. The isolation not only means the suspect is likely among the known characters, but also that it's going to be very difficult to get any help from the outside world, which intensifies the mystery.

Historical or Cultural Richness: A setting with historical significance or cultural richness can add layers to the narrative, allowing the mystery to delve into past events, local legends, or cultural customs that play into the plot. Think Mystic Seaport or Williamsburg Historic Area or South Park City.

A Sense of Community: Beyond the physical location, the ideal setting for a cozy mystery includes a strong sense of community. This might mean festivals, local traditions, or communal activities that bring characters together and provide opportunities for the sleuth to investigate.

Charm with a Dash of Mystery: Ultimately, the setting should have a certain charm that entices readers, combined with an undercurrent of mystery or secrets. This balance keeps readers engaged, both by the allure of the setting and the intrigue of the unfolding mystery.

An ideal cozy mystery setting is one that serves as more than just a backdrop; it becomes a character in its own right, contributing to the story's mood, providing clues, and influencing the characters' actions and interactions. The choice of setting can significantly impact the story's dynamics, making it a critical element in crafting a compelling cozy mystery.

Can a cozy mystery take place in the middle of Manhattan? Sure! Take a look at *Only Murders in the Building*.

While the Arconia sits in the middle of one of the largest and busiest cities in the world, all the real action and excitement take place between those four—well, however many—apartment walls. The crimes are small and intimate, as is the cast of suspects and sleuths.

While the charm of cozy mysteries often lies in their settings, some locales have become particularly popular—so much so that they might be considered overused by some readers and writers.

That said, they're popular for a reason:

Small English Village: The quintessential cozy mystery setting, popularized by Agatha Christie's Miss Marple series. Its charm and quaintness are undeniable, but it's been used extensively.

Quaint Seaside Towns: These offer picturesque settings and a tight-knit community feel, but they're a common choice for many cozy series, especially those with themes of hidden treasures or maritime mysteries.

Bookstores and Libraries: No, nobody is living in the bookstore. (Oh. Wait.) But some of these locales are the primary backdrop for the cozy mystery novel's action. They're a natural fit for mystery lovers, featuring protagonists who are booksellers or librarians, and have become a staple of the genre.

Bakeries, Cafés, and Coffee Houses: Food-themed cozies remain super popular, with bakeries and cafés serving as the epicenter for community gossip and, consequently, mystery solving.

Bed and Breakfasts: The idea of a B&B in a lovely setting is appealing. It's a frequently used locale where the proprietors often find themselves embroiled in solving crimes among their guests.

Craft and Antique Shops: These settings lend themselves to stories involving hidden treasures and historical mysteries but have become common scenes for cozy mysteries. I still dream about Rogue's Gallery in Innisdale.

Small New England—okay, Small Anywhere-in-America Towns: Similar to the English village but set in the US, these towns are often characterized by their celebrations, historical landmarks, and local businesses, and are a go-to setting for many series. Amish towns are especially popular (for reasons that escape me).

Historic Mansions or Estates: Settings that include family secrets, hidden rooms, and a touch of the aristocratic have been well-trodden paths in the cozy mystery landscape. I love these so much, but yeah, obviously frequently used.

Gardens and Greenhouses: Twenty years ago, mysteries that involved botany or gardening offered a unique twist. Now, the setting of a garden, greenhouse, or even a flower shop is much more common.

Picturesque European Locations: From the vineyards of France to the canals of Venice, these idyllic European settings are appealing but are often chosen for cozy mystery series looking for an exotic touch.

While these locales are popular for good reasons, offering built-in charm, community, and intrigue, there's a wide world of underexplored settings that could provide fresh and exciting backdrops for cozy mysteries. Exploring less conventional locales could be a great way to stand out in the genre.

The challenge of getting more inventive and original is that in order to run a series, you have to set your series in a locale that could believably be home to a LOT of murder. If it was hard to believe in

Cabot Cove, it's going to be even harder to believe at a space station. HOWEVER...

Venturing into underexplored settings can breathe new life into cozy mysteries, offering fresh and captivating backdrops for your storytelling. Here are some less conventional locales that could provide intriguing settings for cozy mysteries:

A Theater Production Company: The actual venue or physical location might change but the central cast of characters would be largely the same.

A Tour Bus: This cast of victims and suspects would change, of course, but our sleuths could be the regular tour bus staff—a young, quirky crew reveling in their chance to see the world for "free." Too bad about all those murderous tourists!

Scientific Research Stations: Imagine a mystery set in an Antarctic research station or a remote observatory. The isolation and unique challenges of these locales add an interesting layer to solving mysteries. (I know. I hate science, too.)

A Hotel, Hunting Lodge, Expedition, or Safari: Heck, a camping trip in a remote location. The challenge here, as with the tour bus, is that rarely is a cozy mystery a standalone, so you do have to deal with a constantly revolving cast of characters. But it works for *The White Lotus* (which is not a cozy mystery, by the way).

Boarding Schools or Universities: While not entirely untouched, the academic intrigue of boarding schools or universities outside the typical English setting—think different countries or unusual disciplines—can offer a rich tapestry for mysteries. A finishing school, art school, chef school, etc.

Public Markets and Bazaars: Setting a cozy mystery in a bustling market or bazaar, with its array of stalls, merchants, and diverse goods, could provide a colorful and dynamic setting ripe for intrigue and hidden secrets.

Any Place Snowed in or Under Quarantine: THIS COULD WORK FOR A SHORT RUN.

A Reality Show Location: Again, our regular cast and crew would be our sleuths, and the victims would come from the rotating contestants.

Magic Shops, Witch Shops, or Magic Castle-esque Locations: Whether your sleuth is mortal or has supernatural attributes, these can all work.

Classic Cruise Ship, Luxury Train, or River Cruise Ship: While trains and cruise ships have a classic association with mysteries, modern takes or less-explored routes (such as luxury river cruises in exotic locations) can offer new twists.

Theme Parks or Carnivals: As mentioned above, the magic and mystery of theme parks or traveling carnivals provide a backdrop full of potential for hidden agendas, long-held secrets, and intricate puzzles. CREEPY CLOWNS. Enough said.

Historical Reenactment Sites: A small variation on historic venues, a mystery set against the backdrop of a historical reenactment, whether it's a Renaissance fair or a Civil War battlefield, combines historical intrigue with the passion of those who bring history to life.

Eco-Communities or Off-the-Grid Locations: Settings that explore sustainable living or off-the-grid communities can introduce unique lifestyles and philosophies, alongside mysteries that challenge conventional thinking.

Archaeological Digs: Agatha Christie got a lot of mileage out of archeological digs. A cozy mystery set on an archaeological site could unearth ancient secrets alongside the more immediate mystery, blending history with suspense. And, very often, archeological teams work a site for years.

Space Stations or Colonies: For a futuristic twist, setting a cozy mystery in space, whether on a space station or a colony on another planet, can explore the confines of a close-knit community in the vastness of space.

Virtual Realities: As technology advances, mysteries set in virtual reality worlds could explore themes of identity, reality, and the digital footprint, offering a modern take on the genre. Maybe a little too on the nose these days? You decide.

These settings not only provide a theoretically unique backdrop for your mystery but also allow for exploration of different cultures, technologies, and lifestyles, adding depth and variety to the cozy mystery genre.

Each setting offers its own set of rules, community dynamics, and secrets, making for an engaging and fresh narrative experience.

That said, some of the most unique settings listed above would also be the most difficult to use in a long-running series. When choosing your cozy mystery setting, the main things to consider are:

1. How much do you love this place? Will you still love it six books from now? Does it have enough room to grow—meaning, is it large enough (in possibilities not just square footage) for continual discoveries and revelations?

2. Are you going to be able make this location uniquely your own?

3. Is this location going to appeal to a lot of readers?

Yes, cute, quaint villages are WAY overused. But readers still love them—and probably always will (if Hallmark's Christmas season scheduling is anything to judge by). You can make your village feel familiar and beloved yet unique and fresh if you know how to spruce the place up.

Do you?

Or do you typically describe settings with a quick generic description?

Creating a setting that feels real to readers involves weaving together various literary elements that engage the senses, evoke emotions, and build a believable world.

Here are some key elements to consider when crafting a setting that resonates with realism and depth:

Vivid Sensory Details: Use descriptive language that appeals to the five senses—sight, sound, smell, taste, and touch. Describe the way a place looks during different times of the day, the sounds that fill the air, the scents that linger, the textures of objects, and even the taste of the local cuisine. Sensory details immerse readers in the setting, making it feel lived-in and real.

Cultural Nuances (Real or Made Up): Every place has its own culture, traditions, and social norms. Including details about local customs, languages, clothing, festivals, and everyday behaviors can add depth and authenticity to your setting. These elements help readers understand the social dynamics and cultural context in which your characters operate.

Geographical and Environmental Details: The geography and environment of your setting can significantly affect the story's atmosphere and the characters' lives. Describing the landscape, weather patterns, flora, and fauna can ground your story in a specific location and influence the plot and character interactions. What time is sunrise during the summer? How cold does it get during the winter? Do *&&^^%$#@@ing hummingbirds live there? (Yes, the hummingbirds are a little inside joke.)

Historical Background: Even if your story is set in a fantasy or futuristic world, knowing the history of the place can add layers of richness. Mentioning historical events, local legends, or generational tales can provide a sense of timelessness and continuity—whether you made them up five minutes ago or not.

Economic and Political Context: The economic conditions and political landscape can shape the setting's feel and the characters' lives. Describing the local economy, class divisions, political tensions, or governance structures can lend credibility to the setting and motivate character actions. Just stay off the soapbox.

Architecture and Urban Planning: The design of buildings, streets, and public spaces can tell readers a lot about a place's character, history, and the people who live there. Whether it's the opulence of a wealthy neighborhood, the cramped quarters of a bustling city, or the rustic charm of a rural village, architectural details help paint a vivid picture.

Social Interactions and Community Life: How people interact with each other in public and private spaces reveals much about the setting. Describing market scenes, family gatherings, religious services, or nightlife can bring the social fabric of your setting to life.

Everyday Life and Routine: The mundanity of daily life—commuting, working, shopping, eating—though seemingly trivial, can significantly contribute to the realism of a setting. Is there a tourist season? Is there an "off" season? On what industry is the local economy built? Showing characters navigating their everyday routines helps readers relate to the world you've created.

Contrasts and Conflicts: Real places are filled with contrasts and conflicts, whether they're cultural, social, environmental, or political. Including these elements can add tension and drama, making the setting more dynamic and engaging. However, contemporary cozy or not, I'd avoid getting into political specifics. You can still demonstrate the political causes and values important to your character without coming right out and saying it. I mean, if you're writing a gay cozy mystery, we can probably make one or two assumptions.

Finally, don't forget to make the settings where your character works and sleeps feel real. You don't need paragraphs, let alone pages of details.

It's about quality not quantity of detail.

And don't info dump it all at once. You're not a real estate agent giving a house tour. Give the reader a quick snapshot of where your character is—allow the reader to see what you're seeing, what the character is seeing—and consider the lens through which the character views their surroundings. An interior decorator or someone in the process of renovating their house is going to notice different things than an art collector or art restorer. A bookseller is going to notice bookshelves. A cook is going to pay attention to the kitchen. Everybody is going to notice my Christmas decorations are still up in March.

Setting provides clues to character; setting tells us about the characters who inhabit these spaces.

But also, setting is one of the most powerful tools you have in creating an immersive experience for your reader. The more vibrant and real you can make your settings feel the more deeply entranced in the story your reader will be.

Again, it's not about a *lot* of detail. It's the *type* of detail.

Pay attention to backgrounds in the TV shows and movies you watch. Flip through magazines. Direct your telescope toward your neighbors' windows.

I'M KIDDING.

But you get the idea. Talking heads are never a good thing in fiction, but they are especially not a good thing when your goal is to create a snuggly cocoon for the reader.

Take the time to consider whether you can add a bit of sensory detail to each scene—or whether those details are going to distract from the action. People aren't noticing flower arrangements when they've just caught their prime suspect in a lie—unless the flower arrangement *is* the lie.

By considering and integrating these elements thoughtfully, you can create a setting that not only supports your story but also becomes a character in its own right, enriching the narrative and captivating your readers with its originality, realism, and depth.

EXERCISE 1:
THE SENSORY MAP

Crafting charming yet believable settings is key to the allure of cozy mysteries. Here are two exercises designed to help aspiring authors develop such settings with depth and authenticity.

Objective: *This exercise encourages authors to create a multi-sensory experience of their setting, making it come alive for readers by engaging all five senses.*

Instructions:

Select Your Setting: Begin with a general idea of your setting, whether it's a quaint village, a seaside town, or a unique establishment like a bookstore or café.

Create a Sensory Chart: Make a chart with five columns, one for each of the senses: sight, sound, smell, taste, and touch.

Fill in the Chart: For each sense, list details specific to your setting. For example, for a small village, you might include the sight of colorful cottages, the sound of a local festival, the smell of fresh bread from the bakery, the taste of the signature dish at the local pub, and the touch of hand-woven textiles at the market.

Expand Each Detail: Take each sensory detail and write a short paragraph expanding on it. Describe a scene or a moment in your story where this detail comes to the forefront, making the setting feel real and vibrant.

Integrate the Details: Look for ways to weave these sensory details into your narrative, setting descriptions, and character interactions to enrich the atmosphere and depth of your setting.

EXERCISE 2:
THE SETTING'S BIOGRAPHY

Objective: This exercise aims to develop the history and personality of the setting, treating it as if it were a character in your story. HUMOR ME.

Instructions:

Outline the Setting's History: Start by jotting down key historical events that have shaped your setting. Consider founding stories, notable inhabitants, significant changes over time, and any legends or mysteries associated with it.

Describe the Setting's Personality: Just as you would with a character, describe your setting's personality. Is it warm and welcoming? Mysterious and secretive? Bustling and energetic? Consider how the setting's "personality" affects the mood of your story and the lives of your characters.

Identify Key Landmarks: Choose a few landmarks or focal points in your setting (e.g., a historic inn, a mysterious forest, a charming art gallery) and write a brief backstory for each. Explain their significance to the community and how they contribute to the setting's charm and mystery.

Develop the Social Dynamics: Describe the social fabric and community life in your setting. How do residents interact? What are the local traditions, festivals, or events? How do these social dynamics influence the mysteries in your story?

Reflect on Change: Consider how your setting has evolved over time and how it continues to change. Reflect on how these changes impact the setting's character and the storylines it inspires.

By completing these exercises, aspiring authors can craft settings for their cozy mysteries that are not only charming and inviting but also richly detailed and believably woven into the fabric of their stories. These settings will become more than just backdrops; they'll be integral components that enrich the narrative and captivate readers.

P.S. You can cannibalize these notes later on.

- 4 -
A SERIES OF UNFORTUNATE EVENTS – SERIES

THE MAJORITY OF COZY MYSTERIES—IN FACT, ONE OF THE MAJOR selling points of cozy mysteries—is that these books are largely *series* books. So, before we go any further, we need to discuss the elements of writing a series.

The decision to write a series is ideally made *before* the first book is even written. This is for reasons both creative and strategic.

Here are key reasons why this foresight can be beneficial:

Character Development: Remember our discussion of character arc? Planning for a series allows you to design characters with depth and complexity that can evolve over time. You can introduce backgrounds, traits, and multiple story and character arcs that unfold gradually, keeping readers engaged and eager to see how characters grow across books.

World-Building: With a series in mind, it makes sense to invest time in research and world-building to create a rich and detailed setting that serves as more than just a backdrop for the initial story. This world can expand and deepen with each book, becoming a character in its own right that readers grow to love and look forward to revisiting.

Plot Planning: Knowing you have multiple books allows you to plot not only the arc of each individual book but also an overarching narrative that spans the series. It reminds you to pace yourself and resist the temptation to throw everything you've got into the first book. And it gives you so many more tools, including foreshadowing, developing long-term mysteries, and weaving in subplots that can be explored in more detail in later books to entice and tantalize readers.

Reader Investment: See above. A series offers readers the chance to invest in your characters and the world you've created, building a loyal fan base. If readers know from the start that there's more to come, they're more likely to commit to the first book and anticipate subsequent entries.

Marketing and Sales Potential: From a practical perspective, series have strong marketing and sales potential. They offer multiple points of entry for new readers and provide ongoing opportunities for promotion. Each new book can rejuvenate interest in earlier ones, helping to sustain sales over time.

Creative Momentum: Writing a series can give you, as the author, a clear sense of direction and purpose. Knowing where your story is headed in the long term can fuel your creativity and motivation, making the writing process more focused and enjoyable.

Setting Up Intrigue: The initial book can plant seeds of intrigue that bloom in later volumes, setting up mysteries, character dilemmas, or world secrets that tantalize readers and keep them coming back for more.

Efficient Use of Research: If your series involves extensive research (as is often the case with mystery and crime fiction, especially those involving art crime or historical elements), planning ahead means you can leverage your research across multiple books, making the most of your efforts.

Deciding to write a series from the outset allows for a strategic approach to storytelling, character development, and marketing. It offers the opportunity to build a more compelling and immersive world that can captivate readers over time, establishing a lasting legacy for your work.

Does every idea for a cozy mystery have the potential to turn into the first book in a series? NO.

Is it okay to write a standalone cozy mystery? YES.

But you've already seen there are obvious advantages to writing a series.

Readers adore series books for a multitude of reasons, many of which are rooted in the immersive and evolving nature of extended storytelling.

While it's certainly true that there's an increasing pushback from readers who feel cheated by series that have been milked dry or by books being turned into series when there isn't enough story to support a long run, there are several key factors that contribute to the overall popularity of series among readers, especially in genres like mystery and crime fiction:

Character Development: Series allow for deeper exploration and development of characters. Readers become invested in the characters' journeys, watching them grow, change, and face challenges over time. This investment creates a strong emotional bond between readers and characters, making them eager to follow their stories across multiple books.

Extended World-Building: A series offers the space to build rich, detailed worlds that readers can lose themselves in. The more time readers spend in a world, the more real and vivid it becomes to them. This depth of setting is particularly appealing in genres where the setting plays a crucial role, such as fantasy, science fiction, and certain types of mystery and crime fiction.

Complex Plots: With more room to unfold, series can tackle complex, multi-layered plots that wouldn't fit within the confines of a single book. This complexity, with intertwining subplots and long arcs, keeps readers hooked and guessing, eager to see how everything resolves in the end.

Satisfying Payoffs: Series allow for the setup and payoff of long-term story arcs. The anticipation of resolution, and the satisfaction when it finally arrives, is a powerful draw for readers. The delayed gratification of watching plot threads weave together over time adds to the reading experience.

Sense of Community: Following a series often involves joining a community of fans. Readers enjoy discussing theories, sharing their favorite moments, and anticipating the next installment together. This sense of community and shared experience can enhance the enjoyment of the series.

Emotional Investment: Spending time across several books allows readers to become emotionally invested in the characters and their world. This investment makes triumphs more thrilling and setbacks more heart-wrenching, engaging readers on a deeper level.

Reliable Entertainment: Once readers find a series they love, it becomes a reliable source of entertainment. Knowing there are more books to look forward to can be comforting and exciting, offering a guaranteed escape into a familiar world.

Character Familiarity: Returning to a series is like visiting old friends. Readers enjoy the familiarity of characters and settings, taking pleasure in experiencing new adventures with well-loved characters.

Discovery and Exploration: Each new book in a series offers the opportunity to discover more about the characters, the world, and the overarching story. This continuous exploration keeps the series fresh and engaging.

Completion and Closure: For many readers, there's a deep satisfaction in seeing a series through to its conclusion. The journey with the characters and the buildup of plot culminate in a final resolution that, ideally, provides a sense of closure and completion.

Series books offer a unique, immersive experience that standalone novels can't match. They provide a complex, evolving narrative that allows readers to dive deep into the worlds and lives of their favorite characters, making series a beloved format for many.

Are there "bad" reasons for creating a series? Maybe not *bad*, per se, but weak reasons, yes. Definitely.

1. Emotional Attachment

One of the very weakest reasons is because you really love those characters and that world, and you just aren't ready to give them up. Yeah. No. That's not enough of a reason to keep writing in that universe. Especially if you've already wrapped everything up with a neat bow or chose to end on a powerful but ambiguous note.

Don't second guess yourself. There will be other worlds and other characters you love just as much. Know when to say goodbye.

2. Readers Are Asking for More

Who the hell is driving this car? *Readers are asking for more* is probably the poorest of reasons. If a book is good, readers ALWAYS ask for more. That's not sufficient reason to try to turn a standalone into a series. Beware the trap of the disappointing sequel. A weak sequel actually diffuses the power of the first book. Do you really want to hear twenty years of *Yeah, the first book was great, but the second...*

3. The First Book Did Really Well

I should hope so. I should hope all your books do really well. Having a book do really well should not be a rarity in your writing career. I refer you to my original point: If you've already wrapped everything up with a neat bow *or* chose to end on a powerful but ambiguous note, scrambling to come up with enough story for a sequel, let alone a series, is going to be an exercise in frustration for you and your readers. Come on, we've all seen that disappointing movie, the confusing and rushed sequel to the film we loved so much. Unless you've still got a whole lot of story left to tell, don't try to recreate history.

So how do you know if your story idea has what it takes to turn into a series?

Story Potential: Consider whether your central concept has the legs to span multiple books. Does the world you're creating have enough depth, intrigue, and unexplored corners to sustain readers' interest over several volumes? A series requires a rich setting, complex characters, and evolving plot lines that can keep the narrative fresh and engaging.

Character Depth and Development: Are your characters compelling and complex enough to grow and evolve across multiple books? Readers return to series partly because they're invested in the characters. Your protagonist and supporting cast need to have enough potential for development to carry them through various challenges and arcs. That means they have to start with problems or challenges that cannot be completely solved within the first book.

Author Commitment: Writing a series is a significant commitment. Are you passionate enough about the story and characters to spend *years* working with them? Consider your long-term interest and whether you have the dedication to see the series through to its conclusion. Maybe start with a trilogy? See where that leaves you.

Market Viability: Research the market to determine if there's an audience for your series. Cozy mysteries are *extremely* friendly to series. However, there are a lot of cozy mystery series out there already. Does your concept have what it takes to compete in that crowded marketplace?

Structural Planning: Think about whether you prefer the structure and planning involved in series writing. Not everyone has the attention span for a series. Which is fine. A series can demand intricate plotting to weave threads across books while ensuring each installment offers a satisfying conclusion. Are you prepared for the challenge of balancing overarching storylines with the self-contained narratives of individual books?

Financial Considerations: Series can be financially advantageous, as each book can drive sales of others in the series. However, the initial investment in time before seeing a return might be significant. It typically takes until books 5–8 to see really strong financial returns on a series. Assess your financial expectations and how a series fits into them.

Creative Flexibility: Consider whether you enjoy working within the same world and with the same characters over time. While a series can provide a rich canvas for storytelling, it requires consistency and a certain level of creative constraint compared to standalone projects. While there is a level of comfort and familiarity in writing a series, you're going to find yourself boxed in by what you've already created. Not to mention, there are A LOT of details to keep track of when writing a series, especially a series with a large cast such as the typical cozy entails.

Reader Engagement: Series have the advantage of building a loyal readership. Think about whether you're ready to engage with a community of readers who will have expectations and hopes for your series' direction. There's nothing like having a reader inform you your character would never do something you've planned for them to do for the past three years.

Publishing Strategy: Decide on your publishing strategy early on. If you're aiming for traditional publishing, consider that publishers often look for series potential in mystery and crime fiction. If you're all about self-publishing, think about your capacity to produce books at a pace that keeps readers engaged.

Deciding to write a series is a significant but potentially rewarding decision. It requires careful consideration to ensure that both you and your readers find the journey fulfilling and enjoyable.

If you do decide to write a series, you will *definitely* have to have a series bible.

A series bible is essentially a comprehensive guidebook that writers use to maintain consistency across a series. It's a treasure trove of information on characters, settings, plot points, themes, and anything else relevant to the series. Think of it as a map or a reference tool that helps you keep track of all the intricate details of your world, ensuring that characters stay true to their development and the series remains coherent from book to book. It's particularly handy for avoiding contradictions and for keeping the small details that enrich a story consistent throughout your writing, especially useful in genres like mystery and crime fiction, where complexity and detail are key.

You don't have to maintain the bible yourself (I hire someone for that), but *someone* has to keep it updated—and updated accurately.

Creating a series bible ahead of time offers numerous advantages for authors, especially when tackling a series with intricate plots, a large cast of characters, and a detailed setting. A series bible is essentially a reference document that contains all the crucial information about your series, ensuring consistency and aiding in the development of your story. Here are some key advantages of having a series bible from the outset:

Maintains Consistency: One of the primary benefits is the maintenance of consistency across books. A series bible helps keep track of character details (such as physical descriptions, backgrounds, and relationships), settings (geographic details, cultural norms), and plot points (key events, timelines) to prevent discrepancies that could confuse readers or undermine the story's believability.

Enhances Continuity: For series with complex plots and long character arcs, a bible ensures continuity of storylines and character development. It helps you remember what has already happened and what's been hinted at, allowing for the seamless weaving of narratives across multiple volumes.

Facilitates Efficient Writing: With a comprehensive guide at your fingertips, you spend less time searching through previous manuscripts for details, making the writing process more efficient. It reduces the need for extensive revisions due to inconsistencies and helps speed up the writing of subsequent books.

Aids in World-Building: A series set in a richly detailed world benefits greatly from a bible that catalogs its complexities. This includes geography, political systems, social norms, and cultural practices. A well-constructed bible can make the world more vivid and immersive for readers. The very act of creating the bible often leads to more and better ideas. It's a form of brainstorming with yourself.

Supports Character Development: Tracking character growth and changes becomes simpler with a series bible. This is especially useful for series with large ensembles or where characters undergo significant development. It helps ensure that changes in characters are deliberate and consistent with their arcs.

Encourages Creative Exploration: A series bible can also be a creative tool, offering a space to explore ideas for future plots, characters, and settings that can be integrated into the series. This can lead to richer storytelling and more cohesive narratives.

Improves Planning and Plotting: For authors who plot their series in advance, a series bible is invaluable for planning out story arcs, character trajectories, and major events. It allows you to see the big picture and make adjustments as needed to serve the overall narrative.

Eases Collaboration: If you're working with editors, co-authors, or other contributors, a series bible ensures everyone has the same understanding of the series' elements. This can be crucial for maintaining a unified vision and voice across the series.

Streamlines Fact-Checking: Before publication, a series bible serves as a quick reference for fact-checking, ensuring that all details align with what's been previously established, which is crucial for maintaining reader trust and immersion.

Supports Marketing and Adaptations: A detailed series bible can also be a useful tool for marketing efforts or if your series is considered for adaptation into other media. It provides a comprehensive overview of your series' universe, characters, and plot, which can be invaluable for promotional or development purposes.

In summary, a series bible is not just a tool for keeping track of details; it's an essential asset for crafting a cohesive, engaging, and believable series. It supports the creative process, enhances productivity, and ensures a high-quality reading experience.

STEP-BY-STEP GUIDE TO CREATING A COMPREHENSIVE SERIES BIBLE

1. Choose Your Format

Digital vs. Physical: Decide whether you prefer a digital document (using software like Scrivener, OneNote, or a simple Word document) or a physical binder. Digital formats are easily searchable and accessible from multiple devices, while physical bibles can be satisfying to flip through and annotate by hand.

Template: Consider starting with a basic template that you can customize as your series develops. There are many templates available online, or you can create your own based on the categories most relevant to your series.

2. Organize Your Bible into Sections

Your series bible should include sections for all the critical elements of your series. Common sections include:

Character Profiles: Include detailed descriptions, backgrounds, relationships, character arcs, and any changes that occur throughout the series.

Setting Descriptions: Document the settings of your series, including geographical details, maps, political structures, cultural norms, and significant locations within your story's world.

Plot Summaries: Write summaries of each book or major story arc, including key events, twists, and how they contribute to the overall series narrative.

Timeline: Maintain a timeline of events within your series to keep track of when things happen, ensuring chronological consistency.

Themes and Motifs: Note recurring themes, motifs, and symbols throughout your series to maintain thematic consistency.

Rules of Magic/Technology: If your series includes elements of fantasy or sci-fi, outline the rules governing magic, technology, or other speculative elements to ensure they're applied consistently.

Language and Dialects: Document any unique languages, dialects, or jargon used in your series, including pronunciation guides or glossaries if necessary.

Research: Keep a section for research notes relevant to your series, such as historical details, scientific explanations, or cultural references.

3. Update Regularly or Hire Someone To Do That

Dynamic Document: Your series bible is a living document that should evolve with your series. Regularly update it with new characters, plot developments, and changes to your world.

Review Before Writing: Before starting each new book or story arc, review your bible to refresh your memory and ensure consistency.

4. Include Visuals (Optional)

Maps and Images: Adding maps, character sketches, or mood boards can help visualize elements of your series and inspire your writing.

5. Utilize Tools and Resources

Writing Software: Tools like Scrivener are designed for managing large writing projects and can be excellent for creating a digital series bible.

Cloud Storage: If you choose a digital format, consider using cloud storage (such as Google Drive or Dropbox) to ensure your bible is backed up and accessible from anywhere.

6. Share with Trusted Readers/Editors (Optional)

Feedback: Share your series bible with trusted beta readers, editors, or writing partners to get feedback or help in maintaining consistency.

Creating a series bible is an ongoing process that requires dedication, but the payoff in terms of consistency, depth, and richness of your series is immense. It not only serves as an invaluable reference as you write but also deepens your engagement with your own creation, enhancing the writing process and the reader's experience.

5

YOUR SUPPORTING CAST – OTHER PLAYERS

Y OUR GAY PROTAGONIST CANNOT BE ONE OF THE ONLY TWO GAY people in your cozy little world. At the same time, a village full of gay folks is going to seem like a government experiment, not a naturally occurring organic population.

Here's a tip: When you begin creating that supporting cast of characters, take a look at the demographics of your setting location. Even if your New England village is entirely fictional, you know it's in New England, right?

Well, let's take a look at New England.

New England, a region in the northeastern United States comprising six states (Maine, New Hampshire, Vermont, Massachusetts, Connecticut, and Rhode Island), has a *diverse* population. As of 2023, the resident population in New England was approximately 15.16 million people. This region is known for its significant historical impact, varying demographics, and a blend of urban and rural areas, which contribute to its unique cultural and social landscape.

The most populous state in New England is Massachusetts, with nearly 6.8 million people, while Vermont is the least populous, having just over 626,000 inhabitants. The population density across New England is notably higher than the national average, with urban centers like Boston, Worcester, Providence, Springfield, and Bridgeport ranking among the top largest cities by population in the region.

In terms of demographics, about 80.4 percent of residents speak only English at home, with a notable Spanish-speaking population making up about 8.4 percent. The area has a rich ethnic *diversity*, with significant populations identifying as Irish (17.4%), Italian (11.9%), English (11.4%), German (6.7%), French (6.5%), Polish (4.3%), French Canadian (4.0%), Portuguese (2.8%), Scottish (2.2%), Sub-Saharan

African (1.7%), West Indian (1.7%), Swedish (1.4%), and Russian (1.2%). This *diverse* cultural makeup is reflected in the region's traditions, cuisine, and social practices.

Economically, New England has a vibrant mix of industries, including tourism, education, financial services, manufacturing, and natural resources like lobster and granite. It's also a hub for exports such as maple syrup, fish, and potatoes.

Despite the lower birth rate compared to other US regions, New England has seen steady population growth, indicating a continued trend of development and attraction. This growth and demographic variety contribute to New England's reputation as a region with a rich history, *cultural diversity*, and economic vitality.

There's your starting point.

In New England, the African American population varies across the region, with the percentages being lower compared to the national average. Specifically, Maine and New Hampshire have about 2.0 percent and Vermont about 1.5 percent of their populations identifying as African American. Massachusetts has a significantly higher percentage, with approximately 9.5 percent of its population identifying as African American.

Finding specific numbers on the LGBTQ+ population in New England or any region can be more challenging due to the variability in data collection and reporting. The US Census Bureau and other demographic surveys often don't directly measure sexual orientation and gender identity across every region with the same granularity as they do racial and ethnic demographics. However, general estimates from various surveys suggest that the LGBTQ+ population in the US accounts for about 4.5 to 5 percent of the population, but this percentage can vary widely depending on the source and methodology.

Sure, for more detailed insights and updates, you could refer to specialized studies or surveys focused on LGBTQ+ demographics, such as those conducted by the Williams Institute at UCLA or local organizations that may have more specific data for New England, but you're not writing a thesis. You're trying to figure out what the cast of characters in your New England village should realistically look and sound like.

That said, it's your village. If you want your demographics to be based on wishful thinking, you go right ahead. Some readers will love it. Some readers will roll their eyes.

Either way, creating a diverse cast of characters in a cozy mystery is important for enhancing the storytelling, enriching the narrative landscape, and reflecting the complexity of the real world.

But let's keep in mind what *diversity* actually means.

di·ver·si·ty
/dəˈvərsədē, dīˈvərsədē/
noun
noun: diversity

1.
the state of being diverse; variety.
- "there was considerable diversity in the papers my students handed in"

a range of different things.

plural noun: diversities

- "the editorial section displayed a diversity of views from the community"

2.
the practice or quality of including or involving people from a range of different social and ethnic backgrounds and of different genders, sexual orientations, etc.
"equality and diversity create a stronger workforce"

Ideally, diversity in cozy mysteries will reflect realistic, setting-based demographics as well as some calculated choices.

Why is this type of diversity important?

Reflects Real-World Diversity: Our message is stronger and therefore more believable when it reflects reality. Incorporating characters from various backgrounds, cultures, orientations, and experiences makes the story more authentic and reflective of the real world. This realism—versus magical thinking—can make the narrative more relatable and engaging for a wider audience, allowing more readers to see themselves represented in the story.

Enriches the Storytelling: Diversity introduces a range of perspectives, motivations, and interactions, adding depth and complexity to the plot and character dynamics. It allows for a richer exploration of themes and conflicts, moving beyond surface-level narratives to delve into stories that challenge, entertain, and provoke thought.

Expands Audience Reach: A diverse cast can attract a broader readership, appealing to a wide range of people with different backgrounds and experiences. This inclusivity can broaden the book's appeal, drawing in readers who might not typically explore the cozy mystery genre.

Challenges Stereotypes: By presenting well-rounded, diverse characters, cozy mysteries can challenge and subvert stereotypes, offering more nuanced portrayals that break away from clichés. Not every old person is wise. Not every African American woman votes Democrat. Not every gay man loves musicals. Characters defying stereotypes not only make for more interesting and unpredictable stories but also contribute to a more inclusive and understanding society.

Fosters Empathy and Understanding: Reading about characters who are different from oneself can foster empathy and understanding, promoting a greater appreciation of diversity. When I was in junior high, I read a Scholastic book titled *Mary Jane*. That book, written by Dorothy Sterling in 1971, had a huge influence on me, although I didn't even remember reading it until quite recently. Cozy mysteries, with their focus on community and connection, provide an ideal setting to explore the lives and experiences of a varied cast, encouraging readers to empathize with and understand perspectives different from their own.

Innovates the Genre: Introducing diversity into cozy mysteries can bring fresh ideas, settings, and themes to the genre, keeping it vibrant and relevant. As societal norms and values evolve, so too should the stories we tell, ensuring that the genre continues to captivate and resonate with contemporary readers.

Builds a Sense of Community: Cozy mysteries often revolve around small communities where everyone knows each other. A diverse cast reinforces the idea that communities are made up of individuals with unique stories, backgrounds, and contributions, emphasizing the strength found in diversity.

Enhances Character Development: Diversity allows for more complex character development as individuals navigate their identities, cultures, and relationships within the story. This can lead to more compelling character arcs and interactions, driving the narrative forward in unexpected ways.

Promotes Inclusivity in Literature: Including a diverse cast of characters contributes to the broader goal of promoting inclusivity in literature, ensuring that diverse voices and stories are heard and valued. This inclusivity enriches the literary landscape, making it more representative of the varied tapestry of human experience.

In summary, a diverse cast in cozy mysteries not only enriches the narrative and broadens its appeal but also plays a crucial role in reflecting and fostering a more inclusive, empathetic, and understanding world.

However, try to avoid the temptations of "one from every column," not least because it feels fake and can come off like a marketing ploy.

How big should your supporting cast be? Who should be in that supporting cast? There's no hard and fast rule about the size of your supporting cast—other than there has to be one.

Unlike protagonists in other subgenres of crime and mystery fiction, the cozy mystery protagonist must be a socially well-adjusted human. They will have an assortment of close friends and friendly acquaintances.

There's a very good practical reason for this.

Because your cozy protag is not a trained investigator or a law enforcement officer with plenty of tools and resources, their main source of information and clues must come through (often casual) conversations with a variety of people. Which means…they have to have plenty of people to talk to.

A number of these people will be series regulars. Those are your supporting cast members.

Your supporting cast has to be large enough to provide a variety of voices and experiences, but not be so large that readers—and you—can't keep everyone straight…er, keep track of who everyone is.

One of your series regulars will be your protagonist's romantic interest, though that particular character is a very different animal from the rest of the gang.

Speaking of which, one of your series regulars might very well be an animal. A pet. In particular, a dog or cat.

Finally, and perhaps controversially, one or two of your series "villains" should *also* be in the supporting or extended supporting cast lineup. I don't mean every week, one of your protag's besties turns out to be a murderer. But I also don't mean long-running antagonist when I say "villain." I mean, occasionally, someone your protagonist knows pretty well is going to be driven to commit the ultimate crime.

But the majority of these cast members exist to provide comic relief, to act as a sounding board for your sleuth, and to supply your sleuth with useful information and clues amidst all the chatter. When you do it right, these characters often develop their own fan base within your readership.

Now, is it possible that a family member fills in the role of confidant? Sure. Wacky siblings and overbearing but loving mothers are a staple in the genre. But your protag cannot be housebound or live in a vacuum. They have to be out in the world, working and interacting within a community—even if it is a small and temporary community.

To reiterate: In cozy mysteries, the supporting cast plays a crucial role in enriching the story, providing humor, depth, and sometimes even red herrings to keep readers engaged and guessing.

Inevitably, these characters follow certain tropes that have become beloved—YMMV—staples of the genre:

The Wise Elder: Often a grandparent, elderly neighbor, or local historian, this character provides wisdom, guidance, and sometimes crucial clues from the past. They're a source of support and often have a keen understanding of human nature.

The Comic Relief: This character brings humor to the story, lightening the mood with their quips, eccentricities, or clumsy antics. They often find themselves in amusing predicaments but can also have moments of unexpected insight. (Personally, I think every member of the supporting cast should provide some level of comic relief.)

The Tech Whiz: The go-to person for anything tech-related, this character can hack into systems, recover deleted files, or provide the protagonist with the latest gadgets. They help navigate the modern challenges of sleuthing. Maybe yes, maybe no. This is the dawn of the internet sleuth, and very few of us do not know how to conduct a thorough search on the world wide web.

The Best Friend: Loyal and supportive, the best friend is always there to lend an ear, offer advice, or assist with the investigation. They're often more than just a sidekick, providing emotional depth and sometimes serving as a sounding board for theories. In particular, this person is useful for providing counseling and insight when the protag's relationship with their romantic interest hits the shoals, as it must periodically do.

The Four-Footed Sidekick: An adorable animal companion. Frequently a rescue or inherited along the way. The Four-Footed Sidekick can be a plot catalyst, inadvertently leading the protagonist to clues or crimes in progress.

The Love Interest: Whether a simmering slow burn or an established relationship, the love interest adds romantic tension and personal stakes for the protagonist. Their relationship can also offer insights into the protagonist's character. In an LGBTQ+ cozy, this character is not optional. A little later, we'll discuss why in depth.

The Just-the-Normal-Noises Antagonist: Often a business competitor or romantic rival. Not quite an enemy, the series antagonist provides competitive tension, challenging the protagonist either in their personal or professional life. This rivalry can add a dynamic layer to the story, especially if the antagonist and the protagonist must occasionally join forces. Also, the antagonist may change throughout the series.

The Local Law Enforcement: Often skeptical of the protagonist's sleuthing, the local police or detective can be a foil or an unwilling ally. Their relationship with the protagonist can range from adversarial to cooperative, frequently evolving over the course of the series into romantic interest. Not least because it gives the protagonist information on the case they could not otherwise access.

The Gossip: With their ear always to the ground, this character knows everything about everyone in the town. They're a valuable source of information, though sifting through what's useful among the rumors can be a challenge. But let's face it, in small communities, everybody has a little bit of a gossip.

The Mysterious Stranger: A new face in town or someone with an unclear past, this character adds intrigue and suspicion. Their unknown motives and background provide fertile ground for red herrings and plot twists. You do not need a Mysterious Stranger in every book, but every couple of installments, it's useful to introduce new blood. Meaning, you don't always have to kill off the Mysterious Stranger.

These tropes, while familiar, offer a comforting framework within which you can explore a wide range of characters and dynamics.

My advice is to *blend* these tropes across your cast members. Don't be afraid to defy expectation and create unique twists on these characters. Perhaps your elderly historian is a gossip *and* a computer whiz. Perhaps *all* the supporting characters provide comic relief.

Remember, your cozy mystery protag is both guide and *observer* in this world, so allow them to appreciate the humorous side of their quirky friends and neighbors.

Ideas for possible character types to flesh out your cozy mystery community? We haz 'em! These character descriptions can provide occupations/roles for series regulars *or* provide ideas for (*and serve as potential victims*) in future story installments:

The Culinary Genius: Whether running a local café, bakery, or being a friend with incredible cooking skills, this character adds a warm, homey element, often providing a setting for gatherings or moments of reflection.

The Eccentric Inventor: A local genius whose inventions either cause chaos or provide unexpected solutions. Their gadgets could play a pivotal role in solving the mystery or add humorous complications to the investigation.

The Retired Performer: Once a star in a niche field (think retired magician, circus performer, or opera singer), this character brings a flair for the dramatic and a network of equally colorful former colleagues who can offer help or hindrance.

The Conspiracy Theorist: Always ready with an outlandish theory, this character can throw the investigation off with their wild speculations or, surprisingly, be right when least expected, leading to a pivotal plot twist.

The Time Capsule Keeper: Someone who lives as if they're in another era, providing a living link to the past and possibly key historical insights related to the mystery. Their anachronistic lifestyle and perspective offer both charm and clues.

The Nomadic Traveler: A character who's seen the world and brings back stories, artifacts, and possibly a few unsolved mysteries of their own. Their global perspective and connections can open up international angles to your cozy setting.

The Urban Escapee: A former city dweller who has moved to the countryside to escape the rat race, bringing a fresh perspective and perhaps some unintended sophistication to solving rural mysteries.

The Botanical Wizard: With a deep knowledge of plants, this character can offer insights based on the flora involved in the mystery, be it poison, an obscure clue left at a crime scene, or a plant-based remedy that plays a crucial role.

The Animal Whisperer: Someone with a special connection to animals, who can interpret the behaviors or reactions of pets and wildlife to uncover clues or even solve parts of the mystery.

The Ghost Hunter: Whether or not ghosts are real in your story's universe, this character is obsessed with the supernatural and can introduce eerie elements, historical mysteries, or misinterpretations that lead to red herrings.

The Artisan: Whether they're a brewer, a bookbinder, a glassblower, or any other type of craftsperson, this character's deep knowledge of their craft offers unique insights and solutions, as well as a window into a fascinating world of tradition and skill.

At the same time, focusing on real-life character types that toe the line between annoying and indispensable can also be useful, adding both relatability and depth to your cozy mystery:

The Overzealous Volunteer: Always the first to sign up and the last to leave, this character's boundless energy and need to be involved in everything can be overwhelming. They often overhear crucial information or stumble upon key evidence due to their omnipresence at community events.

The Micro-Manager: A micro-manager character is a boss or manager who closely observes and controls the work of your protagonist (or their employees), often with excessive attention to minor details. This management style can lead to a lack of autonomy for employees, potentially stifling creativity and motivation. It can also, understandably perhaps, lead to murder.

The Nosey Neighbor: This character knows exactly when you leave for work, what you're planting in your garden, and the "proper" way to sort recycling. Their attention to detail and insistence on order can annoyingly lead to noticing something amiss that's crucial to the plot.

The Unsolicited Advice Giver: Hey, it's me!!! Seriously, full of life hacks, health tips, and relationship advice, this character can't help but share their wisdom, whether you want it or not. Occasionally, their offhand comments can provide an unexpected breakthrough.

The Constant Complainer: Nothing is ever right for this character—service is too slow, weather too dreary, and don't get them started on the youth of today. Their grievances might seem tiresome until they complain about something genuinely out of the ordinary that hints at a deeper mystery.

The Armchair Detective: Fueled by true crime podcasts and detective novels, this character is convinced they can solve the mystery before the protagonist. Annoyingly, they sometimes do piece together a valuable clue amidst their many theories.

The Bragger: Ugh. But we all know one. Always one-upping everyone with tales of their accomplishments, travels, or Amazon ranking, this character's incessant need to impress can inadvertently reveal important facts or connections that no one else knows.

The Social Media Oversharer: Whether it's live-tweeting every moment and meal or chronicling neighborhood drama on Facebook, their oversharing habit is eye-roll-inducing but proves to be a treasure trove of timelines, alibis, and maybe even photographic evidence.

The Perpetual Skeptic or Pessimist: Doubting every piece of news and questioning every decision, this character's relentless skepticism can be tiresome but also prompts others to look closer at details they might otherwise accept at face value. This is the character who looks for the cloud in every silver lining.

The Networking Nuisance: Always looking to hand out a business card or connect on LinkedIn, their relentless self-promotion and networking can uncover unexpected links between seemingly unrelated characters or events.

The Old-School Luddite: Eschewing technology for "the good old days" of pen and paper, this character's disdain for modern conveniences is a source of frustration. However, their preference for analog methods uncovers clues that tech-reliant characters might overlook.

Incorporating these character types into your story adds layers of realism and complexity, making your fictional world more vibrant and engaging. They mirror the everyday challenges of dealing with diverse personalities but also highlight how each person, no matter how quirky or annoying, has the potential to contribute meaningfully to the community and the unfolding mystery.

Now, if you are writing a gay cozy mystery, you already know that your main character will identify as a member of the LGBTQ+ community. Which means that there is at least one other person in their cozy world who identifies as LGBTQ+. That person is your protag's romantic interest.

However, these two cannot be the only two LGBTQ+ people in this world.

For one thing, that undercuts the power of their emotional connection.

On the other hand, they might not be acquainted with all the LGBTQ+ people in their community.

Gallup released a poll in February 2022 indicating that 7.1 percent of US adults identified as something other than heterosexual, which includes identities such as lesbian, gay, bisexual, and transgender, et al. This marked an increase from previous years, reflecting a growing willingness among Americans to identify as part of the LGBTQ+ community. These numbers will rise (or fall) with societal attitudes. Ideally, they will evolve as more people feel comfortable openly identifying with non-heterosexual orientation.

That said, it's safe to assume that 7.1 percent did not jump to 50 percent in the span of three years—and I highly doubt it will in ten years. But diversity, as previously discussed, is not just one thing. So yes, you want to include people—characters—who serve as representatives for all kinds of different experiences and viewpoints. People of different ages, backgrounds, races, ethnicities, sexualities, spiritualities.

Why is diversity so important?

Frankly, for a whole host of reasons both philosophical and practical.

Diversity enhances relatability. It broadens perspectives, deepens character dynamics, increases realism, fuels creativity and innovation—I'm serious about this! Drawing from a wide range of cultures, experiences, and backgrounds can inspire fresh plot ideas, unique character arcs, and unexpected twists. Diversity can be a wellspring of creativity, pushing the cozy subgenre in new and exciting directions.

But also, diversity in fiction can gently, persuasively challenge stereotypes, enhance world-building, expand market appeal, promote inclusivity, and encourage reflective thinking. A diverse cast subtly encourages readers to reflect on their own biases, assumptions, and worldviews. Through engaging with characters who may be different from themselves, readers can explore new ways of thinking and being in the world.

Let me ask you this. Is there a good reason *not* to strive for diversity?

You're trying to populate this imaginary world in a way that feels recognizably real. Because *that* is the way to create the most satisfying and convincing reading experience.

Striving for diversity in literature, including cozy mysteries, is necessary for the richness and authenticity it brings to storytelling. However, it's crucial to approach diversity with sincerity and depth rather than treating characters as checkboxes to fulfill a diversity quota. Let's explore the issues with an artificial approach to diversity and how it can be navigated.

Tokenism and Lack of Depth

Tokenism: When characters from diverse backgrounds are included merely to meet a diversity "quota" without genuinely integrating them into the narrative, it can lead to tokenism. Token characters are typically one-dimensional and defined solely by their race, ethnicity, gender identity, or sexual orientation, rather than being fully fleshed-out individuals.

Lack of Depth: Artificial attempts at diversity can result in characters who lack depth and authenticity. Without meaningful backstories, motivations, and character development, these characters can feel like afterthoughts, undermining the richness that true diversity brings to a story.

Stereotyping and Simplification

Stereotyping: There's a risk of falling into stereotypes when diversity is approached superficially. Characters might end up representing clichéd or simplistic views of a particular group, which not only disrespects the complexity of real people's lives but also perpetuates misconceptions.

Simplification: Reducing characters to their demographic characteristics can oversimplify the diversity of experiences within any given group. Real people are shaped by an intersection of factors, including but not limited to their cultural background, and these nuances may be lost in a superficially diverse cast.

Reader Alienation and Misrepresentation

Alienation: Readers are increasingly discerning and value authenticity in representation. An artificial or forced diversity can alienate readers, especially those from the very communities being represented, if they feel that the portrayal is inaccurate, superficial, or exploitative.

Misrepresentation: There's a significant responsibility in portraying characters from backgrounds different from one's own. Missteps in representation can spread misinformation or reinforce harmful stereotypes, contributing to a broader cultural misunderstanding.

STRATEGIES FOR AUTHENTIC DIVERSITY
AKA *IS THERE AN ECHO IN HERE?*

You've heard it once, but that's not going to stop me.

Research and Sensitivity: Undertake thorough research and engage with sensitivity readers to ensure that the portrayal of diverse characters is respectful, accurate, and nuanced.

Character Development: Focus on developing well-rounded characters whose identities inform but do not solely define their roles in the story. Each character should have their own arc, motivations, and personality, beyond their demographic characteristics.

Integration into the Narrative: Ensure that diverse characters are integral to the narrative, with their backgrounds and experiences enriching the plot and themes of the story, rather than feeling tacked on or peripheral.

Avoiding Stereotypes: Be vigilant against stereotypes and seek to represent the diversity within communities, acknowledging that there is no single way to be part of any demographic group.

In summary, while achieving diversity in cozy mysteries is essential, it must be approached with care, respect, and a commitment to authenticity. The goal is to reflect the real world's complexity and richness, providing all readers with characters they can relate to, learn from, and see themselves in, without reducing those characters to mere tokens or stereotypes.

Incorporating diversity into your cozy mystery series not only makes for richer, more engaging storytelling but also aligns your work with broader social values of inclusivity and representation. It's an opportunity to entertain and enlighten, to challenge and charm—all key ingredients for a memorable and meaningful series.

WHODUNIT – YOUR VILLAIN

The murderer in a cozy mystery novel is not an evil mastermind.

He or she is not a serial killer, a hired assassin, a mob enforcer, or a violent vagrant who just happened to be passing through. He or she is not legally insane.

Much like our hero or heroine, our villain is an ordinary person caught in extraordinary circumstances. Unlike our hero or heroine, they are making all the wrong choices. Their moral compass has reversed polarity. The villain is convinced that what they want or need is more important than what anyone else wants or needs.

Ultimately, they make the grim choice that what they want or need is more important than someone else's life.

This choice reflects the genre's focus on the human condition, societal norms, and the belief that evil deeds can spring from common sources. In a perhaps peculiar way, the concept of a normal person pushed to dreadful and drastic lengths is part of what contributes to the genre's appeal. Frankly, it's relatable.

Cozy mysteries often explore the idea that anyone is capable of crime under the right (or wrong) pressures. This premise adds a layer of psychological intrigue, as it prompts readers to consider the moral complexities and ethical dilemmas that can drive a seemingly average person to commit a crime.

Unlike the premeditated crimes often seen in thrillers or crime dramas, cozy mystery crimes tend to be more spontaneous or born out of a moment of weakness. This can make the crime—and by extension, the story—more recognizable.

It reflects real-life situations where people might make a split-second decision they later regret, driven by fear, jealousy, greed, or a desperate attempt to cover up a mistake.

When you're creating your killer, it's important to remember that very often the cozy mystery villain was not always a villain.

They frequently feel great guilt, even remorse for their actions.

Granted, that doesn't always keep them from trying to do even more terrible things to cover up the first terrible thing.

Because cozy mysteries eschew graphic violence, serial killers, and organized crime, the focus is instead on the puzzle-solving aspect of the crime and the community's response to it. This decision aligns with the genre's aim to provide a more restrained and comforting form of escapism, where the emphasis is on the intellectual challenge and the restoration of social order rather than on violence or the darker aspects of human nature.

Part of both the horror and appeal in this setup is that the villain is usually someone within the protagonist's social circle or community. This setup enhances the story's tension and drama, as it underscores the betrayal and disruption of social harmony caused by the crime. It also allows for a deeper exploration of relationships and character dynamics, as the protagonist must navigate their personal connections to solve the mystery.

Finally, the resolution of a cozy mystery often involves not just the unmasking of the villain but also an element of moral resolution. Since the villains are ordinary people who have erred, there's sometimes a path to understanding their motives and, in some cases, a chance for redemption. This aspect underscores the genre's often optimistic or forgiving view of human nature.

The portrayal of villains in cozy mysteries reflects the genre's broader themes: the belief in the basic goodness of people, the importance of community, and the idea that disorder can be restored through intelligence and empathy rather than through violence or force. This commonsense approach to villainy adds depth to the cozy mystery genre, making it a rich and rewarding field for both writers and readers.

In cozy mysteries, the reasons behind murder often differ from those in darker crime genres, reflecting the genre's unique tone and setting. While cozy mysteries revolve around murder, the motives are usually intertwined with the community, relationships, and human emotions rather than with random acts of violence or psychopathy.

That said, the motives for murder in cozy mysteries are pretty much the same motives we see in all crime fiction—and, frankly, real life:

Financial Gain or Inheritance: A classic motive, where the murderer stands to inherit money, property, or valuable items. The prospect of financial gain can push someone to commit murder, especially if they are desperate, greedy, or feel entitled.

Jealousy or Love Triangle: Romantic entanglements and jealousy frequently serve as motives. A character might kill out of jealousy, to eliminate a rival, or because of unrequited love, setting the stage for an emotionally charged investigation.

Revenge: A character seeks vengeance for a real or perceived wrong. This could stem from a variety of sources, such as a business dispute, a personal betrayal, or an old grudge, and often ties into the community's history. I didn't use to put a lot of credence in revenge as a motive until I became a regular viewer of *Dateline*.

Cover-Up of Another Crime: The murderer might kill someone to prevent the exposure of a past crime, scandal, or secret that could ruin their reputation, career, or relationships. This motive layers the mystery, revealing deeper secrets as the protagonist investigates.

Self-Defense or Defense of Another: In some cases, the murder is the result of a confrontation that escalates, where the character claims they acted in self-defense or to protect someone else. The ambiguity of these situations can add complexity to the mystery.

Protection of Status or Reputation: A character might commit murder to protect their social standing, reputation, or a secret that, if revealed, could lead to their downfall. This is often seen in settings where community image is everything.

Fear of Exposure: Similar to covering up another crime but more focused on personal secrets, such as hidden pasts, relationships, or compromising information. The fear of being exposed can drive a character to extreme actions. Note: unless you're writing a historical cozy, modern audiences are going to have trouble swallowing the idea that your villain committed all those murders to hide the truth of their sexuality.

Accidental or In the Heat of the Moment: Sometimes, murder in cozy mysteries occurs almost by accident—an impulsive act in a moment of high emotion or a plan gone terribly wrong. These cases often involve characters who are otherwise seen as good people, adding to the tragedy and complexity of the situation.

Business or Professional Rivalry: Competition in business or professional life can lead to murder, especially if a character feels their livelihood, legacy, or life's work is threatened by someone else's actions or existence.

Obsession or Madness: While less common in the cozy genre, which tends to shy away from depicting graphic violence or deep psychological disturbances, characters might still be driven to murder by an obsession that has taken over their rational thought processes, though this is often portrayed with a lighter touch compared to other genres. The key difference here is that the villain is never in doubt that what they are doing is illegal or wrong, but their obsession leads them to feel justified in breaking the law.

These motives are woven into the fabric of the cozy mystery's setting—be it a small town, a tight-knit community, or a specific hobby or interest group—highlighting human relationships and the often-surprising darkness that can lurk beneath the surface of ordinary life. The key in cozy mysteries is to balance the seriousness of the crime with the warmth and charm of the genre.

Let's say you want to make your villain more sympathetic, or perhaps you want a more original motive for the crime.

Creating a scenario where a generally good person is driven to commit a serious crime, including murder, can add significant depth to your cozy mystery, engaging the reader with complex moral questions and emotional dilemmas. Sometimes good people do bad things for good reasons.

Add these emotional drivers, and your motives for murder will resonate more deeply with readers:

Protection of a Loved One: A character might be driven to extreme measures if they believe it's the only way to protect someone they love from an imminent threat. This could be a parent protecting their child from an abuser, or someone acting to prevent harm to a vulnerable friend or family member. The primal instinct to protect can override moral codes under perceived dire circumstances.

Desperation and Despair: A character overwhelmed by desperate circumstances—such as financial ruin, a health crisis without access to necessary treatment, or being trapped in an abusive situation—might see crime as their only escape. Desperation can cloud judgment, making extreme actions seem like the only viable solutions. The challenge here, of course, is that in a cozy mystery, the desperate circumstances can't be *too* desperate without shattering the safe and sane world you've created for your characters. You need a deft and delicate hand with this one.

Accidental Consequences: A character could commit a serious crime unintentionally. A fatal hit and run with (apparently) no witnesses. Or an attempt at self-defense that goes too far. Or any variety of tense situations that spiral out of control, leading to tragic consequences. The guilt and fear of the aftermath could compel these characters to make more questionable decisions.

A Quest for Justice: A character might take the law into their own hands if they feel the legal system has failed them or their loved ones. This vigilantism can stem from a place of righteousness, where the character believes that their actions, however extreme, are necessary to serve justice where formal channels have failed.

Blackmail or Coercion: A character could be coerced into committing a crime due to blackmail or the threat of harm to themselves or someone they care about. The perpetrator might leverage a secret or vulnerability, pushing the character into a corner where they see compliance with the criminal act as the lesser of two evils.

Each of these scenarios offers a rich tapestry for storytelling, allowing you to explore the shades of gray in human morality and the complexities of decision-making under pressure. They also provide a pathway to empathy for the reader, who can engage with the character's dilemma, understanding how a fundamentally good person might be driven to commit an act that is otherwise out of character for them.

Remember, heinous crimes can be committed out of love as well as hate.

Hiding your murderer effectively among your cast of characters in a cozy mystery is crucial for maintaining suspense and delivering a satisfying reveal.

Here are three strategic approaches to keep your readers guessing until the end:

The Likable Red Herring: Craft a character so charming and seemingly helpful that readers and the protagonist alike would never suspect them. This character can be involved in the investigation, offering crucial insights or helping to divert suspicion onto others. Their likability serves as the perfect cover, making their eventual unmasking as the murderer both shocking and compelling. Throughout the story, drop subtle hints of their guilt, careful not to make them too obvious until the pieces come together in the end.

The Background Presence: Introduce the murderer early on but keep them somewhat in the background—present enough so their eventual reveal doesn't feel like a cheat, but not so involved that they attract much attention. They might be someone the community sees every day, like a mail carrier, a librarian, or a café owner, whose routine presence makes them blend into the fabric of the setting. Give them a solid alibi or an apparent lack of motive by carefully weaving their backstory and interactions with other characters to mislead both your protagonist and your readers.

The Sympathetic Motive: Design a character with a compelling, sympathetic backstory that seemingly distances them from any motive for murder. This could be a character who has suffered a great loss, someone who has been wronged in the past, or a person who is universally regarded as too kind or gentle to commit such a crime. The sympathy they garner serves as a natural deterrent against suspicion. As the story unfolds, reveal how their seemingly unrelated backstory directly motivates the crime, flipping the narrative in a way that is both surprising and believable, and showing how extreme circumstances can push even the most unlikely person to the edge.

In all these approaches, the key is *balance*.

You want to provide just enough hints or discrepancies in the character's story to allow for an "aha!" moment upon reveal, without giving the game away too early.

Effective use of misdirection, coupled with deep character development, ensures that when the murderer is finally revealed, readers experience the satisfaction of a mystery well solved, reflecting back on the clues you've artfully laid out.

This strategy not only keeps readers engaged and guessing but also deepens the complexity and enjoyment of your cozy mystery.

BE STILL MY HEART – YOUR LOVE INTEREST

Traditionally, the decision to include a romantic subplot in your cozy mystery series has been optional. In my opinion, in a gay cozy mystery series, the decision is not optional. You must eventually have some kind of happy, healthy romantic relationship.

Including a healthy, happy romantic relationship subplot for the protagonist in a gay cozy mystery series adds depth to the character, making them more relatable and multi-dimensional to readers. It also provides a contrasting backdrop of warmth and personal growth against the tension of the mystery, enriching the overall narrative with emotional layers and offering moments of reprieve and happiness amidst the intrigue.

But there are broader and more important societal implications.

I mean, is there really a lot of point to creating a gay main character if he's going to live his life as a monk? Well, I mean, unless he *is* a monk. (Which is fine, too.)

Anyway, adding a healthy, happy romantic relationship for a gay protagonist in a cozy mystery series does more than just enrich the narrative; it carries broader societal implications. It normalizes LGBTQ+ relationships, presenting them as just as rich, complex, and deserving of happiness as any others.

This representation can foster greater acceptance and understanding in society, challenging stereotypes and prejudices— something particularly valuable at this moment in time. Moreover, for LGBTQ+ readers, it provides valuable visibility and affirmation, potentially offering comfort and a sense of belonging. Through such narratives, literature becomes a powerful tool for cultural change, subtly influencing perceptions and promoting inclusivity.

Get it? Got it? Good.

Far too often, the romantic interest in a cozy mystery series is simply a good-looking cipher. NOT THAT THERE'S ANYTHING

WRONG WITH THAT. But actually, yes, there is. True, the star of our show is our protagonist, absolutely, and most of our page time will be spent in that character's company, but a well-developed and attractive romantic foil can add a whole lot of dimension and excitement to our—er, your story.

In fact, very often, that romantic subplot provides the appeal of one cozy mystery series over another.

Who should this person be?

It's helpful, but not mandatory, that the person be someone of help to our sleuth in his investigations. Perhaps this person is the main suspect in one of investigations. Perhaps they are a victim. Not *the* victim, obviously—a romantic relationship with a ghost is a bit of a dead end—but a secondary victim.

However, a member of law enforcement, a former FBI agent, a computer whiz, or local historian—someone with connections, resources, or skills—could be a useful ally, and if the romantic partner has some involvement in the investigation, there's less chance that they fade into the scenic background.

Whatever their background, give them something useful to do in the plot and series besides make our protag's heart beat faster.

At the same time, regardless of expertise or resources, the romantic interest cannot swoop in and solve the crime for our protag. They cannot always be running to the rescue of the protagonist. The romantic interest is *not* the protagonist. Their primary role is just that: a character who provides romantic interest to the plot.

If you do it right, this character will wind up being as popular or even more popular than your protagonist.

If you do it wrong, readers will openly wish on book forums that you kill the character off.

Here are seven suggestions for a cozy mystery's romantic interest's occupation (remember, you want occupations that can either complement the protagonist's sleuthing activities or add an interesting dynamic to the story):

1. Librarian, Historian, or Archivist: They have access to a wealth of information, and their skills in research and uncovering hidden gems in old texts could be invaluable for solving mysteries. Plus, there's the romantic allure of quiet moments among the stacks of books or ancient archives. Sexy spectacles, people! Hear me now, believe me later.

2. Antique Dealer: They have a keen eye for the valuable and the fake, knowledge of historical objects, and a network of collectors and sellers. Their expertise could lead to uncovering clues hidden in plain sight or within the provenance of an item. Plus they often live in cool old mansions with secret passages.

3. Local Police Officer or Detective: While this might seem a bit on the nose, it offers a direct link to official investigations and can provide a realistic way for your protagonist to gain access to crime scenes or confidential information. The dynamic between a civilian sleuth and a law enforcement officer can also add tension and depth to the relationship.

4. Journalist or Crime Reporter: They're always on the hunt for the truth and have a knack for digging deeper. This profession allows them to be naturally curious and often gives them a broad network of contacts and sources, which could prove useful in solving mysteries. Their quest for a good story could align with the protagonist's pursuit of justice.

5. Chef or Restaurateur: Food brings people together, and a setting around a restaurant or bakery offers a cozy backdrop for romance and mystery. A chef could have a unique perspective on the local community, access to gossip, and an understanding of the finer things in life, including poisons. Plus, there's potential for deliciously descriptive passages that can add sensory depth to your stories. Take it from me, a man who can cook well is worth his weight in gold.

6. Doctor: With their access to confidential information, medical expertise, and trust and influence within the community, doctors are an excellent choice. Incorporating a local doctor as the romantic interest is a good choice, offering both logistical support and emotional depth to the protagonist's endeavors. Plus, the caregiving aspect of their personality can be quite appealing, providing a soft counterpoint to the darker elements of mystery and crime in your stories. Hurt/Comfort anyone? Besides, your protag's mom always wanted him to marry a doctor.

7. Lawyer: A local lawyer as the romantic interest in a cozy mystery also brings a wealth of potential to the narrative. Their legal insights and access to resources are extremely useful. Also, there's potential for conflict between their professional responsibilities and their personal involvement in the mystery, especially if their client is a suspect (this is also true of doctors when one of their patients becomes the sleuth's prime suspect). Lawyers often need to be persuasive and quick-thinking, qualities that can make for a charismatic and appealing character.

Let's consider some of the character traits we look for in potential (long-term) romantic partners (while keeping in mind that what is considered attractive can vary significantly across different cultures). Most of us in the Western Hemisphere consider the following personality traits to be appealing:

Confidence: Confidence influences how a man or woman carries themself, how they speak, and how they interact with others, contributing to a charismatic presence. Confidence is consistently seen as an attractive trait, as it suggests a sense of self-assurance and competence. Confident people are often perceived as more capable and reliable, but it's important to distinguish between genuine self-confidence and arrogance.

Sense of Humor: A good sense of humor is highly attractive because it indicates intelligence and the ability to navigate social situations with ease. Humor can lighten difficult moments and put others at ease. The ability to laugh, make others laugh, and not take life too seriously all the time is a universally appealing trait. It's especially attractive in a character who might otherwise seem a bit remote or hard-nosed.

Kindness and Empathy: Emotional intelligence, the capacity to understand and share the feelings of others, showing compassion and emotional depth, is increasingly recognized as an attractive trait in men as well as women. It allows for meaningful connections and shows a caring nature. The ability to empathize with others, a man's capacity for understanding and compassion, is especially appealing in characters who initially present as inflexible and uncaring.

Intelligence: Intelligence, both in the traditional sense and in terms of emotional intelligence, is attractive. It suggests a curiosity about the world, a capacity for problem-solving, and the ability to connect with others on a deeper level. Intellectual prowess and a sharp mind are attractive qualities. Being knowledgeable, curious, and thoughtful can spark engaging conversations and foster deep connections.

Ambition and Passion: We like people who are driven to be successful and are passionate about their pursuits, whether in career, hobbies, or personal goals. Ambition and passion demonstrate a zest for life that many find appealing. Ambition reflects a desire to grow and achieve. Passion indicates the power to feel deeply and pursue the things that matter. Ambition and a passion for life indicate goals and a desire to achieve them. This drive is often associated with a sense of purpose and determination, which many find appealing.

Physical Fitness: Not as shallow as you might think. Physical attractiveness usually includes fitness, and physical fitness is an attractive trait for most of us, especially when it seems to stem from organic endeavor versus vanity. While societal standards for physical attractiveness vary, taking care of one's body and valuing health and fitness generally contributes to a man's appeal. It reflects discipline and self-respect.

Reliability and Responsibility: Being reliable and taking responsibility for one's actions are attractive traits that indicate maturity and the ability to be a supportive partner in a relationship. Dependability is sometimes portrayed as boring, but being reliable and trustworthy in both small and significant matters is actually a big deal in adult relationships. A dependable partner provides a sense of security and stability, qualities that are often sought after in emotional partnerships.

Respectfulness: Respect for others, including listening and valuing different opinions, is a key trait that contributes to a person's attractiveness—and bodes well for negotiating the inevitable conflicts of a romantic relationship. It shows a capacity for understanding and co-existing with others harmoniously.

Generosity: Generosity, not just in terms of material things but also with one's time and attention, is attractive. It suggests a giving nature and a willingness to support others. Acts of kindness and a generous spirit can significantly enhance a man's attractiveness. Compassion toward others, willingness to help, and showing respect are traits that contribute to a positive and appealing character.

Leadership Abilities: The ability to lead, combined with fairness and the capacity to inspire others, is often seen as attractive. It suggests someone can take charge when necessary but also values the contributions of others.

These traits highlight a combination of characteristics that contribute to a person's overall attractiveness and emphasize the importance of both inner qualities and outward behaviors. While societal standards and personal preferences can influence what traits are considered most attractive, the qualities listed above tend to be universally valued for their role in fostering healthy, positive relationships and interactions.

While societal norms and expectations can vary widely across different cultures and communities, there are certain traits that are commonly frowned upon in many societies. These negative perceptions often stem from how these traits affect interpersonal relationships, professional environments, and societal well-being.

That said, lightly sprinkling your protag's significant other with a bit of the following can add natural conflict to a relationship and give your romantic foil room to grow within the series.

Just don't go overboard. Nobody wants their best friend to date a psycho.

1. Aggressiveness

While assertiveness can be a positive trait, crossing into aggressiveness, especially when it leads to domineering or what might feel like bullying behavior, is generally frowned upon. We want our romantic others to be able to handle disputes and conflicts in a controlled and respectful manner.

2. Emotional Unavailability

This can read as weirdly attractive, especially in the initial chapters of a developing romance. Men are often stereotypically expected to be stoic or to suppress their emotions. However, emotional unavailability can hinder deep, meaningful relationships, and society is increasingly recognizing the importance of emotional intelligence and vulnerability in men.

3. Irresponsibility

I'm not sure this trait is going to do anything for your romantic interest. Failing to take responsibility for one's actions, especially in roles such as parenthood, partnership, and professional obligations, is widely criticized. Society values people who are reliable and accountable.

4. Sexism

It happens, and it can even be slightly amusing in very small doses, especially if your protagonist delivers a timely and loud wake-up call. But attitudes and behaviors that perpetuate gender inequality or disrespect, particularly toward women, are increasingly being called out and condemned in many societies, so go easy. Equality and respect are becoming more central to societal expectations of men.

Also, there's a big, crucial difference between sexism and misogyny. One is curable. One is terminal.

5. Entitlement

It's possible that a character might start out with a sense of entitlement, or expecting certain privileges, and then experience a wake-up call, but unless you're writing very young characters, this is a pretty unattractive quality in a fellow human. Especially when it manifests in disregard for others' rights or feelings.

6. Lack of Ambition

While this can be subjective, a perceived lack of ambition or drive is often frowned upon, particularly in men. Yes, that's tied to traditional expectations of men as providers and achievers. These expectations can be nuanced by increasing recognition of the value of work-life balance and personal fulfillment over traditional success metrics. That said, no one likes a layabout.

7. Inflexibility

Oh, those Harlequin heroes of old! Remember those guys? Granted, they were so often comtes or earls or billionaires or reclusive writers. It was understandable that they were used to having everything their own way. Anyway, an unwillingness to adapt to change or consider other viewpoints is generally viewed negatively. Societies value people who can be flexible and open-minded, especially in rapidly changing global and local contexts. But, I mean, I could think of a way or two to make an inflexible romantic interest...interesting.

8. Dishonesty

Ugh. Unless your protag is a retired professional jewel thief, or a retired spy whose safety depends on hiding certain truths, this is not going to be very charming. Dishonesty is *particularly* frowned upon in one's significant other. Being truthful and transparent is valued in personal relationships, professional settings, and societal interactions. With good reason.

9. Lack of Compassion

I'm not sure a lack of empathy or compassion for others is anything but appalling. Societies are increasingly valuing empathy and caring behaviors in men as well as women, challenging old stereotypes of emotional detachment.

10. Dependency

Excessive dependency, whether financial, emotional, or otherwise, without striving for self-sufficiency, is often viewed negatively. Independence and self-reliance are traits that are generally encouraged. We want to follow fully autonomous characters pursuing relationships with other fully autonomous characters.

This is just as important for female characters as male. Princess Charming isn't coming, Sleeping Beauty. Wake up!

Many traits considered socially undesirable are also often viewed as unattractive in personal relationships, but with a focus on how they impact intimacy, compatibility, and mutual understanding.

It's important to recognize that societal expectations are constantly evolving, and what is frowned upon in one culture or generation might be viewed differently in another. Increasingly, there's a push toward valuing traits such as empathy, emotional intelligence, and respect for equality, reflecting broader shifts in how masculinity is understood and expressed. At the same time, it's safe to assume traits like self-centeredness, vanity, and cruelty are never going to be considered plusses in a prospective mate.

The attraction to traits of masculinity and strength in Western society is rooted in a complex interplay of historical, cultural, and psychological factors. These traits have been valorized across various cultures and epochs, often associated with leadership, protection, and competence.

Since there's at least a 50/50 chance your gay protagonist is going to be male, and a more than 50/50 chance that you are *not* male, let's analyze the traits of masculinity and strength and consider why we find these particular traits attractive, even essential in our protagonist's romantic interest.

Historical and Cultural Foundations

Protector Role: Historically, men have often been cast in the role of the protector, responsible for the safety and well-being of their families and communities. This role has emphasized physical strength and assertiveness, traits that have become deeply associated with the ideal of masculinity.

Social and Economic Leadership: Men have traditionally held positions of power and leadership in many Western societies. Strength (both physical and character-based) and masculinity have been seen as essential traits for leaders, reinforcing their desirability.

Cultural Heroes and Myths: Many Western myths, legends, and cultural narratives celebrate masculine heroes who embody strength, bravery, and resilience. These stories, passed down through generations, shape societal expectations and ideals around masculinity.

Psychological and Evolutionary Perspectives

Attraction to Competence: From an evolutionary psychology standpoint, traits associated with strength and masculinity may be interpreted as indicators of a mate's ability to provide and protect. This can translate into a subconscious attraction to these traits, perceived as beneficial for survival and offspring well-being.

Social Status and Confidence: Masculinity and strength often correlate with higher social status and confidence, traits that are generally attractive because they suggest a capacity for resource acquisition and social influence.

Safety and Security: On a psychological level, the association of masculinity and strength with protection can evoke feelings of safety and security, making these traits attractive to those seeking emotional and physical reassurance in their relationships.

Modern Interpretations and Shifts

Expanding Definitions: Contemporary Western society is increasingly recognizing and valuing diverse expressions of masculinity and strength, including emotional resilience, intellectual strength, and the courage to defy traditional norms.

Social and Gender Dynamics: There's growing awareness of the limitations and pressures imposed by traditional gender roles. This has sparked conversations about the attractiveness of traits such as vulnerability, empathy, and emotional intelligence in men, alongside or instead of traditional markers of masculinity and strength.

Media and Representation: Media representations influence societal perceptions of attractiveness. While traditional depictions of masculinity and strength persist, there's a growing presence of alternative models that challenge and expand these norms.

The attraction to traits of masculinity and strength in Western society is multifaceted, influenced by historical roles, psychological tendencies, and cultural narratives. While these traits have been and continue to be seen as attractive and essential by many, there's a dynamic conversation about what masculinity and strength mean in the modern world. This conversation reflects a broader cultural shift toward a more inclusive and nuanced understanding of gender, where strength is recognized in its many forms, and masculinity is freed from rigid definitions, allowing for a fuller expression of human potential and diversity.

Bottom line, try to create a potential romantic partner for your protagonist who makes your heart flutter. It's the best way of ensuring your reader's heart will flutter, too.

THE RETRO LOVE QUIZ

If you're writing an old-school cozy with more mature characters, this quiz might be helpful. If these questions feel a little dated, just skip to the next exercise.

Instructions: *Answer these ten questions in the voice of your protagonist and your protagonist's love interest.*

What is your idea of a perfect date?

    a) A moonlit stroll along the beach.
    b) A romantic dinner at a fancy restaurant.
    c) Cozying up by the fireplace with a good book.

How do you feel about love at first sight?

    a) It's a fairy tale come true!
    b) It's possible, but rare.
    c) True love takes time to develop.

Which movie best represents your ideal love story?

    a) *Casablanca*
    b) *Gone with the Wind*
    c) *It Happened One Night*

What's your opinion on public displays of affection?

    a) I adore them! The more, the better.
    b) A little hand-holding is nice, but nothing too extravagant.
    c) I prefer to keep my affection private.

What's your favorite romantic gesture?

    a) Sending cards. Writing love letters.
    b) Surprising your partner with flowers.
    c) Cooking a special dinner together.

How important is it for partners to have similar interests?

    a)   Extremely important! We should share everything.

    b)   It's nice to have some common ground, but differences can be exciting, too.

    c)   Compatibility is key, but a little diversity keeps things interesting.

What's your take on traditional gender roles in relationships?

    a)   I believe in the man being the provider and protector.

    b)   I think roles should be flexible and based on individual strengths.

    c)   I prefer a more traditional dynamic with clear roles.

How do you handle conflicts in a relationship?

    a)   I believe in passionately expressing my feelings.

    b)   I prefer to calmly discuss and find a compromise.

    c)   I tend to avoid confrontation altogether.

What's your dream honeymoon destination?

    a)   Paris, the City of Love.

    b)   A tropical island getaway.

    c)   Exploring historic European cit es.

What's the most important quality in a partner?

    a)   Passion.

    b)   Trustworthiness.

    c)   Compatibility.

THE CONTEMPORARY LOVE QUIZ

Instructions: *Answer these ten questions in the voice of your protagonist and your protagonist's love interest.*

If your love story was a current hit series, which would it be?

a) *Stranger Things* – Adventurous with a touch of supernatural mystery.
b) *The Crown* – Elegantly dramatic with historical flair.
c) *Brooklyn Nine-Nine* – Full of laughs and unexpected heartwarming moments.
d) *This Is Us* – Deeply emotional with real-life challenges.

What's your go-to modern date night activity?

a) Escape room challenge, testing your teamwork and wits.
b) A trendy new food truck park for a culinary adventure.
c) Binge-watching a new streaming series under a comfy blanket.
d) Virtual reality arcade for a futuristic fun time.

Which contemporary love song encapsulates your feelings right now?

a) "Adore You" by Harry Styles.
b) "Lover" by Taylor Swift.
c) "Thinkin Bout You" by Frank Ocean.
d) "All of Me" by John Legend.

If you could send a love DM (Direct Message), what would it say?

a) "Just saw something that made me think of you. Now I can't stop smiling. 😊"
b) "Counting down the minutes until I see you again. 🤍🖤"
c) "If I could send you a kiss through the phone, I'd be spamming you all day. 😘"
d) "You've got a permanent residency in my thoughts. 🏠 "

Your modern love potion includes...

a) A screenshot of your first text conversation.
b) A playlist of songs you both love.
c) A meme that always makes you both laugh.
d) The location pin of where you first met.

Which contemporary TV couple do you and your significant other mimic?

a) Eleanor and Chidi from *The Good Place* – Philosophical and unexpectedly perfect for each other.
b) David and Patrick from *Schitt's Creek* – Heartwarming with a journey of self-discovery.
c) Jake and Amy from *Brooklyn Nine-Nine* – Competitive yet deeply supportive.
d) Randall and Beth from *This Is Us* – Strong, facing life's challenges together with grace.

Choose a modern love token to give to your sweetheart:

a) A custom playlist of love songs on Spotify.
b) A heartfelt video message recounting your favorite moments together.
c) Matching phone cases that complement each other.
d) A book you've annotated with notes and thoughts for them.

What's your current relationship status?

a) "It's Complicated" – Navigating the ups and downs, but hopelessly devoted.
b) "Swiping Right" – Just discovered each other and excited to see where it goes.
c) "Netflix and Commitment" – Comfortable and content in each other's company.
d) "In a Relationship" – Facebook official and going strong.

The soundtrack to your romantic evening is...

a) A curated Spotify playlist of indie love songs.
b) The latest lo-fi hip-hop beats to relax/study to.
c) A live-streamed concert of your favorite band.
d) An immersive sound bath experience for two.

The modern love advice column you'd write to asks...

a) "Is ghosting really the new norm, or can we bring back breakup texts?"
b) "How do you keep the spark alive in a long-distance relationship with different time zones?"
c) "In a sea of dating apps, how do you know when you've found 'the one'?"
d) "What are the new rules for defining the relationship in a world where labels feel so 2010?"

EXERCISE:
DEVELOPING YOUR COZY MYSTERY VILLAIN

Step 1: Character Sketch

Begin by writing a brief character sketch of your villain, including basic details such as their name, age, occupation, and role in the community. How do they present themselves to the world? What facade do they maintain?

Step 2: Motivation and Goals

Write a paragraph detailing your villain's primary motivation. What drives them to commit the crime(s) in your story? Consider motivations that are relatable or understandable, even if the reader doesn't agree with their actions. This could include fear, desire for protection, a sense of injustice, or a desperate need.

Next, outline their specific goals. What do they hope to achieve through their actions? How do they justify their actions to themselves?

Step 3: Relationship Dynamics

Create a list of relationships your villain has with other key characters in your story, including the protagonist, potential victims, and allies. For each relationship, note the public perception versus the reality of their interaction. How do these dynamics mask or reveal the villain's true nature?

Step 4: The Turning Point

Describe a pivotal moment in the villain's past that set them on their current path. This could be a backstory event that deeply affected their choices and motivations. How does this event influence their actions in the mystery?

Step 5: Flaws and Vulnerabilities

Identify at least two significant flaws or vulnerabilities in your villain's character. How do these weaknesses contribute to their downfall or lead to their unmasking? Consider how these aspects can be woven into the plot to provide clues for the protagonist and the reader. By the way, human villains with recognizable motivations and flaws are far more interesting—and frightening—than cartoon bad guys.

Step 6: A Moment of Sympathy

Craft a scene or a monologue in which the villain elicits sympathy from the reader. Show a side of them that is human, vulnerable, or regretful. This can add complexity to their character and make the conflict more emotionally engaging.

Step 7: The Reveal

Plan the reveal scene where the villain's true identity and motives come to light. How is the reveal executed? Consider the setting, the characters present, and the reaction of both the protagonist and the community. How does the villain react to being caught?

Step 8: Reflection and Integration

Reflect on how the villain's actions and motivations are integrated into the larger narrative. How do they influence the development of the protagonist and the community? Write a brief outline of how the villain's presence weaves through the mystery, affecting the plot and the growth of other characters.

By completing this exercise, you'll develop a villain who is not just a foil for the protagonist but a fully realized character in their own right, whose actions and motivations drive the story forward and add depth to your cozy mystery.

EXERCISE:
CREATING THE PERFECT ROMANTIC FOIL

Creating the perfect romantic foil for your cozy mystery protagonist involves crafting a character who complements and challenges your protagonist in equal measure.

Objective: *This writing exercise will guide you through developing a romantic interest whose relationship with the protagonist evolves, with all the requisite bumps and growth, over the course of your series.*

Step 1: Character Foundation

Begin with a basic profile of your romantic foil. Include physical descriptions, occupation, hobbies, and any quirks that make them unique. How do these elements contrast with or complement your protagonist's characteristics?

Step 2: Initial Attraction

Write a scene or a series of interactions that spark the initial attraction between your protagonist and the romantic foil. Consider what draws them to each other. Is it physical attraction, a shared sense of humor, intellectual compatibility, or something unexpected?

Step 3: Complementary Strengths and Weaknesses

List the strengths and weaknesses of both your protagonist and the romantic foil. How do their strengths support each other's weaknesses? Develop scenarios or plot points where these complementary traits come into play, especially in moments of tension or conflict within the story.

Step 4: Conflicting Values or Goals

Identify at least one major area of conflict between your protagonist and the romantic foil. This could be a difference in values, life goals, or approaches to problem-solving. Plan how this conflict will initially create tension in their relationship and how they might work to resolve or come to terms with these differences over time.

Step 5: Growth and Change

Outline key moments in the series where the romantic foil and the protagonist individually experience growth or change. How do these moments affect their relationship? Consider both setbacks and breakthroughs that test and ultimately strengthen their bond.

Step 6: Romantic and Mystery Plot Interweaving

Develop plot points where the romantic subplot and the mystery plot intersect. How do the challenges of solving the mystery impact the romantic relationship? Conversely, how does their relationship provide new insights or solutions to the mystery?

Step 7: External Obstacles

Create external obstacles to the relationship that are beyond the control of either character. This could include family objections, societal pressures, or external threats related to the mystery plot. How do these obstacles challenge the relationship, and how are they addressed or overcome?

Step 8: Moments of Vulnerability

Craft scenes where the protagonist and the romantic foil show vulnerability to each other. These moments should deepen their connection and understanding, revealing new layers to their characters and relationship.

Step 9: The Role of Humor

Inject humor into their relationship through banter, inside jokes, or amusing situations. How does humor play a role in keeping their relationship dynamic and resilient through the ups and downs?

Step 10: Future Teasers

Finally, brainstorm ways to tease the future development of the relationship at the end of each book. These could be unresolved tensions, upcoming challenges, or hints at deeper commitments. How do you keep readers invested in their relationship throughout the series?

Completing this exercise will help you create a romantic foil who not only serves as a captivating love interest but also enriches your protagonist's journey and the overall narrative. The evolving relationship should add depth to your cozy mysteries, providing readers with emotional investment ard a compelling reason to follow the series.

6

FOOTPRINTS LEFT IN THE SNOW – PLOT

Y OU MIGHT BE WONDERING WHY, WHEN COZY MYSTERIES ARE DRIVEN by plot, it's taken us so long to get to this foundational building block.

Though it is true the cozy mystery is plot driven, the appeal of the cozy lies in the characters and world-building. You can have the best plots in the world, but if the cozy reader doesn't cotton to your main characters or love the world you've created, they won't be back for more.

While I'm not saying your plots can be generic, there are only so many plots in the world. The success of your series is *largely* going to lean on your characters and setting, not least because your plots will often arise *out* of your setting and characters.

For example, if you've set your series in the Deep South, several plots could easily and instantly arise from that rich and colorful past: haunted plantations, lost confederate gold, a long-missing famous jazz musician…

How about a story that taps into the rich tapestry of the Deep South, steering clear of the usual tropes and instead diving into a lesser-explored facet of its history—a mystery centered around the Prohibition era, speakeasies, and the birth of jazz, set in a small but lively town in Louisiana?

The next thing to understand is that a cozy mystery is—well, all mysteries, really—simply a series of interviews.

These interviews must be interesting. They can also be funny, thrilling, surprising, touching—but they *must* be interesting.

Also, they need not be formal "interviews." Your protagonist cannot drag potential suspects down to their ice cream parlor to interrogate them. Every conversation your protagonist has with a potential witness or suspect is actually an interview—even if it is simply bumping into the murder victim's widow at a coffee house.

Every interview must move the story forward—whether the protagonist initially realizes it or not.

Which means, in every single conversation, there will be at least one nugget of useful information, as well as lots of extra chatter that may amuse, confuse, or simply add to local color and our understanding of other characters.

Roughly 90 percent of the detection in a cozy mystery occurs during interviews/conversations with other characters. And by *other characters*, I do not mean a law enforcement significant other. Certainly, *some* information can come that route, but having a cop boyfriend or brother-in-law or father cannot be how your sleuth solves all her cases.

Also, though cozy mystery protagonists are frequently intuitive, the solution to the mystery cannot come simply through a flash of intuition (let alone, a dream). It's fine for the intuition to come once a ton of information has been gathered and analyzed, but the deduction still has to arise from logic and reason. It has to be able to hold up in a court of law.

Which is to say, your detective cannot have a flash of intuition and confront the main suspect, who immediately breaks down and conveniently confesses all—even though there's zero proof and a first-year public defender could surely get him off.

A sleuth has to sleuth.

FOUR MANDATORY PLOT ELEMENTS IN A COZY MYSTERY NOVEL

1. The Hook

Pirate's treasure, a body in a snowman, a lost manuscript by Lord Byron, a stolen mummy, a murder in a locked room, someone vanished twenty years ago, an onstage murder, a long-lost heir returns… Basically, something exciting, unusual, and interesting has occurred. This intriguing inciting incident will ultimately, even if tangentially, tie into the murder investigation.

2. The Crime

Almost always murder. Even if murder is not the original crime, at some point, a violent or mysterious death should occur. SOMEONE HAS TO DIE. No, it's not absolutely mandatory, but the gentle readers of the cozy mystery subgenre are a blood-thirsty lot. Defy their expectations at your peril.

Oh, and two murders are better than one. But you can't just dispatch characters willy-nilly. There must be valid, understandable reasons for all the murder and mayhem. Typically, the second murder occurs in order to cover up the first murder. Although sometimes the second murder victim was the intended target all along.

3. Suspects

Ideally, two to three characters should have strong reasons for getting rid of your victim. In fact, those reasons should be strong enough that, were you to change your mind about the culprit late in the book, the story would still hang together. Fewer than three suspects isn't going to be much of a challenge for your readers. More than five strong suspects would probably just be confusing. One of the suspects cannot always be the protagonist, though sometimes it can be (especially in the first book of the series). One of the suspects is ideally someone we really don't want to be guilty.

Sometimes the murderer will be someone from our regular extended cast of characters, someone readers feel they know but don't think a lot about. This adds tension and suspense to future installments. However, avoid the tiresome cliché of the lifelong friend or family member suddenly and without warning turning into a complete lunatic.

I cannot stress enough: *your murderer must have a valid motive.* Meaning, a reason for committing murder that your reader can recognize though, obviously, not agree with. Being "crazy," on its own, will not cut it.

4. Clues and Red Herrings

In a cozy mystery, a red herring is an intentionally misleading clue or a piece of information that leads the protagonist (and the reader) astray, diverting attention from the true culprit or the actual solution to the mystery. Red herrings are designed to make the investigation more challenging by introducing clues and suspects that usually end up being unrelated to the crime. It's a classic misdirection technique used by mystery writers to add complexity to the plot and keep readers engaged and guessing until the very end

In real life, detectives follow the clues of evidence, both direct and circumstantial. In cozy mysteries, sleuths follow clues *and* red herrings—the more colorful, weird, and mysterious, the better.

Red herrings are a huge part of the fun in cozy mysteries, but they needn't always be dusty footprints beside an empty mummy case or the fingerprints of someone who disappeared in 1908. A red herring could be an intriguing character with a mysterious past who seems to have a motive for the crime but turns out to be completely unrelated to it.

The use of red herrings adds depth to the story, allowing for twists and turns that keep the narrative interesting. They also can fill up a lot of page time if your mystery is fairly slight. And they enhance the satisfaction for readers when they (or the protagonist) finally unravel the true mystery, having navigated through the maze of distractions and misleads.

Clues, on the other hand, do, in fact, lead the reader and the protagonist to the correct conclusion and the identity of the villain. Professionals and amateurs alike pay attention to the following clues:

Physical Evidence: This includes items found at the crime scene or in the victim's possession that can be directly linked to the murderer or the motive, such as a unique piece of jewelry, a handwritten note, or a distinctive weapon. It's the kind of clue that's hard to ignore but might need some puzzle-solving to understand its significance. Typically, your protagonist has access to these because they found the body or the victim has sent them this item for safekeeping.

Alibis and Timelines: Statements from characters that establish their whereabouts at the time of the crime. An obvious clue could be a seemingly solid alibi that, upon closer inspection, has holes or relies on unverified information, hinting at a suspect's possible guilt.

Overheard Conversations: Eavesdropped dialogues that hint at motives, secrets, or conflicts. These can provide direct insights into the relationships and tensions between characters, sometimes revealing more than intended by the speakers.

Behavioral Changes: A character acting out of character or showing unusual nervousness, hostility, guilt, or evasiveness can be an obvious clue, signaling their involvement in the mystery or knowledge of crucial information.

Forensic Results: While cozy mysteries often focus less on the technical aspects of crime-solving, simple forensic clues such as fingerprints, footprints, or the absence/presence of certain substances can provide clear pointers toward solving the case.

Motive-Revealing Clues: Discoveries that unveil possible motives for the crime, such as financial difficulties, romantic entanglements, rivalries, or revenge plots. These clues often come from digging into the victim's background or the relationships between characters.

Inconsistencies: Contradictions in stories or evidence that don't add up. This could be something as simple as a character claiming to have been somewhere they couldn't possibly have been or facts about the crime scene that don't match the supposed sequence of events.

Symbolic or Thematic Clues: Sometimes, clues can be more symbolic, tied to the theme of the book or the victim's personality. For example, a clue might be hidden within a piece of art or a book that was significant to the victim, offering insights into the nature of the crime or the identity of the murderer.

Cozy mysteries have their own unique flavor, and while they follow the basic plot structure of all mysteries, there are a few adjustments and nuances worth noting:

Introduction/Exposition: We know cozies often take place in a small, tightly knit community or a charming setting. The introduction is key in establishing this sense of place and the close-knit group of characters, often including a likable amateur sleuth with a personal stake in the mystery.

The Previously Mentioned Hook: Something interesting or unusual has happened that everyone is talking about. In fairness, sometimes there is no real hook. Sometimes the hook is simply the murder. Sometimes that's enough.

Inciting Incident: While this remains the discovery of a crime, typically a murder, it's usually sanitized. Remember, cozies tend to focus less on the gore and more on the puzzle. The crime disrupts the peaceful setting, and our amateur detective feels compelled to solve it, often because they or someone they care about is implicated.

Rising Action: As the sleuth investigates, they navigate through the community's quirks and secrets. There's a big emphasis on interpersonal relationships and character development. Puzzling out the mystery involves more social engineering and understanding of human nature than forensic science. The obstacles and conflicts often come in the form of local politics, gossip, and the personal challenges of the sleuth. In other words, up the ante.

Climax: The climax in a cozy mystery tends to be less violent or dangerous than in other mystery genres, focusing more on the intellectual triumph of solving the puzzle. The sleuth has a moment of revelation, often in a very personal or intimate setting, rather than a high-stakes confrontation. There will probably not be a climactic car chase or shoot-out—unless the chase takes place in golf carts and the shoot-out is with paint guns.

Falling Action: This phase involves the sleuth explaining how they solved the mystery, often gathering the key characters together for the big reveal. It's more about the satisfaction of the intellectual exercise and the restoration of social order than the adrenaline of the chase.

Resolution/Denouement: The resolution reinforces the restored order and community bonds. Relationships are mended, and the sleuth's role in the community is often celebrated—if only by their significant other. The ending usually aims to leave readers with a warm feeling, looking forward to the next adventure in this delightful world.

CONFLICT

Cozy mysteries, with their focus on character, setting, and puzzle over procedural details or violent crime, require a slightly different touch in each of these plot stages to maintain their distinctive charm and appeal. However, this does not mean the stories are without conflict.

I'm not sure why the word "conflict" makes so many writers anxious, but without conflict there is no story—even in the comfortable and generally peaceful world of the cozy mystery.

In literary terms, "conflict" is simply the struggle between opposing forces. It's the heart of *any* story, driving the narrative forward and keeping readers engaged. Without conflict, a story would lack tension, stakes, and, ultimately, interest.

The necessity of conflict in storytelling, especially in cozy mysteries, goes beyond the surface-level understanding of conflict as merely arguments or violence. Here's why conflict is indispensable and how it enriches a story, particularly from the cozy mystery perspective.

1. Conflict Drives the Plot

You want a plot, right? At its core, conflict propels the narrative forward. Without conflict, there's no story, just a series of events. Conflict introduces challenges and obstacles that the protagonist must overcome, which keeps readers turning the pages. In a cozy mystery, the conflict often starts with a crime that disrupts the peace of the community, setting the stage for the mystery that the protagonist needs to solve. This isn't just about arguments or unpleasantness; it's about setting up a puzzle that needs solving, creating a goal for the protagonist, and engaging the reader's curiosity.

2. Conflict Reveals Character

Characters are revealed through how they respond to conflict. Their reactions, decisions, and development are all influenced by the challenges they face. In cozy mysteries, it can be as subtle as a moral dilemma, a personal struggle to decide whether to investigate a crime, or even the internal conflict of balancing personal relationships with the pursuit of justice. These moments of conflict provide depth to characters and make them more relatable and human.

3. Conflict Engages Readers

Conflict creates tension and suspense, essential ingredients for keeping readers engaged. It raises questions that readers want to see answered: Who did it? Why? How will our protagonist solve the mystery? Even in the amiable environs of a cozy mystery, where the mood is generally more playful and the violence is offstage, conflict in the form of a puzzle or mystery keeps readers hooked. It's the engine of curiosity that drives the narrative.

4. Conflict Facilitates Growth and Change

The challenges characters face and the conflicts they navigate lead to growth and change, providing a satisfying character arc and narrative progression. This evolution is crucial for stories to feel complete and rewarding. In cozy mysteries, the protagonist's journey to solve the mystery often leads to personal growth, insights into human nature, and a deeper connection with their community. It's a testament to the idea that facing and overcoming challenges, even in a fictional setting, can lead to profound personal development.

5. Conflict Enhances Themes

Conflict allows writers to explore and reinforce the themes of their stories. Whether it's justice, truth, community, or the importance of knowledge, conflict brings these themes to the forefront and makes them more impactful. In cozy mysteries, the conflict arising from a crime introduces themes of right versus wrong, the importance of community, and the quest for truth, all of which are explored in a context that emphasizes the power of the individual to make a difference.

For beginning writers, especially those crafting cozy mysteries, it's vital to understand that conflict is not synonymous with aggression, negativity, or discomfort. Instead, it's a dynamic tool that adds complexity, engages the reader, and brings the story to life. It's about balancing the scales, solving puzzles, and restoring harmony, all of which are achieved through the resolution of conflict. Embrace conflict as a narrative necessity that opens up a whole new world of storytelling possibilities.

In the context of cozy mysteries, and indeed all genres, conflict comes in several delicious flavors:

Character vs. Character: This is one of the most common types of conflict, involving direct confrontation between characters. It could be the protagonist against the antagonist, such as a detective squaring off against a clever criminal, or interpersonal conflicts among characters that drive the narrative and develop character arcs. Cozy mysteries thrive on the dynamics between characters. Conflicts between the sleuth and suspects, or between townsfolk with long-standing feuds, add layers of intrigue. These interpersonal conflicts are usually more subdued and less violent than in other mystery genres, focusing on motives rooted in human emotions and relationships. The sleuth often has to navigate these troubled waters with tact and empathy.

Character vs. Society: Here, the protagonist is in conflict with societal norms, laws, or expectations. This type of conflict explores themes of individuality, freedom, and the struggle to effect change within a community or society at large. In cozies, this might manifest as the protagonist challenging local traditions or confronting societal issues. This is a common conflict in cozies, where your amateur sleuth is often pitted against the norms, expectations, or secrets of the small community. The sleuth's quest for truth might ruffle feathers, challenge local hierarchies, or expose hidden societal issues. This conflict adds depth to the narrative, showing the protagonist's determination to seek justice, even at the cost of personal comfort or social standing.

Character vs. Self: Internal conflict occurs within the character's mind, involving struggles of conscience, decisions, fears, or conflicting desires. This deeply personal conflict is crucial for character development, showing growth, and making characters more relatable and multidimensional. Your sleuth might grapple with self-doubt, ethical dilemmas, or personal growth challenges. This internal conflict is crucial for character development, making the sleuth relatable and human. They might question their own abilities, the moral implications of snooping around, or how their actions affect their relationships. Overcoming these internal hurdles can be as satisfying for the reader as solving the mystery.

Character vs. Nature: In this type of conflict, characters face natural disasters, extreme weather, or the environment itself as a formidable opponent. While not as common in cozy mysteries, it can add dramatic tension and force characters into survival mode, revealing their resilience and adaptability. Though less common in cozies, conflicts with natural elements can occur, especially if they highlight the setting's role in the story. A snowstorm might trap everyone in a manor, or a power outage could heighten tension at a crucial moment. These scenarios force the sleuth to adapt and often bring characters together in interesting ways, providing new opportunities for clues to emerge or for the sleuth to demonstrate ingenuity.

Character vs. Supernatural: This involves characters battling supernatural forces, such as ghosts, monsters, or curses. This appears in cozies that lean toward the paranormal, adding an intriguing layer to the mystery. Typically, in cozy mysteries, the ghosts aren't real. If they are real, your protagonist is not locked in mortal battle with them. That is more the realm of fantasy and horror. Although, I suppose if your main character is a witch, this type of conflict might come into play. However, even if your character is a witch, if she's in a cozy mystery, she's supposed to be solving mortal crimes with mortal victims and mortal antagonists who can face human justice.

Character vs. Technology: This conflict emerges when characters confront artificial intelligence, machines, or the internet. It can explore themes of dependency, the ethics of technology, and the impact of technological advancements on society. In modern cozies, technology can play a role in the conflict—whether it's the sleuth struggling with it, the community divided by it, or technology being the means through which a crime is committed or solved. This can add a contemporary twist to the traditional cozy formula, appealing to readers who enjoy a mix of old and new.

Character vs. Fate/Destiny: Here, characters struggle against forces of destiny or fate. They might try to outrun or change their predestined paths, raising questions about free will and determinism. You don't see much of this in cozy mysteries as it's a bit antithetical to the theme of these stories, although presumably a victim or antagonist might buy into the notion of predestined rights or outcomes. Again, a witch protagonist might experience this conflict.

While several of these conflicts can—and should—appear in one book, you do not need every conflict to pop up in every book. Pick and choose. Mix up the challenges your protagonist will face in each installment.

Just remember that the resolution of these conflicts should lead to personal growth for the sleuth, a deeper understanding of human nature for the reader, and the restoration of harmony in the sleuth's community.

Using the made-up character (yes, I know all characters are made up) of a gay antiques dealer by the name of Robin living in the New England village of Witches Bridge, MA, let's consider scenarios for potential conflict within a cozy mystery.

1. Character vs. Society

Robin stumbles upon a hidden piece of art rumored to be cursed, which he decides to display in his shop. The village is abuzz with whispers and warnings, as many believe the piece brings misfortune. Robin, initially skeptical, faces ostracism from the superstitious community. He must navigate the fine line between respecting local beliefs and proving there's a logical explanation behind the so-called curse, all while uncovering the real story behind the artwork.

2. Character vs. Character

During an annual antique fair in Witches Bridge, a rival dealer accuses Robin of selling counterfeit antiques. The accusation threatens Robin's reputation and his cherished relationships within the village. To clear his name, Robin needs to solve the mystery of the alleged counterfeit item, a journey that pits him directly against his accuser. This conflict delves into themes of professional jealousy, the value of reputation, and the lengths to which people will go to protect what they hold dear.

3. Character vs. Self

After purchasing a collection from an estate sale, Robin discovers a diary hidden within a secret compartment of an antique desk. The diary contains sensitive information that could ruin the reputation of a prominent Witches Bridge family. Robin is torn between his desire for historical preservation and his ethical duty to protect privacy. This internal struggle tests his principles and forces him to decide what kind of man he wants to be, highlighting his growth and the personal cost of uncovering secrets.

4. Character vs. Nature

A severe winter storm hits Witches Bridge, isolating the village from the outside world. During the blackout, a valuable antique goes missing from Robin's shop. With no way to call for outside help and the snow preventing anyone from leaving or entering the village, Robin must rely on his own resourcefulness and the help of his neighbors to find the thief. The storm's relentless force brings the community together, showcasing the resilience of Robin and the villagers, as well as the strength found in unity.

5. Character vs. Technology

Robin introduces an online auction as a modern twist to his antique business, but the launch is marred by a cyberattack that not only shuts down the auction but also leaks his clients' private information. Accusations fly, and trust in Robin wanes. He has to delve into the digital world, a place in which he's not entirely comfortable, to track down the hacker. Along the way, he learns about the vulnerabilities and strengths of embracing new technologies, balancing his love for the old with the realities of the modern world.

Each scenario presents Robin with unique challenges, pushing him to solve mysteries that not only involve external puzzles but also require him to reflect on his values, relationships, and place within the community of Witches Bridge. These conflicts enrich the cozy mystery narrative, making Robin's adventures in antique dealing as much about personal growth and community as they are about solving crimes.

When it comes to making trouble for our protagonist, we have so many terrific options for creating conflicts that feel organic rather than manufactured.

1. Develop Rich Characters with Hidden Depths

Create Complex Characters: Even in a cozy setting, characters should have secrets, desires, and fears that can lead to internal or interpersonal conflicts. A well-loved community member might have a hidden past, or a seemingly happy couple might have unseen tensions.

Use Relationships: Relationships are fertile ground for conflict. Rivalries, old grudges, or misunderstandings among characters can provide ongoing sources of tension that propel the plot and add depth.

2. Incorporate Community Dynamics

Small-Town Secrets: The close-knit nature of cozy mystery settings is perfect for brewing conflict. The history and dynamics of a small community can be a rich source of conflict as past incidents and local gossip come to light.

Community Roles: The protagonist's role in the community (such as a bookstore owner, librarian, or café owner) can naturally lead to conflicts with other community members, be it through competition, community projects, or local politics.

3. Use the Setting as a Character

Atmospheric Tension: The setting of your cozy mystery can add layers of conflict. An impending storm, a power outage in a critical moment, or a local festival can all serve as backdrops that heighten the tension.

Setting-Related Conflicts: Conflicts arising from the setting itself, such as disputes over land, historical buildings, or community traditions, can provide a continuous thread of tension throughout your story.

4. Weave in Subplots

Subplots as Conflict Sources: Subplots involving secondary characters can introduce conflicts that intersect with or run parallel to the main mystery. These can add complexity to the story and provide opportunities for character development.

Romantic Tension: A romantic subplot can offer a different kind of conflict, especially if the course of true love does not run smooth—which, frankly, it never should. In fiction, I mean. The balance between romantic developments and the main mystery plot can keep readers engaged.

5. Employ Misdirection and Red Herrings

Clues and False Leads: Skillfully placed clues and red herrings can create conflict by leading the protagonist and the reader astray. Our sleuth and her helpers can hold opposing views on what these clues mean, who they really implicate. The challenge of deciphering which clues are genuine adds an intellectual conflict to the mix.

Character Misdirection: Characters who are not what they seem can introduce conflict. A trustworthy friend might hide a secret agenda, or a suspected antagonist could turn out to be an ally.

6. Focus on Personal Growth and Challenges

Internal Conflict: Your protagonist's personal growth can be a source of conflict. Facing fears, overcoming personal flaws, or making difficult ethical choices can all add depth to the cozy mystery.

Challenges to Beliefs: Characters faced with situations that challenge their beliefs or moral compass can create engaging internal conflicts that resonate with readers.

7. Layer Conflicts

Vary Degrees of Conflict: Not all conflicts need to be high stakes. Not all conflicts have to be completely resolved in every book. A mix of serious and lighter conflicts can maintain tension without overwhelming the cozy atmosphere. Balancing a serious investigation with minor but amusing disputes keeps the tone in check. Your protagonist need not be the only conflicted character in your story. Because readers come to care about your supporting cast, the trials and tribulations of those characters are important to them. They *care*.

8. Feedback and Revision

Beta Readers and Critique Groups: Use feedback from readers familiar with the cozy mystery genre to identify if the conflicts feel genuine and engaging without crossing into the territory of more intense mystery genres.

By weaving together these elements, you can create a cozy mystery that delights and surprises readers, offering them a puzzle to solve alongside engaging characters and settings. Remember, the goal is to maintain the cozy atmosphere while still providing enough conflict to drive the narrative forward and keep readers turning the pages.

PACING

It is hard to write a satisfying and stimulating plot if you don't understand the role of pacing.

"Pacing" in literature refers to the speed or rhythm at which a story unfolds.

Pacing is how quickly or slowly events in the narrative occur and how much time the author devotes to developing scenes, characters, and conflicts.

Pacing is crucial because it affects how engaged readers are with the story; it's the tempo that keeps readers turning pages, eager to find out what happens next.

Here's a breakdown of how pacing works and why it's important, especially in genres like mystery and crime fiction:

1. Pacing Controls Reader Engagement

Pacing is a tool to control reader engagement and emotional response. Fast pacing, with quick scenes, swift action, and rapid dialog, can create excitement and tension, pulling readers along. Slow pacing allows for deeper exploration of characters, settings, and themes, letting readers immerse themselves in the complexities of the narrative. A well-paced story balances these elements to maintain interest without overwhelming or boring the reader.

2. Pacing Drives the Narrative Forward

Effective pacing ensures that the narrative moves forward compellingly. It involves the strategic arrangement of action scenes, exposition, character development, and cliffhangers to maintain momentum. In a cozy mystery, for instance, pacing might involve the careful placement of clues, red herrings, and character interactions to keep readers guessing without revealing too much too soon.

3. Pacing Enhances Tension and Suspense

In mystery and crime fiction, pacing is essential for building tension and suspense. The timing of reveals, the pace at which clues are discovered, and the intervals between key events all contribute to a sense of suspense, urging readers to solve the puzzle alongside the protagonist. Too fast, and the mystery may feel rushed; too slow, and the tension might wane.

4. Pacing Supports Theme and Tone

Pacing can also reflect the theme and tone of the story. A leisurely pace might suit a narrative with a reflective, introspective theme, while a fast-paced story might complement themes of urgency or danger. The pacing should match the overall atmosphere the writer wants to create, whether it's the cozy, gentle tempo of a small-town mystery or the brisk pace of a thriller. Know how to pace yourself.

5. Pacing Facilitates Structural Balance

Good pacing requires a balance between different parts of the story—beginning, middle, and end. Each section has its pacing needs; for example: a quick start to hook the reader, a middle that weaves in complexity without sagging, and an end that accelerates toward the climax and resolution. Managing pacing across these sections ensures that the story remains engaging throughout.

How do you know if your pacing is off?

If you can be objective about your own work, it's easier than you might think. Watch for these, and if, as you're reading through, you feel a little niggle of doubt, *go with it.*

Long Stretches of Uninterrupted Action or Exposition: Beware the info dump. However, nonstop action can be as tiring as long-winded exposition. If your story jumps from one high-tension scene to another without giving the reader a moment to breathe or process what they've learned so far, or if it dwells too long on background information without advancing the plot, the pacing might be off.

Character Development Feels Rushed or Shallow: We've talked A LOT about character development, so hopefully this isn't going to be your downfall. However, pacing isn't just about the speed of the plot; it's also about giving characters time to grow and reveal themselves. If key moments of character development feel hurried or occur without enough buildup, it might indicate pacing issues.

The Stakes Don't Escalate Smoothly: In a well-paced story, the tension and stakes should gradually increase, leading to a climax. If your story plateaus, with the stakes remaining constant or jumping erratically, it can disrupt the pacing and lessen the impact of the climax.

Certain Scenes Feel Out of Place: Listen to that little voice in the back of your mind! If some scenes seem too slow or too fast compared to the rest of the story, or if they don't contribute to advancing the plot or developing the characters, it can indicate pacing issues. These scenes might need to be revised or cut to maintain a consistent flow.

Loss of Interest in the Middle: Ugh. Middle-aged sag. The middle of a story is often where pacing issues are most evident. If the narrative sags or feels like it's meandering without direction, it's a sign that the pacing is off. This is sometimes referred to as the "muddy middle."

Climax Feels Anticlimactic: The kiss of death. If the climax of your story arrives too suddenly, without sufficient buildup, the pacing may need to be adjusted. At the same time, don't drag the ending out. If there is nothing left to resolve, it's time to wrap it up. Yes, there will always be the readers out there who wanted a little more time with the characters just because. IGNORE THEM. A well-paced story builds smoothly to its climax, maintaining tension and interest to the end, and then the bubble pops, the spell is broken. The reader should always be left wanting more.

Reader Feedback Indicates Confusion or Boredom: Better this happens before than after publication! If beta readers or early reviewers mention that they're confused about the plot or the characters, or if they're skipping sections because they're bored, it's a strong indicator that the pacing is uneven.

To check the pacing in your stories, consider the rhythm of scenes, how you alternate between action and reflection, and whether each chapter moves the story forward. A well-paced story, like a well-composed piece of music, has variations in tempo that enhance the overall experience, leading to a satisfying crescendo and resolution. Adjusting pacing might involve cutting unnecessary parts, adding scenes to develop characters or plot points more fully, or reordering scenes to improve the flow and buildup of tension.

How do you adjust your pacing?

Do not be afraid to cut anything that raises a question in your mind. That's first and foremost. Not everything we write is golden. In fact, sometimes the lines and scenes we love the most don't add anything to the story. But scissors aren't your only tool. Writers can adjust pacing through sentence structure, paragraph length, chapter breaks, and the detail level. Short, sharp sentences and chapters can speed things up, while longer, more descriptive passages can slow things down. Action scenes should be brisk. Romantic scenes should be leisurely. The key is to use pacing deliberately, shaping the reader's experience and maintaining control over the narrative flow.

Understanding and mastering pacing allows writers to craft stories that captivate and resonate, making it a vital aspect of storytelling, especially in genres that rely heavily on engagement and suspense, like mystery and crime fiction.

BOTH DEATH AND DANGER SCORNING

Sleuthing is a hazardous business. Especially for amateurs. Cozy mystery protagonists do not carry guns. If they have to fight for their lives, they will have to use their wits and whatever weapons lie in reach.

In the cozy mystery genre, balancing the threat of violence or disaster with lighter, cozier elements like humor and romance is a delicate art. This balance is crucial for maintaining the genre's hallmark—providing a comfortable, engaging read while still delivering the suspense and excitement of a mystery.

1. Subtlety in Threat and Violence

As discussed, cozy mysteries inherently downplay violence and direct threats. The crime, often a murder, happens off-page, and any violence is implied rather than graphically described. Subsequent threats are often more psychological or situational. The threat should feel real but not terrifying. You're not going for a nail-biter.

2. Incorporating Humor and Romance

Humor and romance are integral to cozy mysteries, providing a counterbalance to the central mystery. Humorous interactions, quirky characters, and romantic subplots are woven throughout the narrative, offering readers moments of relief and enjoyment amidst the sleuthing. The key is to integrate these lighter moments at points where the narrative tension naturally dips, allowing for a pacing rhythm that feels organic and satisfying.

3. Maintaining Engagement Without Overwhelm

Hey, overwhelm is a real word. It's a noun. Anyway, the pace of a cozy mystery should engage without overwhelming with too much action or complexity. Cozy mystery readers aren't looking for a high-octane thriller. Your goal is the steady drip of clues and developments, interspersed with character-driven scenes that offer insight, humor, or romantic tension. The goal is to keep readers turning pages, eager to see how the protagonist navigates both the investigation and their personal life.

4. Building Tension Through Character and Setting

Instead of relying on action-packed sequences or graphic danger to build tension, cozy mysteries often use character relationships and the setting itself as sources of suspense. The pacing of character interactions and the revelation of secrets tied to the setting (such as a small town's historical feud or a hidden aspect of a quaint business) are timed to build suspense in a way that feels true to the cozy genre. This approach ensures that the tension rises at a pace that complements the story's tone.

5. Leading to a Satisfying Conclusion

The conclusion of a cozy mystery typically sees an acceleration in pacing as the pieces of the puzzle come together. This increase in pace toward the climax ensures that the resolution feels earned and satisfying, tying up not just the mystery but also advancing character arcs, humor, and romance subplots. The pacing here is crucial; it must gather all the threads of the story, from the carefree to the suspenseful, and weave them into a conclusion that feels both exciting and true to the cozy atmosphere. You've got to move fast, but not so fast that the reader's head is spinning, wondering what the heck just happened.

In crafting a cozy mystery, the writer's challenge is to juggle the elements of threat and coziness in a way that feels seamless and engaging. Pacing is the tool that allows for this balance, ensuring that the story provides a comfortable escape with just the right amount of suspense and intrigue.

Here are some practical tips and tools for beginning cozy mystery writers to create and maintain the ideal pacing:

1. Plan Your Plot Points

Outline Major Events: You don't have to do a full-on outline with bullet points. But at least consider sketching out the key events of your mystery, including the crime, major clues, red herrings, character development milestones, and the resolution. This helps ensure your story has a clear direction and that you evenly distribute these elements for consistent pacing.

OR

Use a Timeline: A visual timeline can help you see how your plot points are spaced and allow you to adjust the pacing before you get too deep into writing.

2. Balance Action with Character Moments

Interweave Character Development: Use quieter moments of character interaction, humor, and romance to offer readers a breather between the twists and turns of the mystery. These moments can deepen engagement without necessarily pushing the plot forward at breakneck speed.

Character-Driven Subplots: Incorporate subplots that explore your characters' backgrounds, relationships, or personal growth. These can run parallel to the main mystery and provide pacing variety.

3. Master the Chapter Cliffhanger

End Chapters with Questions OR on an exciting development: Leave a question hanging at the end of chapters to propel readers into the next. It doesn't always have to be dramatic; even a small mystery or an unexpected arrival can keep readers turning pages.

Vary Chapter Lengths: Playing with chapter lengths can affect pacing. Shorter chapters can quicken the pace, while longer chapters can slow it down for more in-depth exploration. (Personally, I like all my chapters to be about the same length, but a lot of people recommend this.)

4. Incorporate Pacing Through Setting and Atmosphere

Use Setting to Control Tempo: Descriptions of your cozy setting can slow down the pace, offering a sense of place and atmosphere, while scenes with minimal setting details can speed things up. Choose where to elaborate and where to streamline based on the pacing needs of your narrative.

Atmospheric Details: Use the unique elements of your setting (a failing resort, a magic shop, a mysterious old mansion) to create moments of suspense or relief, influencing the pacing indirectly through mood.

5. Monitor Dialogue and Narrative Balance

Dialogue to Accelerate Pace: Quick exchanges of dialogue can speed up the pace, making scenes feel lively and immediate. Use dialogue for key revelations or to increase tension subtly.

Narrative Passages for Depth: Longer narrative passages can slow the pacing, allowing for backstory, clue analysis, or the sleuth's reflections. Use these sections judiciously to ensure they contribute to the story without stalling momentum.

6. Feedback and Revision

Beta Readers and Critique Partners: Use feedback from trusted readers to identify pacing issues. They can tell you where the story lags or feels rushed.

Read Aloud: Reading your manuscript aloud can help you catch pacing issues by feeling the rhythm of your story. You'll naturally notice when things feel too slow or too fast.

7. Study Cozy Mysteries

I know! What a concept. Read in the genre you want to write in?! REVOLUTIONARY. Anyway.

Analyze Your Favorites: Pay attention to how your favorite cozy mysteries handle pacing. Note how they balance the investigation with character development, the distribution of clues, and how they maintain suspense without overwhelming the reader.

Remember, *pacing is not just about speed*; it's about rhythm and flow. The goal is to keep your readers engaged and moving smoothly through the story, balancing moments of tension with those of character-driven warmth and humor. Mastering pacing is a skill developed over time, so keep experimenting.

TO OUTLINE OR NOT TO OUTLINE

The debate over outlining versus "pantsing" (writing by the seat of your pants) is a perennial one among writers, but when it comes to genres with intricate plots like cozy mysteries, outlines can be invaluable.

Here's why an outline is not just useful but often essential in crafting a well-written cozy mystery series, and how it actually fosters creativity rather than stifles it:

1. Structure and Coherence

Keeps the Mystery Tight: Cozy mysteries thrive on tight, coherent plots where every detail matters. An outline ensures that clues, red herrings, and character arcs are introduced and resolved at the right moments, keeping the story engaging and satisfying for readers.

Series Continuity: For series writing, outlines help maintain consistency and continuity across books. They allow you to track character development, recurring themes, and overarching series plots, ensuring that each book fits well within the larger narrative.

2. Efficiency and Problem-Solving

Saves Time: Outlines act as a roadmap, saving you from dead ends and major rewrites. Knowing where your story is headed allows you to write more efficiently and confidently. It's the difference between setting out with a well-packed suitcase and a map versus stumbling out the front door with a bindle and broken compass.

Preemptive Problem-Solving: By plotting out the story beforehand, you can identify potential plot holes, pacing issues, and character inconsistencies early on. This preemptive problem-solving is much easier than fixing structural issues after the fact.

3. Creative Freedom Within Boundaries

A Framework for Creativity: Far from stifling creativity, an outline provides a framework within which creativity can flourish. Knowing the major plot points frees you to explore character development, dialogue, and the nuances of the mystery with the confidence that you're always moving the story forward.

Flexibility: An outline isn't a straitjacket. (Unless you want it to be.) It's a living document that can evolve as you write. If you come up with new ideas or directions for your story, you can adjust your outline accordingly. This flexibility encourages creativity while keeping the story on track.

4. Pacing and Tension

Control Pacing: Outlines allow you to plan the pacing of your story, ensuring that the narrative builds tension effectively and keeps readers engaged from beginning to end.

Strategic Reveals: By plotting out when to reveal certain pieces of information, you can better manage suspense and surprise, key elements of a cozy mystery.

5. Character Arcs and Development

Consistent Character Growth: Outlines help you track character development across the narrative, ensuring that each character's growth is consistent and believable.

Interweaving Arcs: For a series, outlines enable you to weave character arcs across books, planning long-term growth and changes that contribute to the series' depth and appeal.

6. Focus and Motivation

A Clear Goal: Having a clear outline can keep you motivated and focused. It's easier to tackle a large project like a novel when you know what you need to write next.

Measurable Progress: Outlines allow you to set and achieve short-term goals (like finishing a chapter or a key scene), which can be incredibly motivating during the long process of writing a book.

CONCLUSION

If you're allergic to the idea of an outline, then that's that. You have to do what works for you. However, I do get tired of hearing comments about how outlining kills creativity from people who don't actually outline.

Outlining a cozy mystery—or any book, really—is about laying down a flexible framework that guides your storytelling. It ensures that your narrative is coherent, your characters are well-developed, and your mystery unfolds in a satisfying way, all while providing the freedom to explore and be creative within that structure.

For many writers, the outline becomes a creative tool that brings clarity, focus, and confidence to the writing process, turning the daunting task of novel-writing into a manageable and even enjoyable journey.

MURDER IN THREE ACTS

You've probably heard of the Three Act Structure. If you don't like the idea of outlining, then you might consider the three-act structure. This is a classic story model used in narrative fiction that divides a story into three distinct parts: the Setup, the Confrontation, and the Resolution.

This simple structure helps in organizing the plot and character development in a coherent and accessible manner. It's particularly popular in screenwriting, but it's equally valuable for novels and short stories, including mystery and crime fiction.

Act 1: Setup

Introduction: Introduces the main characters, setting, and the story's world. It establishes the protagonist's normal life before the main plot kicks in.

Inciting Incident: A pivotal event that disrupts the protagonist's normal life and sets the main story in motion. It's the hook that pulls the protagonist (and the readers) into the conflict.

Plot Point One: Often ends Act 1. This is a significant event that fully commits the protagonist to their journey, clearly defining the story's direction. It transitions the narrative from the setup to the confrontation phase.

Act 2: Confrontation

Rising Action: The bulk of the story takes place here, featuring challenges, obstacles, and further development of the plot and characters. The protagonist faces increasing difficulties, and the stakes become higher.

Midpoint: A crucial moment in the middle of the story that often changes the game: revealing new information, shifting the protagonist's understanding of the situation, or intensifying the conflict.

Plot Point Two: Also known as the climax of Act 2, this is a critical turning point where the protagonist's goals are furthest from reach, often leading to their lowest moment. It sets the stage for the final act by presenting a seemingly insurmountable challenge.

Act 3: Resolution

Climax: The peak of the story, where the tension and conflict reach their highest point. The protagonist faces the main conflict head-on, and the outcome is decided.

Falling Action: After the climax, the story begins to wrap up. The consequences of the climax are explored, and loose ends start to tie up.

Denouement/Resolution: The story concludes, and the narrative comes full circle. The protagonist's journey is resolved, whether through success, failure, or a mix of both. The new status quo is established, showing how the characters have changed from the beginning.

The three-act structure provides a solid framework for constructing a well-paced and compelling narrative. It helps in pacing the story correctly, ensuring that there's a clear arc of tension and development, and making the storyline more satisfying for readers.

EXERCISE:
CHECKLIST FOR LOOSE ENDS

Tying up loose ends is crucial in cozy mystery writing to ensure a satisfying resolution for readers. Here's a practical exercise that can help writers ensure they've addressed all necessary points in their story.

This checklist might seem daunting, but it's an effective way to ensure your cozy mystery is satisfyingly complete, leaving no stone unturned and no question unanswered. It not only enhances the quality of your manuscript but also your skills as a storyteller when you're first starting out.

1. Create a Plot Element List:

Characters: List all major and minor characters, including suspects, victims, and side characters involved in subplots.

Clues: Note every clue introduced, no matter how small or misleading (red herrings).

Subplots: Outline each subplot, including romantic elements, personal growth challenges, community issues, etc.

Questions Raised: Write down every question your story poses, both directly (through characters) and indirectly (through narrative).

2. Review and Resolve:

Go through your Plot Element List and ask the following for each item:

Characters: Have all character arcs been resolved? Are their roles in the main plot and subplots clear by the end? Have any characters introduced mysteries or questions that haven't been addressed?

Clues: Has each clue been explained or connected to the resolution of the mystery? Are there any loose ends with the red herrings that might confuse readers?

Subplots: Have all subplots been resolved satisfactorily? Does each subplot tie back into the main story in some way, contributing to the overall narrative or character development?

Questions Raised: Ensure every question posed in your story has an answer by the end. This includes mysteries, character backgrounds, relationship outcomes, etc.

3. Cross-Reference with the Manuscript:

With your checklist in hand, go through your manuscript. Mark off each item as you verify its resolution in the text. Pay special attention to the last few chapters, where most resolutions occur, but don't neglect earlier chapters—some resolutions might be spread out or hinted at before the final reveal.

4. Seek External Feedback:

Once you've gone through the checklist yourself, it can be incredibly helpful to have beta readers or a writing group review your story with the same list in mind. They might catch unresolved elements you've overlooked. Now, I basically rely on my editors for this, but if you're very new, it might be a good idea to have a few people read your manuscript before you summon the help of a paid professional.

5. Final Review:

After adjustments based on feedback, go through your list one last time to ensure all elements have been addressed. This final review is your safety net before considering the manuscript ready for submission or publication.

Additional Tips:

Keep Detailed Notes: Throughout the writing process, keep detailed notes on all elements introduced in your story. This makes the Loose Ends Checklist easier to compile and more comprehensive.

Timeline: Consider creating a timeline alongside your checklist to visually track when each plot element is introduced and resolved. This can help identify any pacing issues related to the resolution of plot points.

SAMPLE COZY MYSTERY OUTLINE: "THE CURSE OF WITCHES BRIDGE"

This will be a great exercise in blending character vs. society conflict with the charming quirks of a cozy mystery. I'll include points on conflict and pacing to guide beginners through crafting a compelling narrative.

Introduction

Setting: Introduce the quaint village of Witches Bridge, a place with rich history and superstitions, during its annual art and antiques fair.

Characters: Present Robin, our gay antiques dealer with a keen eye for unique finds, and introduce key village characters (e.g., the skeptical local historian, the supportive but worried love interest—as a matter of fact, the historian could be the love interest—Robin's assistant Ivy, and a few superstitious townsfolk).

Inciting Incident: Robin unveils a newly acquired piece of art rumored to be cursed. His excitement over the find is met with immediate concern and warnings from the community. We learn the artwork's previous owner died under mysterious circumstances.

Early Developments

Conflict Introduction: Highlight the village's reaction. A series of minor misfortunes (a broken window, a boyfriend who wants him to stay out of trouble, a mysterious illness, a series of bad luck events) begins, and the villagers blame the cursed artwork. Robin faces social ostracism.

> **Pacing Tip:** *Start with a gentle pace, introducing the conflict slowly, to build the atmosphere and deepen the reader's connection to the setting and characters.*

Middle Section

Deepening Conflict: As Robin insists on keeping the artwork—he needs a good reason for this—the ostracism worsens. Robin discovers historical inconsistencies about the artwork's provenance and the nature of the curse. As he delves deeper, he begins to recognize (2–3) possible suspects in the previous owner's death.

Introduce Subplots: Weave in subplots to explore village life and relationships, such as a more problems in his romance—perhaps someone's old boyfriend shows up?—and a village elder with secret knowledge about the art's history.

> *Pacing Tip: The pacing should pick up here, alternating between moments of conflict escalation and quieter, character-driven scenes to maintain engagement without overwhelming the reader.*

Climax

Revelation: Robin, with the help of the village elder and his friends and boyfriend, uncovers the truth behind the artwork—a tale of lost love and a misunderstood curse, perhaps tied to a historic village scandal—and the discovery that the previous owner's death was indeed accidental. (Please note, in an actual cozy mystery, this is going to irritate the heck out of readers—ideally, you want your suspicious deaths to be homicides).

Turning Point: A major event (e.g., a fire or a dramatic confrontation during a village meeting) forces the community to confront their superstitions and Robin's ostracism.

> *Pacing Tip: This section should be fast-paced, with shorter scenes and chapters to build tension and drive toward the resolution.*

Falling Action

Resolution of Subplots: Address the subplots (e.g., the romance finds stability, and the villagers start to accept Robin again).

Community Reflection: The village reflects on the events, considering the balance between tradition and progress, superstition and science.

> *Pacing Tip: Slow the pace to allow readers to absorb the climax's aftermath and begin to see the story's resolution.*

Conclusion

The Artwork's Fate: Robin decides what to do with the artwork now that its story is known, perhaps leading to a museum donation or a special village display.

Character Growth: Show how Robin has grown from the experience, gaining a deeper understanding and respect for the village's traditions and earning a place in the community. He has also learned to deal with his boyfriend's concerns and skepticism in a way that will leave their relationship stronger.

> **Pacing Tip:** *Conclude with a gentle, reflective pace, offering closure to the story and character arcs, leaving readers with a sense of satisfaction and completion.*

Remember, **Conflict** is the story's heartbeat, driving the narrative and character development. In the above outline, the primary conflict is Robin's struggle against societal superstitions. This conflict is personal, affecting his business and social standing, and it's also broader, touching on themes of tradition vs. change.

Meanwhile, **Pacing** controls the story's rhythm, ensuring readers are engaged but not overwhelmed. Start slow to build the world, pick up speed as conflicts intensify, then slow down again to let readers reflect on the resolution.

The key is balance, ensuring each scene and chapter contributes to moving the story forward or deepening the reader's understanding of characters and setting.

By focusing on these key elements, beginners to the subgenre can craft a cozy mystery that's compelling, character-driven, and satisfying, all while navigating the intricate dance of conflict and pacing.

A CRASH COURSE ON CRIMINAL INVESTIGATION BASICS

Although there are no graphic violence or forensic details in the cozy mystery, and taking into account that police procedure specifics can change from jurisdiction to jurisdiction, it's helpful to at least understand some of the universal basics of any homicide investigation.

By which I mean, there are certain things aspiring cozy mystery writers should keep in mind, so as to add the *appearance* of realism and credibility to the narrative. You don't have to—in fact, you should not—get into the weeds are far as the details of the law enforcement side of the investigation goes.

You're not writing a police procedural. In fact, you are writing the absolute opposite of that because you're writing the viewpoint of amateurs. But it's still helpful to know what happens when someone drops dead under mysterious circumstances.

INITIAL RESPONSE AND SECURING THE SCENE

The first officers on the scene secure it to prevent contamination of evidence. This is crucial for maintaining the integrity of the investigation. Here's a quick rundown of what the police do when they first arrive at a crime scene:

1. Assess the Scene for Safety: First things first, they ensure the scene is safe for themselves and others. This means checking for any ongoing threats or hazards.

2. Provide Assistance: They offer immediate aid to any victims or injured persons if necessary.

3. Secure the Perimeter: Officers set up barriers or tape to define the crime scene's boundaries, keeping unauthorized persons out to prevent contamination of evidence.

4. Preserve Evidence: They take steps to protect evidence from being altered, destroyed, or lost. This could mean covering physical evidence to protect it from the elements or ensuring nothing is moved unnecessarily.

5. *Document Initial Observations:* Officers make initial observations about the scene, noting anything immediately noticeable or out of place. They might start taking photos or jotting down notes about the environment and any visible evidence.

6. *Call for Backup and Specialists:* Depending on the crime, they might call in detectives, forensic teams, or other specialists to further investigate and collect evidence.

7. *Witness Coordination:* They identify and separate witnesses to prevent them from talking to each other, thereby preserving individual accounts of the event.

8. *Establish a Log:* A log or record of everyone who enters and exits the scene is kept to maintain the integrity of the scene and track potential sources of contamination.

These steps can vary based on the specifics of the crime and the scene, but generally, this initial approach is about balancing the preservation of life and evidence with the need to start piecing together what happened.

DOCUMENTATION

Every aspect of the crime scene is documented thoroughly, including photographs, sketches, and written descriptions. This includes the position of the body, any items found near the body, and potential signs of struggle or entry. Both first responders and detectives play roles in this, albeit in slightly different capacities.

1. First Responders

The first officers on the scene begin the documentation process. Their primary focus is on securing the scene and making initial observations. They might take preliminary photos or make quick sketches to capture the scene's initial state, noting positions of bodies, weapons, and any other evidence in sight. Their documentation provides a crucial first look before any changes occur, even unintentional ones by emergency personnel. These notes will later be reviewed by the detectives.

2. Detectives and Crime Scene Investigators (CSIs)

Once the scene is secure, detectives and CSIs take over the thorough documentation process. This involves several detailed steps:

1. Photography: Detailed photographs are taken from multiple angles and distances to capture the entire scene and specific pieces of evidence in their original state. This often includes a progression from general to specific: wide shots of the area, mid-range shots, and close-ups of individual pieces of evidence.

2. Sketches and Diagrams: Detailed sketches and diagrams complement photographs, providing measurements and spatial relationships that photos alone might not convey. These can include dimensions of the room, distances between objects, and the exact position of evidence within the scene.

3. Videography: Video recordings offer a continuous, flowing documentation of the crime scene, capturing details that still photographs might miss. It provides a real-time walkthrough of the scene, giving viewers a comprehensive understanding of the spatial relationships and layout.

4. Notes and Reports: Detailed notes and reports are compiled, including descriptions of the scene, the condition and position of evidence, environmental conditions, and any initial observations or changes made to the scene for safety or evidence preservation. These notes often include the observations of the first officers on the scene, interviews with witnesses or first responders, and any preliminary findings or hypotheses about what occurred.

5. Evidence Collection and Cataloging: As evidence is collected, detailed records are kept of where each item was found, its condition, and any changes made during its collection. This process is meticulously documented through photographs, notes, and chain-of-custody forms to ensure the integrity and admissibility of evidence in court.

Detectives and CSIs work closely together, using their documentation to build a comprehensive, detailed picture of the crime scene. This documentation is crucial for the ongoing investigation, allowing for the reconstruction of events and providing essential evidence for prosecution. The initial documentation by first responders sets the stage, but the detailed work of detectives and CSIs deepens and expands that initial picture into a full narrative of the crime.

COLLECTION OF PHYSICAL EVIDENCE

Evidence is collected systematically, including fingerprints, blood samples, fibers, and any items that could be related to the crime. The chain of custody is meticulously maintained. While you're probably not going to be writing about the collection of physical evidence at a crime scene, you do want to at least understand how it works and who's involved in the process.

1. Who Collects the Evidence

Crime scene investigators or forensic technicians are usually responsible for collecting physical evidence. These professionals have specialized training in handling and preserving various types of evidence to prevent contamination or degradation.

2. How Physical Evidence is Collected

Preparation: Before collecting evidence, CSIs wear protective gear to prevent contamination. They also ensure they have the appropriate collection tools and containers for different types of evidence (e.g., gloves, tweezers, swabs, paper bags, plastic containers).

3. Identification and Documentation

Each piece of evidence is first identified and documented in its original location. Photos are taken, and the item may be marked with an evidence number. This step is crucial for maintaining the context of where each piece of evidence was found.

4. Collection Techniques

The technique for collecting evidence depends on its nature. For example:

Fingerprints are lifted using dusting powders and lift tape.

Biological materials (like blood or bodily fluids) are collected with swabs and stored in breathable containers to prevent degradation.

Firearms and bullets are carefully handled to preserve markings, with firearms being secured in boxes or gun bags.

Digital evidence (like computers or phones) is collected with precautions to prevent data loss or corruption.

Packaging and Labeling: Each piece of evidence is packaged separately to avoid cross-contamination. It's then labeled with details about the evidence, where it was found, who collected it, and the date and time of collection.

5. Chain of Custody

A log is maintained to record everyone who handles the evidence from the scene to the lab and eventually to the courtroom. This chain of custody is critical for ensuring the integrity of the evidence and its admissibility in court.

6. Difficulty of the Process

The difficulty can vary widely depending on the type of evidence and the conditions of the crime scene. For instance, collecting DNA evidence in a clean indoor environment might be straightforward, while collecting evidence from an outdoor scene affected by weather can be challenging. The process requires meticulous attention to detail, patience, and sometimes creativity to preserve the integrity of the evidence.

7. Recording the Process

NOTE: The entire process is meticulously recorded:

Photographs are taken before and after collecting evidence to show its original state and how it was handled.

Notes and Forms detail each step taken during collection, including descriptions of the evidence, how it was collected, and any observations made by the CSIs.

Evidence Logs track the chain of custody, documenting every person who has handled the evidence and when.

Collecting physical evidence is a crucial and often intricate part of the investigative process, requiring specialized skills and tools to ensure evidence is preserved in a way that it can be effectively used in legal proceedings.

AUTOPSY

An autopsy is usually conducted to determine the cause of death, time of death, and any other details that might be apparent from the body. This can provide critical information about the murderer's methods and intentions. You will not be describing autopsies. Your characters will not be attending autopsies. Random citizens are not invited to attend autopsies.

However, you should know what helpful facts about the crime might be discovered during the autopsy.

1. Cause of Death: This is the primary goal, determining what caused the person's death. It could be a disease, a physical injury, poisoning, or another condition.

2. Manner of Death: The autopsy can help establish whether the death was natural, accidental, suicidal, homicidal, or undetermined. This is especially crucial in criminal investigations.

3. Time of Death: While often not as precise as depicted in fiction, estimates can be made based on body temperature, rigor mortis (the stiffening of muscles after death), and livor mortis (the settling of blood in the lowest parts of the body).

4. Injury Analysis: The pathologist examines the body for injuries or signs of violence, such as stab wounds, gunshot wounds, signs of strangulation, or evidence of blunt force trauma. The characteristics of these injuries can indicate the type of weapon used and sometimes the sequence of events.

5. Toxicology Results: Chemical analysis of tissues and fluids can reveal the presence of drugs, alcohol, poisons, or other substances, which can be crucial in determining cause and manner of death.

6. Identification of Diseases: Autopsies often uncover diseases or medical conditions that might have contributed to the person's death or were simply undiagnosed during their life. Detailed examination of organs and tissues can reveal signs of diseases such as heart disease, cancer, or infections, providing insights into the person's health prior to death.

7. *Confirmation of Identity:* Though usually known before the autopsy, in some cases, the process can help confirm the deceased's identity through dental records, surgical implants, or unique physical characteristics.

The findings from an autopsy can be pivotal in criminal investigations, helping to clarify the circumstances of the death and providing crucial evidence for legal proceedings. Moreover, in non-criminal cases, autopsies can provide families with closure or understanding about their loved ones' final moments and contribute to medical knowledge.

However, while autopsies provide a wealth of information, there are limits to what they can reveal: exact time of death; psychological state of the victim or perpetrator; detailed circumstances of death; exact cause in complex cases; long-term effects of injuries or poisonings; some neurological conditions; privacy and personal experiences.

In other words, the results of an autopsy must be combined with other investigative techniques to form a complete picture of the events leading to death.

WITNESS INTERVIEWS

Your character will almost certainly be interviewed by the police at least once. If they become a prime suspect, they will be interviewed again, and possibly even interrogated (which is a much more intense experience). It's important to understand what information detectives are trying to gather during those initial interviews. They are not expecting to hear a confession, although in real life that does occasionally happen.

Through the interview process, detectives attempt to gather comprehensive information to piece together what happened before, during, and after a crime. Each witness can offer a unique perspective, so detectives try to cover a wide range of questions to construct a detailed picture.

Here are some of the key facts detectives attempt to learn during these interviews:

1. Witness Identification and Background: Basic details about the witness, including their name, age, address, and relationship to the crime scene or victim. This helps establish their potential bias or reliability.

2. Details of the Event: Detectives ask for a step-by-step account of what the witness saw, heard, or experienced. This includes actions, conversations, or any specific details about the crime itself.

3. Sequence of Events: Understanding the timeline is crucial. Detectives try to pinpoint when each aspect of the incident occurred to establish a sequence of events and identify any possible discrepancies with other accounts.

4. Descriptions of Suspects: Witnesses can provide descriptions of any suspects involved, including physical appearance, clothing, distinctive marks, or behaviors. This information is vital for identifying and locating the person(s) responsible.

5. Descriptions of Vehicles: If vehicles were involved, details about their make, model, color, license plate, and any noticeable damage or distinguishing features are collected.

6. Possible Motive: Witnesses might offer insights into the potential motive behind the crime, especially if they know the victim or the suspect. Understanding the motive can help detectives narrow down their list of suspects.

7. Relationships and Interactions: Information about the relationships between involved parties can shed light on possible reasons for the crime. Detectives explore any known conflicts, recent encounters, or relevant history between the victim(s) and others.

8. Evidence and Artifacts: Witnesses may be aware of physical evidence left at the scene or have information about objects related to the crime, which can lead to critical evidence or corroborate other findings.

9. *Alibis and Corroboration:* Detectives verify the witness's whereabouts at the time of the crime to confirm their account and potentially corroborate the timelines and activities of others involved.

10. *Witness's Condition:* The mental and emotional state of the witness during the event can affect their perception and recall. Detectives assess this to gauge the reliability of their account.

11. *Any Changes in Story:* Detectives pay attention to any inconsistencies or changes in the witness's story over time or when compared to other accounts, which can indicate areas needing further investigation or clarification.

12. *Additional Witnesses or Participants:* Detectives ask if the witness noticed anyone else at the scene who might provide further information or if they know of anyone else with relevant knowledge about the incident.

Remember, anything that a member of law enforcement would be interested in knowing, is something your sleuth *should also be trying to figure out*. When your sleuth is asking questions, these are the types of information he should be trying to learn.

The process is as much about reading between the lines and noting nonverbal cues as it is about the facts stated, which is where your sleuth's knowledge of her neighbors or his extensive study of local customs comes into play. Witness interviews enable detectives to fill in gaps and identify new avenues of investigation—that is as true for your protagonist as it is for the professionals.

USE OF FORENSIC ANALYSIS

While not delving into the graphic details, acknowledging the role of forensics in solving a crime is important. This includes analysis of DNA, blood spatter, ballistic evidence, and digital footprints. It encompasses a wide range of techniques and disciplines aimed at analyzing physical evidence collected from a crime scene to support investigations and legal proceedings.

Uses of Forensic Analysis

1. Identification of Substances: Forensic analysis can identify unknown substances found at a crime scene, such as drugs, chemicals, or toxins, through chemical and toxicological tests.

2. Analysis of Biological Evidence: DNA profiling is a critical aspect of forensic analysis, allowing investigators to identify or exclude suspects and connect victims and suspects to crime scenes.

3. Trace Evidence Examination: This includes the analysis of fibers, hair, glass, soil, and other microscopic evidence that can link suspects to crime scenes or victims.

4. Ballistics: Forensic ballistics involves the study of bullets and bullet impacts to determine the type of firearm used, the trajectory of bullets, and potentially the shooter's location.

5. Digital Forensics: The examination of digital devices such as computers, smartphones, and storage media to recover and analyze digital evidence like emails, texts, and files.

6. Fingerprint Analysis: Examining fingerprints found at the crime scene to identify individuals who were present.

7. Document Examination: Analyzing handwriting, paper, ink, and other aspects of documents to ascertain their authenticity, origin, or any alterations.

8. Reconstruction: Forensic analysts can reconstruct crime scenes or events based on the evidence gathered, helping to establish sequences of events or how a crime was committed.

How Forensic Analysis Differs from an Autopsy

1. Scope: An autopsy is a specific type of forensic examination focused on a deceased body to determine the cause and manner of death. Forensic analysis, however, covers a broader range of scientific techniques applied to a wide array of evidence types, not just human remains.

2. Purpose: While the primary goal of an autopsy is to uncover how and why a person died, forensic analysis aims to identify, collect, preserve, and examine physical evidence from crime scenes to support legal investigations and proceedings.

3. Process: Autopsies are performed by forensic pathologists and focus on internal and external examinations of the body, including organ analyses, toxicology tests, and injury assessments. Forensic analysis involves various specialists (e.g., forensic biologists, chemists, digital forensic experts) working on different types of evidence using specific methodologies relevant to their fields.

4. Outcome: The outcome of an autopsy is a detailed report on the cause and manner of death, contributing to the overall investigation. Forensic analysis, on the other hand, produces a range of results depending on the type of evidence analyzed, which can link suspects to crimes, corroborate witness statements, and provide insights into the modus operandi.

In essence, while an autopsy is a crucial part of forensic science focusing on the deceased, forensic analysis encompasses a broader spectrum of scientific disciplines applied to diverse forms of evidence, each contributing unique insights to unravel the mysteries of a crime.

POINTS FOR WRITERS TO KEEP IN MIND

1. Jurisdictional Variations: Acknowledge that procedures can vary greatly by location. A little research into the specific setting of your story can add authenticity.

2. Investigator Expertise: While your sleuth might be an amateur, interactions with law enforcement should reflect a realistic understanding of investigation procedures. Officers and detectives are trained professionals.

3. Legal Constraints: Be aware of legal procedures and rights, such as the Miranda rights in the United States or the need for search warrants. These details matter to the credibility of police actions in your story.

4. Technological Limitations: Remember that while technology plays a significant role in modern investigations, it has its limits. Not every case is solved with a clear-cut DNA match or digital trace.

5. Community Relations: In many cozy mysteries, the close-knit community plays a significant role. Consider how local law enforcement interacts with the community and how this dynamic can impact the investigation.

6. Keeping the Cozy Tone: While incorporating police procedures, maintain the cozy tone by focusing on the puzzle-solving aspect and community dynamics rather than the grim details of the crime.

Incorporating these elements thoughtfully can help create a murder mystery that feels grounded in reality while still preserving the charm and gentleness of the cozy genre. As you blend factual police procedures with the creative liberties of fiction, you'll strike the perfect balance that keeps readers engaged and respects the conventions of the genre.

Avoiding embarrassing mistakes regarding police investigations in writing requires a blend of research, understanding of legal procedures, and a touch of common sense. Here are some of the most common pitfalls writers can fall into, turning potentially gripping scenes into moments of unintended comedy or disbelief:

1. Ignoring Jurisdictional Boundaries

For the record, your character has ZERO jurisdiction anywhere. But there are limitations for your law enforcement characters, too. They can't act outside their jurisdiction without proper authorization or collaboration with local authorities. Detectives from one city can't just start investigating a crime in another without going through the correct channels.

2. Overestimating Forensic Capabilities

The "CSI Effect" leads writers to overstate the speed and efficacy of forensic analysis. In reality, tests like DNA analysis can take weeks or longer, and not all evidence is as conclusive as television shows might suggest. Obviously, you're going to have to streamline a few procedures since few cozy mysteries take place over the course of months. But you should still keep this in mind.

3. Underestimating the Importance of Paperwork

Investigations involve a significant amount of paperwork and procedural steps that are often glossed over or ignored in fiction. Skipping these can make a story feel unrealistic to those in the know. Not that you have to actually detail this stuff, but you should occasionally at least *mention* that the cop boyfriend has a pile of paperwork to get through.

4. Miranda Rights Misunderstandings

A frequent mistake is having law enforcement officers recite Miranda rights at the wrong time, such as upon discovery of a suspect, rather than at the point of arrest when the suspect is taken into custody for interrogation. Understanding when and how these rights are applied is crucial.

5. Unrealistic Interrogation Tactics

Granted, your protagonist is already stretching the boundaries of reality by questioning anyone at any time. But when your protag is questioned, you should be mindful of interrogation tactics that are illegal or ethically dubious, without any narrative consequence. Torture, threats, and other forms of coercion are not only illegal in a cozy mystery (okay, yes, I'm kidding) but can also render confessions inadmissible in court.

6. Lack of Legal Procedure

Again, you don't need tons of detail, but the details you choose to include need to be accurate. Oversimplifying or misunderstanding legal procedures, such as how evidence is obtained, the role of warrants, and the process of charging someone with a crime, can undermine the credibility of the investigation portrayed.

7. Inaccurate Portrayal of Autopsies

Autopsies are a key part of many investigations, but writers sometimes misrepresent how they're conducted, who is present, and what information can realistically be gleaned from them.

8. Inappropriate Officer Conduct

Unless one of the villains in your cozy mystery is a police officer, members of law enforcement engaging in behavior that would realistically get them suspended or fired, such as tampering with evidence, going rogue without consequences, dating the prime suspect without so much as a qualm, or using excessive force without provocation, is going to irritate cozy mystery readers.

9. Instant Tech Solutions

Technology definitely plays a role in the contemporary cozy mystery. But assuming that technology can instantly track people, hack into any system, or solve crimes with a few keystrokes overlooks the complexities and legalities of using technology in investigations, plus it takes all the fun out of the game. It's a little anticlimactic for your sleuth to spend two hundred pages asking shrewd questions and drawing clever conclusions if, in the end, the case is going to be solved by a couple of clicks of the computer keyboard.

10. Solving Crimes Single-Handedly

While cozy mysteries often feature an amateur sleuth, it's important to avoid portraying them as outsmarting law enforcement at every turn, especially without showcasing a realistic collaboration or sharing of information between the sleuth and the police.

Avoiding these mistakes doesn't mean your narrative has to become bogged down in procedural detail. Instead, it's about striking the right balance between dramatic license and realism, ensuring that the police investigation elements enhance the story's credibility and engagement. A little research and consultation with law enforcement professionals can go a long way in making your story feel vivid and real.

- 7 -

LOVE AND ROMANCE

DO CHARACTERS IN COZY MYSTERIES HAVE SEX?

GOOD GRACIOUS, YES! MY *DEARS*, THEY ARE GOING AT IT HAMMER and tongs!

The crucial difference between romance in a cozy mystery (and this includes gay cozy mysteries) and a subgenre like romantic suspense is that all sexual activity occurs behind closed doors. Many things, pleasant and unpleasant, occur behind the pretty painted doors of the cozy mystery.

That is one of the rules of the genre.

That doesn't mean that your gay cozy mystery can't have a strong and emotionally resonant romantic subplot. In fact, I would argue that having a strong and emotionally resonant subplot is mandatory for a gay cozy mystery.

In my opinion, the gay cozy mystery is where the cozy mystery subgenre and the subgenres of M/M or F/F romance intersect.

In case you aren't aware, M/M romance focuses on romantic same-sex relationships between male characters. It's a very popular category within the broader romance genre, appealing to a broad swath of readers, including those in the LGBTQ+ community as well as straight women and others who enjoy exploring the dynamics of romantic relationships between men through fiction.

The same is mostly true of the F/F romance subgenre. However, this is a smaller subgenre, largely lacking the powerhouse readership of straight women.

M/M romance spans various settings, time periods, and subgenres, including contemporary, historical, fantasy, paranormal, and more. The stories typically center on the development of the *romantic* relationship between the protagonists, navigating the challenges they face, from societal pressures and personal conflicts to external obstacles that test their love.

Key aspects of M/M romance include character development, emotional depth, and the exploration of themes such as identity, acceptance, and the power of love to overcome adversity. Like other romance genres, M/M romance offers a range of heat levels, from sweet and closed-door romances to more explicit content.

The popularity of M/M romance has grown significantly, with a thriving community of readers and authors contributing to the genre. It's celebrated for its diversity and inclusivity, providing space for stories that affirm LGBTQ+ experiences and offer varied representations of love and relationships, although many M/M readers will insist that they aren't interested in books without erotic content.

Ruh-roh.

Now, if you know anything about cozy mysteries, you know that there will never be any onscreen erotic content, gay or straight. That's not up for debate.

Which means, to some extent, the range of LGBTQ+ experience you can explore within your cozy mystery is limited.

Very simply, while your protagonist's sexual identity is crucial to the development of their character, the journey to get to where they are when the story begins is *not* crucial or even relevant to the plot of a cozy mystery. It is no more appropriate in an LGBTQ+ cozy mystery than in a cozy mystery with a heterosexual protagonist.

Cozy mysteries aren't about the protagonist's backstory (barring the occasional Very Special Episode). They are about the protagonist solving crimes in the here and now.

Your character can identify in whatever way is true to them and meaningful to you. However, there is a limit to how much of their experience you may share on the page.

To reiterate, you may write anything you want. But if you plan to target a cozy mystery reading audience, if you plan to market your book to cozy mystery readers, you have to follow the rules of the genre.

Otherwise, it's an exercise in frustration for everyone. But mostly you.

WHAT ROLE DOES ROMANCE PLAY IN THE COZY MYSTERY?

Regardless of what I think, it is *not* mandatory to include romance in your cozy mystery; however, the modern trend is to create some kind of romantic interest for your protagonist. Which is why I advise you to adhere to this trend.

Romance in cozy mysteries serves several key roles, augmenting the narrative and adding layers to character development and reader engagement. Unlike in pure romance novels where the love story is the central plot, romance in cozy mysteries complements the main storyline, offering an engrossing subplot that supplements the overall reading experience.

Romance subplots provide a means to explore the protagonist's character beyond their sleuthing skills. Romantic relationships can reveal vulnerabilities, strengths, desires, and fears, offering a more rounded and relatable character portrait. As the protagonist navigates the ups and downs of romance, readers see their growth and evolution, making them more invested in the character's journey.

A romantic subplot can introduce additional motives, suspects, and red herrings, making the mystery more complex and engaging. Romance can intertwine with the main plot in surprising ways, where romantic interests might become suspects or unwittingly provide crucial clues, keeping readers guessing until the end.

Cozy mysteries are known for their warm, community-oriented settings that offer a contrast to the darker themes of crime and murder. Romance contributes to this cozy atmosphere by adding elements of love, hope, and human connection, balancing the tension of the mystery with the comfort of interpersonal relationships.

Romantic relationships can heighten the stakes for the protagonist, especially when there are complications along the way, or the love interests are in danger, accused of the crime, or otherwise entangled in the mystery. This added personal stake drives the protagonist's motivation and invests readers more deeply in the outcome, creating a more compelling narrative.

Romance offers moments of levity and respite from the main plot's tension, giving readers an emotional break and adding variety to the pacing of the story. These lighter, romantic moments can endear characters to readers and build anticipation for both the resolution of the mystery and the outcome of the romantic storyline.

In cozy mystery series, ongoing romantic subplots can serve as a thread connecting individual books, enticing readers to follow the series to see how the relationship evolves over time. The slow burn of romance across several books can build a loyal readership eager to see their favorite characters find happiness together.

Finally, successful relationships—romantic, familial, and platonic—are central to the genre's appeal, embodying the warmth and safety that define the cozy mystery genre. A romantic subplot underscores cozy mysteries' themes of community, belonging, and interpersonal connections.

In gay cozy mysteries, romance plays a crucial role, as it does in their heterosexual counterparts, but it can carry additional significance due to its representation and exploration of LGBTQ+ relationships within the genre. Whether romance matters more or less isn't a straightforward question; rather, its importance can be seen in how it enriches the narrative, offers representation, and connects with readers on various levels.

In a genre historically dominated by heterosexual relationships, gay cozy mysteries provide much-needed representation and visibility for LGBTQ+ relationships. Romance in these stories matters greatly because it normalizes and celebrates love in its many forms, contributing to a broader understanding and acceptance of diverse relationships.

For LGBTQ+ readers, the inclusion of a gay romance can significantly enhance the relatability and appeal of the story. It offers a reflection of their own experiences and desires, making the story more engaging and emotionally resonant. For readers outside the LGBTQ+ community, it provides insight into the joys and challenges unique to gay relationships, fostering empathy and understanding.

As with any cozy mystery, the romantic subplot in a gay cozy mystery adds depth to characters and complexity to the plot. The dynamics of a gay romance can introduce unique conflicts, societal pressures, or family tensions that enrich the narrative and provide opportunities for character growth and exploration.

Romance in a gay cozy mystery might *subtly* explore themes of coming out, acceptance, and the search for community, which can add layers of meaning to the story. These themes resonate deeply with many readers, making the romantic elements not just a subplot but a vital aspect of the protagonist's journey and personal growth.

Including gay romance in cozy mysteries is still pretty new. It can push the genre in new and innovative directions, challenging traditional conventions and expanding the scope of stories being told. This innovation makes romance a critical element in diversifying the genre and appealing to a wider audience.

Gay cozy mysteries often emphasize themes of community and belonging, both within the LGBTQ+ community and the wider society. Romance enhances these themes, showcasing the importance of love and support in overcoming adversity and finding one's place in the world.

In sum, romance plays a multifaceted role in cozy mysteries, adding depth, complexity, and warmth to the narrative. Unlike the cozy mysteries of old, the primary focus of the cozy is not a baffling puzzle. Sure, a baffling puzzle is always welcome, but it is the connections formed with other characters within this cozy environment that has propelled the cozy to its current popularity.

One of the deepest connections we form is that romantic partnership with someone we hope to grow old with. Well, I mean, we don't hope for the growing-old part—although, it's better than the alternative. ANYWAY.

Adding a romantic subplot will enrich the reader's experience by offering a more complete picture of the protagonist's world, making the stories not just about solving a mystery, but about finding love, happiness, and belonging within a community.

WHAT MAKES US FALL IN LOVE?

Falling in love is a complex, many-sided process influenced by an interplay of psychological, emotional, and social factors. While the experience of falling in love can vary widely from person to person, there are several common elements that tend to spark this profound emotional response:

Chemical Attraction: On a basic biological level, falling in love triggers a cocktail of chemicals in the brain, including dopamine, oxytocin, and serotonin. These chemicals produce feelings of euphoria, attachment, and happiness, akin to a natural high that draws us toward the object of our affection. Granted, chemical attraction doesn't always lead to love. Sometimes it just leads to lust, which is okay too, though we don't write about that much in cozy mysteries.

Emotional Connection: Sharing personal thoughts, feelings, and experiences with someone can lead to a deep emotional connection, laying the foundation for love. Vulnerability and mutual understanding foster a sense of closeness and intimacy.

Shared Values and Interests: Discovering common values, interests, and goals can play a significant role in the development of romantic feelings. These similarities provide a sense of compatibility and the potential for a shared future.

Physical Attraction: This is partly chemical reaction, sure, but it's a little more subtle and complicated. I'm not going to deep dive into "genetic similarity theory" or "assortative mating," but essentially the idea is humans tend to be attracted to others who are genetically similar to themselves. It's a bit like looking for a mate who could be from the same tribe in ancient times, which, in theory, could lead to stronger offspring due to the reinforcement of genetic traits. Anyway, physical attraction often serves as the initial draw between two people. While it's not the sole basis for a lasting relationship, it can spark interest and desire, leading individuals to explore a deeper connection.

Admiration and Respect: Admiring someone's qualities, achievements, or the way they conduct themselves in the world can be a powerful catalyst for love. Respect for the other person's character and abilities contributes to a foundation of mutual admiration.

Reciprocity: The perception that one's feelings are reciprocated can intensify emotions of love. Knowing that the affection is mutual fosters a sense of security and validation in the relationship.

Timing and Circumstance: Right time right place? Sometimes, yes. Sometimes, the timing and circumstances align perfectly for love to blossom. Being at the right place in one's life emotionally, psychologically, and situationally can make individuals more open to falling in love.

Mystery and Novelty: The excitement of discovering new things about another person can fuel romantic feelings. Mystery keeps the relationship dynamic and engaging, encouraging a deeper exploration of each other's personalities and experiences.

Companionship and Compatibility: Enjoying each other's company and finding ease and comfort in one's presence are crucial for love to grow. Feeling understood and accepted for who you are can reinforce the bond between two people.

Personal Growth: Sometimes, a person might inspire us to become better versions of ourselves. This encouragement toward personal growth and fulfillment can deepen feelings of love and admiration.

Falling in love is a uniquely personal experience shaped by individual preferences, past experiences, and cultural influences. Despite its complexity, at its core, love is about connection, mutual understanding, and the profound bond that develops when two people share their lives with each other.

The stages of intimacy and the stages of falling in love are related but focus on different aspects of relationship development. While there's some overlap, the distinction mainly lies in the emphasis: intimacy stages focus on the deepening of emotional closeness and trust over time, whereas the stages of falling in love are more about the emotional journey from attraction to deep affection. Ideally, you will want to show your protagonist and their romantic interest going through each of these stages, book by book.

Initial Attraction (Infatuation): This is the first spark, where physical attraction, curiosity, or a sense of intrigue draws people together. It's often superficial and based on initial impressions.

Discovery and Exploration: Here, people start sharing personal stories, likes, dislikes, and begin to reveal their vulnerabilities. This stage is where mutual interest and attraction deepen as individuals explore their compatibility.

Deepening Connection and Intimacy: This stage involves building emotional intimacy, trust, and a strong bond. Partners begin to see a future together, share deeper fears, dreams, and establish a strong sense of "us."

Commitment and Stability: At this point, the relationship has a secure foundation, and partners are committed to each other. They have navigated through ups and downs successfully and feel secure in their partnership.

True Partnership and Teamwork: This final stage is about working together toward common goals, supporting each other's ambitions, and continuing to grow both individually and as a couple. It represents a mature, stable relationship where both parties feel valued and understood.

For writers entering this genre by way of M/M romance, the idea of trying to write a romantic subplot without any erotic content might seem a little daunting, or even pointless. In fact, there are many heartfelt and creative ways to illustrate a developing romance by emphasizing emotional connection, affection, and the building of a relationship.

Here are several ideas to show romantic feelings between characters in a way that fits the soft, warm atmosphere of the genre:

Thoughtful Gestures: Characters can express their affection through small, thoughtful acts that show they understand and care for each other. This could be as simple as bringing the other person a cup of their favorite coffee, preparing a meal for them, or helping them solve a problem without being asked.

Meaningful Gifts: Gift-giving that reflects a deep understanding of the other person's interests, needs, or desires can be a powerful expression of love. These gifts don't have to be expensive but should carry personal significance, like a first edition of a book from an author they love or a handmade item that connects to a shared memory.

Support During Tough Times: Showing unwavering support during moments of doubt, fear, or stress can deepen the bond between characters. This could be emotional support, like listening and offering comfort, or practical support, like assisting with an investigation or standing up for them in a difficult situation.

Shared Secrets and Vulnerability: Sharing personal stories, fears, or dreams can be a profound way of showing trust and building intimacy. Moments where characters open up about their past, their insecurities, or their hopes for the future can strengthen their emotional connection.

Protectiveness: A character showing a natural, non-overbearing sense of protectiveness in situations of danger or discomfort can be a sign of deep care and affection, especially in the context of a mystery where risks may be involved.

Playful Teasing and Banter: Friendly teasing and banter that shows familiarity and comfort with each other can be a way to express affection and build rapport without delving into physical intimacy.

Subtle Physical Contact: Small, non-sexual touches like brushing away hair, a hand on the back, holding hands, or a comforting hug can convey deep affection and provide moments of closeness. By the way, your characters can kiss, cuddle, and hug. Just avoid getting too hot and heavy.

Looks and Glances: Much can be said without words. Shared looks, smiles, and glances can convey a wealth of emotion, from amusement and shared secrets to deep longing or concern, allowing for a silent communication of affection.

Collaboration and Partnership: There's nothing like solving a mystery to bring people together. Brainstorming ideas or getting out of tricky situations can strengthen their bond and show their compatibility as a team, highlighting their mutual respect and admiration.

Romantic Settings and Activities: Placing characters in pleasant or attractive settings, such as watching a sunset, stargazing, or a picnic in a secluded spot, can set the stage for intimate conversations and moments of connection without the need for physical intimacy.

Remember, love and romance are about emotional connection. Erotic content is the icing on the cake. We do not always need it. Or, even if we do, sometimes we prefer to lick our frosting off a spoon in private. In the cozy mystery, sex happens behind closed doors.

None of this means you can't show your characters being playful and romantic in plenty of other ways. It's not the 1940s. You can show your main characters in the same bed. Some of the sweetest moments and funniest banter can occur while your sleuths are between the sheets, discussing the case. But when the conversation ends, turn out the light.

THE COURSE OF TRUE LOVE

Falling in love can happen relatively quickly and is often driven by emotional and physical attraction, while the development of intimacy is a slower process that requires vulnerability, trust-building, and ongoing commitment. Realistic conflicts in new romantic relationships often stem from the process of getting to know each other better and navigating the transition from attraction to a deeper, more nuanced connection.

You're going to need some believable dips in the road of your protagonist's romance. These low points should be based on genuine and believable conflict, not some idiotic misunderstanding that could be resolved by five minutes of grown-up conversation. Think about the challenges you've experienced in your own real-life relationships, and see if any of these are applicable to your characters.

Communication Styles: Differences in communication can lead to misunderstandings and frustrations. One person might prefer direct communication, while the other might use hints or be more reserved, leading to confusion and conflict.

Pacing of the Relationship: Disagreements about how quickly the relationship is moving can be a source of tension. One partner might want to advance things faster—meeting family, moving in together— while the other prefers to take things slow. That's believable real-life stuff.

Balancing Time Together and Apart: Finding the right balance between spending time together and maintaining individual independence can be challenging. Conflicts may arise from differing needs for personal space or time spent with friends and family (OR SOLVING MYSTERIES).

Expectations and Assumptions: Each person brings their own set of expectations and assumptions to a relationship, influenced by past experiences, cultural background, and personal values. Conflicts can emerge when these expectations aren't communicated clearly or when reality doesn't match them. This is also known as the first week after moving in together.

Jealousy and Insecurity: Feelings of jealousy and insecurity can surface as partners navigate their new relationship, especially if there are lingering insecurities from past relationships or fears about the relationship's stability. Even confident, self-assured guys have their moments of insecurity or jealousy.

Financial Matters: Even in the early stages, differing attitudes toward money and spending can lead to conflicts. This might involve disagreements over who pays for dates, how much to spend on gifts, or attitudes toward saving and spending.

Intimacy: Differences in desire for physical intimacy, including frequency and preferences, can create tension. Open communication about needs and boundaries is crucial but can be difficult to navigate without causing misunderstandings. Granted, in a cozy mystery you're probably not going to get into this too much, though you can hint at these things.

Social Circles and Family: Integrating into each other's social circles and family can be a BIG source of conflict, especially if there are differing opinions, lifestyles, or if the partner doesn't get along with important people in the other's life.

Life Goals and Ambitions: Diverging life goals, career ambitions, or values can become apparent as the relationship deepens, potentially leading to conflicts if partners feel their paths are not aligned.

Handling Conflict: *How each person deals with conflict can itself be a source of conflict.* One might prefer to address issues head-on, while the other might avoid confrontation, leading to frustrations if not addressed.

These conflicts are legitimately challenging, which means they are realistic opportunities for growth and understanding in your protag's relationship. Showing your characters successfully navigating these challenges makes their relationship feel more believable and engrossing to readers. Navigating them successfully requires open communication, empathy, and a willingness to compromise and understand each other's perspectives. Addressing these issues early on can strengthen the relationship, building a foundation of mutual respect and understanding.

"LOVE QUIZ" FOR YOUR MAIN CHARACTERS

Whether your series begins with your main character already in a meaningful relationship or with your main character meeting the future love of their life, this writing exercise can be a playful yet insightful way to explore and develop the emotional dynamics of this central relationship. Plus, it's a great way of brainstorming some of the key turning points that lie ahead.

Answer these questions from the viewpoint of your protagonist and their significant other.

1. The First Glance

How did your characters feel the first time they saw each other?

- a) Intrigued but indifferent.
- b) Instantly attracted.
- c) Mildly annoyed but curious.
- d) Completely oblivious.

2. The Spark

What ignites the spark between them?

- a) A shared laugh over an inside joke.
- b) A moment of vulnerability.
- c) Working together to solve a problem.
- d) Physical attraction.

3. The Obstacle

What stands in the way of their relationship initially?

- a) External pressures (family, society).
- b) A misunderstanding or miscommunication.
- c) Previous romantic commitments.
- d) Personal insecurities.

4. The Confession

(Not *that* confession! Your protags SO cannot be the killer!)

How does the first confession of feelings occur?

    a) A spontaneous, passionate admission.
    b) During a moment of life-or-death intensity.
    c) A well-planned, romantic gesture.
    d) Accidentally overheard by the other person.

5. The First Date

What would their ideal first date look like, according to each character?

    a) A cozy night in, cooking together.
    b) An adventurous outing, like hiking or exploring a new city.
    c) Attending a cultural event, like a concert or art exhibit.
    d) A simple coffee date with deep conversation.

6. The Misunderstanding

What misunderstanding threatens their relationship?

    a) A secret kept from the past.
    b) A perceived interest in someone else.
    c) A lie told with good intentions.
    d) An overheard conversation taken out of context.

7. The Make-Up

How do they resolve their first major conflict?

    a) A heartfelt apology and honest conversation.
    b) A grand gesture to prove love.
    c) Through a mutual friend's intervention.
    d) A letter or message explaining their feelings.

8. The Deep Connection

What shared experience deepens their bond the most?

    a) Facing and overcoming a danger together.
    b) Discovering a shared passion or interest.
    c) Supporting each other through a personal crisis.
    d) A trip or journey taken together.

9. The Love Test

What ultimate test does their relationship face?

a) Distance or long periods apart.
b) Disapproval from important people in their lives.
c) A betrayal or breach of trust.
d) A significant life change (e.g., career move, illness).

10. The Future Together

How do your characters envision their future together?

a) Building a life in their current setting, surrounded by friends and family.
b) Traveling the world or embarking on new adventures together.
c) Focusing on their careers but making time for each other.
d) Starting a family or community project together.

HOW TO USE THE QUIZ:

Track Progress: Use the quiz to map out the progression of your characters' relationship, identifying key turning points and emotional milestones.

Character Insights: Analyze how each character's answers reflect their personality, fears, and desires, providing deeper insight into their motivations and how they view the relationship.

Plot Development: Let the quiz inspire scenes, conflicts, and resolutions in your story, ensuring the romantic subplot is intertwined with the main narrative in a meaningful way.

Because you're answering from the viewpoint of *both* main characters, this exercise is especially interesting and useful in helping you craft a love story that resonates with readers and adds depth to your narrative.

8

LET'S TALK ABOUT DIALOGUE

DIALOGUE IN LITERATURE IS BASICALLY THE WRITTEN CONVERSATION between two or more characters. It's a vital part of storytelling, bringing characters to life and moving the plot forward. It can reveal their personalities, relationships, and the dynamics between them.

Dialogue also helps to show rather than tell, allowing readers to infer what's happening without explicit description. Dialogue can be a powerful tool to unravel clues, build tension, and develop a mystery. Plus, it's great for pacing, adding realism, and giving readers a break from narrative and description. It's like letting your characters speak directly to the reader, making the story more engaging and dynamic.

Most authors believe that dialogue is their particular strength. But remember Pareto's Principle? Dialogue cannot be EVERY author's strength. So, let's refresh ourselves on what makes for good dialogue by considering the elements that make dialogue stand out, especially in the mystery and crime genres where every word can be a clue:

1. Authenticity

Dialogue should sound real. Think about how people speak in real life, including pauses, beats, and the occasional *ahs*, *ers*, and *ums*. HOWEVER, use restraint. Dialogue is *not* real-life conversation. It must be smarter, sharper, more entertaining, and move the story along. It cannot ramble pointlessly. It must never bore the reader.

2. Character Voice

Each character should have a distinct way of speaking that reflects their background, personality, and current mood. This helps readers distinguish between characters and adds depth to them. HOWEVER, don't get carried away with accents and affectations. Think about the challenges you're presenting to the narrator of your audiobooks. Above all, the cozy mystery must be readable.

3. Advancing the Plot

Good dialogue moves the story forward, revealing plot points, secrets, and conflicts. Especially in mystery writing, dialogue can drop hints and red herrings, keeping the reader engaged. No quibbles here. That is absolutely a must for dialogue.

4. Revealing Information

Beyond plot, dialogue can reveal character motives, relationships, and changes in dynamics. It's a subtle tool for exposition, letting you avoid heavy-handed narration and awkward info dumps. HOWEVER, avoid clumsy and unrealistic conversations that real people would never have, like, "As you know, since we've both lived here and owned small businesses on this island for twenty years…"

5. Conciseness

Each line of dialogue should serve a purpose, whether it's developing character, advancing the plot, or adding tension. While I'm not saying that author voice isn't important in the cozy mystery, cozies have their own clean, straightforward style. Again, it's quality versus quantity of detail. You don't need a lot of literary pirouettes in the cozy. A breezy, conversational tone will serve you well. Trim any dialogue that doesn't add value.

6. Subtext

Often, what's not said is just as important as what is. Good dialogue can have layers of meaning, with characters speaking around issues or through metaphors, adding richness to their interactions. Subtext is where characters say one thing but mean another. For example, when a character answers with that loaded word *fine*. Or where a character's actions and expressions don't line up with what they're saying. Body language can be a kind of subtext.

Subtext can add layers of complexity, revealing hidden motives, emotions, and truths, making it a powerful tool in your storytelling arsenal, especially in emotional scenes or when weaving clues into your mysteries.

7. Conflict and Tension

Dialogue should often reflect or build conflict, creating tension that propels the story forward. This is crucial in mystery and crime fiction, where dialogue can escalate the stakes or reveal conflicts.

8. Natural Flow

The back-and-forth of dialogue should feel natural and dynamic, mimicking real conversation's rhythm. This keeps readers engaged and makes the characters' interactions more believable.

As mentioned earlier, the cozy mystery essentially amounts to a series of entertaining and informative interviews. This means dialogue is where the majority of sleuthing will happen. Clues, red herrings, revelations, and motive are all discovered through character conversation. Striking the delicate balance between dialogue focused on solving the mystery and dialogue that builds characters or relationships is more art than science.

Aim to weave together dialogue that advances the mystery with dialogue that deepens character and relationship development. This can often be achieved simultaneously, with characters revealing their personalities and dynamics even as they discuss clues or speculate about the mystery.

Because clues often come from the community or relationships, every conversation becomes a potential goldmine for both character insights and puzzle pieces. This allows you to focus on character or relationship building while still contributing to the mystery-solving aspect.

The balance might shift throughout the book. Early chapters could focus more on establishment of character and setting, gradually blending more heavily into mystery-solving dialogue as the story progresses, then swinging back toward character resolution and growth toward the end (after the climax).

A rough starting point might be a 60/40 or 70/30 split between mystery-solving and character/relationship development, adjusting based on the particular story and its needs. Remember, the most memorable cozy mysteries often shine brightest in their characters and how they relate to each other and the world around them, with the mystery providing the backdrop for these interactions.

COMMON MISTAKES IN WRITING DIALOGUE

Remember, the first draft of dialogue is often about getting ideas down. Much of it serves as a placeholder. The real magic happens in revision, where you can refine, tighten, and ensure each line of dialogue is doing the work it needs to do. Revision is key to great dialogue. Don't be afraid to second-guess yourself.

With every page, your book changes, evolves. Original ideas give way to better ideas. Themes appear, plot twists present themselves, characters develop in unexpected ways, so it's no surprise that dialogue will be tightened and reworked.

1. Overusing Names

Beginners often have characters frequently address each other by name in dialogue, which can feel unnatural. In real conversations, people rarely use names unless they're calling attention, emphasizing a point, or there are multiple people in the discussion. *Oh*, or if a character is angry. When we're angry, we tend to use the name of the person we're ~~yelling~~—er, talking to.

2. Exposition Dump

I mentioned earlier that dialogue is a valuable tool for exposition, but resist the temptation to unload someone's background information in a single conversation. In the real world, when someone sits down and tries to share their entire life story with us, we edge away as fast as politely possible. Whether through exposition or dialogue, sprinkle information throughout the narrative organically, and let it serve the story's flow.

3. Lack of Distinct Voices

Each character should have a voice, reflecting their background, personality, and current situation. Somewhere between a creative writing exercise on dialects and accents, and dialogue where every character sounds exactly the same, lies a realistic conversational middle ground. You don't want your protagonist and his or her significant other to sound exactly the same. Here, it might be helpful to imagine an audiobook narrator reading their parts. How would you want the narrator to differentiate between them? Is there a way for you to cue the reader to these differences through how the characters speak?

Regular supporting cast members should have their own style of speaking. Maybe one character hems and haws a lot. Another character might interrupt others a lot. Maybe one character requires more exclamation points than the normal person. Maybe someone emphasizes certain words and has a catchphrase. All of this has to be handled with a light hand. You're making pastry not mashing potatoes.

4. On-the-Nose Dialogue

This is when characters say exactly what they think or feel, without any subtlety or subtext. "As you know, I am very upset about being a suspect in Roger's murder." While it's true, that many of us do state the obvious, fictional dialogue is supposed to be better than real-life conversation. But also, in real life, we rarely speak so directly about our emotions or intentions, especially to strangers and especially in situations charged with tension or mystery.

5. Ignoring the Power of Silence

Sometimes, what characters don't say is as powerful as what they do. Don't overlook the strength of pauses, interruptions, or silent reactions, which can add depth and realism to conversations. Timing is everything.

6. Unrealistic Monologues

Long, uninterrupted monologues can feel artificial unless there's a very good reason for a character to speak at length. Even your killer's confession—should you choose to write that scene—is going to feel more legit if the protagonist can occasionally get a word in edgewise. You're not writing *Hamlet*. Dialogue is about exchange and interaction.

7. Too Many Dialogue Tags

"Dialogue tags are extremely useful," she announced.

Which is true. Anybody who tells you that tone and delivery should be obvious from the words themselves, is someone who A – has never worked with a narrator, and B – is not particularly good at crafting dialogue.

"Yep, I said it and I meant it," she said.

For example, let's take the simple phrase, *Go to hell*.

Go to hell is something some of us say when joking with each other. It's also something some of us say when we're not joking at all. It can be whispered fiercely or shouted before a door is slammed. It can be chopped out in little bitty syllables. It can be choked through sobs.

If there is going to be doubt in the reader's mind about how a line is delivered, then a tag can be useful.

That said, the vast majority of dialog will not need a tag because the lines aren't going to require any special delivery.

Tags are about clarity. Clarity in who is speaking and how they are speaking. Use tags sparingly. Too few is probably preferrable to too many. But don't be afraid to use them.

8. Forgetting Body Language

Nonverbal cues are a huge part of communication. Beginners might focus solely on the words spoken, neglecting how body language, tone, and facial expressions can add layers to a conversation.

9. Not Using Contractions or Natural Speech Patterns

This is so obvious but so often overlooked. To make dialogue sound more realistic, it's important to use contractions and mirror natural speech patterns. Overly formal dialogue sounds unnatural and will distance the reader—unless English is a second language for your character, in which case, you can turn it into a specific character trait.

10. Ignoring the Setting

The environment can impact how characters interact. We don't share everything in front of everyone. We don't launch into long, complicated revelations when we've got five minutes before our coffee order is ready. We don't share confidential information where we can be overheard. (Well, hopefully, we don't!) Your setting will determine how much, and in what manner, your characters will exchange information. Use setting effectively to influence the dialogue's tone, pace, or intensity.

11. Forcing Humor or Witty Banter

Banter or repartee refers to the witty and playful exchange of remarks, often animated and humorous, between characters. It's a rapid back-and-forth conversation—often between romantic or potentially romantic partners—where each participant tries to outdo the other with clever comments or retorts. This type of dialogue is not just about being funny; it serves several important purposes in storytelling, especially in genres that thrive on dynamic character interactions, such as mystery, romance, and comedy.

Readers love funny cozy mysteries. While well-executed humor or banter can enrich dialogue, force-feeding it into the conversation will feel strained and unfunny. If you're naturally witty, that's terrific. But you don't have to be a standup comic to infuse lightness and humor into your story. You can mine situations and character quirks for amusement value. And remember, no matter how naturally funny you are, jokes at the wrong time can defuse tension you're trying to build or wreck a romantic scene (much like in real life, if you know what I mean).

How to Craft Effective Banter:

Know Your Characters: Characters engaging in banter should have well-defined voices and personalities. Their exchanges should reflect their backgrounds, attitudes, and the dynamics of their relationship.

Keep It Quick: Banter is all about timing. The exchanges should be quick and to the point, mimicking the natural flow of a playful argument or a teasing conversation.

Balance Between Characters: Effective banter requires a balance, with each character getting their moments to shine. It shouldn't be one-sided; rather, it should feel like a game of tennis, with the dialogue bouncing back and forth equally.

Use Subtext: Good banter often has layers of meaning beneath the surface. Characters might be flirting, jockeying for position, or testing each other's boundaries. The subtext adds depth to what might otherwise be a purely comedic exchange.

Be Witty, Not Mean: There's a fine line between witty banter and characters just being mean to each other. The exchange should feel fun and engaging, not hurtful. Even when characters are rivals, their banter should hint at a mutual respect or an underlying affection.

Practice and Edit: Writing banter can be challenging because it requires a good ear for dialogue and a deep understanding of your characters. Don't be afraid to write a lot of dialogue and then edit down to the best bits. Sometimes, the process of discovery through writing can lead you to the most authentic and engaging exchanges.

Read It Aloud: This helps you catch the rhythm of the exchange and ensure it sounds natural and lively. Banter should have a musical quality, with a rhythm and flow that make it enjoyable to read.

To write banter effectively, it's important to keep it natural, ensure it serves the story, and remember that the best exchanges reveal as much (about the characters and their relationships) as they entertain. Balancing wit with depth and ensuring it flows organically from your characters' personalities and the situation at hand will make your dialogue sparkle with authenticity and engagement.

12. Close Your Eyes and Think of Huck

Dialect and accents are meant to add authenticity and depth, giving characters a distinct voice and cultural background. But when overused or inaccurately depicted, dialect and accents are just plain painful, turning characters into caricatures, potentially offending or alienating readers, and making the dialogue difficult to read. Your goal is to sprinkle your dialogue with a little cultural flavor—not to emulate Huck Finn and Jim sailing on a raft down the Mississippi.

How to Use Dialect and Accents Effectively:

Be Sparing: Use dialect and accents sparingly, choosing a few key phrases or word choices to suggest the accent rather than attempting to phonetically replicate it throughout.

Do your Research: Ensure accuracy and sensitivity by researching dialects and accents thoroughly, understanding the nuances and avoiding stereotypes.

Keep it Readable: Remember, the primary goal is clarity and immersion for the reader. If an accent or dialect pulls them out of the story because it's too hard to decipher, it's counterproductive.

Don't Stereotype: There's a fine line between representing a dialect or accent authentically and veering into caricature. Italian characters need not sound like The Super Mario Brothers' Luigi to get your point across. It's important to respect and understand the speech patterns you're trying to depict, ensuring they add to character development without reducing characters to stereotypes.

13. Too Realistic Dialogue

Realistic dialogue aims to mirror real-life conversations to add believability to your characters and their interactions. However, cozy mysteries are not reality. In addition to profanity and a clutter of *ums* and *ers*, real-life conversation is full of filler content. Readers don't need to hear about the weather, Mrs. McGillicuddy's lumbago, or Mr. Greene's grandkids. Stay on point. Meandering, dull, pointless exchanges bog down narrative pace and bore readers.

INTERNAL DIALOGUE
OR (MORE ACCURATELY) INTERNAL MONOLOGUE

Internal dialogue refers to the thoughts of a character that are not spoken out loud but are shared with the reader. It's a direct window into the character's inner world, revealing their feelings, reactions, secrets, and intentions that might not be apparent through action or spoken dialogue alone.

Internal dialogue reveals the complexities of your characters, showing their vulnerabilities, fears, desires, and motivations. This is especially useful in mystery fiction, where characters' hidden motives can add twists and depth to the plot.

While witty repartee can be difficult, humorous or wry observations often come naturally to us writerly types. Consider sharing your protagonist's inner commentary as a way of infusing scenes and character interactions with humor and insight.

Thoughts can hint at future actions, foreshadow events, or reveal important clues that advance the mystery without directly stating them in dialogue or action.

Internal dialogue can build tension by showing what a character knows, suspects, or fears, especially if it contrasts with what other characters or the reader knows. People are constantly thinking, reacting internally to what happens around them, and this inner monologue helps readers connect with the characters on a deeper level.

Internal dialogue also allows you to explore themes more deeply, such as justice, morality, or identity, by showing how these themes impact the character internally, influencing their decisions and growth.

Things to avoid when writing internal dialogue

1. Overuse: Relying too heavily on internal dialogue can bog down your narrative, making it feel sluggish. It's like adding too many solos in a song or slow songs in a set list; balance is key. Mix internal thoughts with action, dialogue, and description to maintain pace and interest.

2. Telling Instead of Showing: New writers might use internal dialogue to tell readers how a character feels instead of showing it through actions or interactions. While internal dialogue can reveal thoughts directly, it should complement, not replace, more dynamic ways to develop character.

3. Lack of Distinct Voice: Just as every character should have a unique spoken voice, their internal voice should also reflect their personality, background, and experiences. Beginners might write internal dialogue that sounds too similar across different characters, missing an opportunity to deepen character portrayal. Now, in a cozy mystery, the odds are strong you will only be inside the head of your protagonist, so this is probably not a huge concern unless your character's inner voice sounds like they have a split personality.

4. Inconsistency: Internal dialogue must be consistent with the character's development and the story's context. New writers might inadvertently include thoughts that contradict a character's established traits or knowledge, disrupting reader immersion. Your protagonist's inner voice should match their outer voice.

5. Anachronisms or Inappropriate Language: Especially important if your cozy mystery is set in an earlier time. The language and thoughts should be appropriate to the time, place, and world. Also, not to belabor the point, but cozy mystery characters don't *think* swear words any more than they say them aloud.

6. Forgetting the Reader is Listening: Don't make the mistake of having your sleuth reflect on something that has yet to happen in the story! Make sure internal dialogue doesn't reveal too much too soon, undermining suspense or mystery. Conversely, make sure your protagonist's thoughts aren't too cryptic or vague, leaving readers confused. Finding the right balance of revelation and concealment can enhance tension and engagement.

7. Ignoring Subtext: Sometimes, what a character doesn't think about directly—or thinks around—can be as revealing as their explicit thoughts. Beginners might miss the chance to use omission or evasion in thoughts to hint at deeper secrets or internal conflicts.

8. Not Integrating with the Narrative: Internal dialogue should feel like a seamless part of the narrative, enhancing and deepening the story. New writers might insert internal thoughts awkwardly, making them feel like interruptions rather than integral parts of the narrative flow.

9. Unrealistic Thought Processes: Characters' thoughts should mimic real thought processes, including fragments, nonlinear jumps, and emotional reactions. Beginners might write internal dialogue that's too polished or formal, lacking the authenticity of genuine thought.

Crafting effective internal dialogue is about enhancing the reader's connection to your characters and enriching the narrative without overwhelming it.

SPEAK TO ME OF LOVE

Even though cozy mysteries follow the traditions of mystery fiction, in the gay cozy mystery, romance is going to play a nearly equal role to the investigation. Which very likely means romantic dialogue is going to take place at some point. So, let's talk about the dangers of overly lovey-dovey or unrealistically lyrical dialogue, and why it can utterly ruin an otherwise romantic scene.

You know how adding too much sugar to a dessert can overwhelm the palate and detract from the overall delectability of a dish? Too many sweet nothings, dialogue that's too flowery or saccharine, can actually undermine the authenticity and emotional impact of the moment you're trying to create.

Real people rarely speak in poetry or grandiose declarations of love, especially in intimate moments. When characters do, it can make the scene feel disconnected from reality, making it hard for readers to relate or believe in the relationship. My husband and I are both writers, and we've never used metaphors or similes on each other, to my recollection.

The beauty of a romantic scene often lies in its simplicity and the genuine connection between characters. Overly ornate dialogue can create a barrier between the characters and the reader, making the emotion feel manufactured rather than organic.

Also, if the rest of your narrative maintains a certain tone or style— we'll call it the cozy mystery voice—a sudden shift to overly romantic or lyrical dialogue can feel jarring and out of place. Consistency is key to maintaining immersion and emotional investment.

Characters should speak in a way that's true to their development and the story's setting. A gruff and stoic cop suddenly waxing poetic without a good reason is liable to be funny for all the wrong reasons.

Finally, when every romantic interaction is dialed up to eleven, it desensitizes readers to the relationship's emotional peaks. Saving the most heartfelt declarations for pivotal moments helps preserve their impact.

How to Craft Authentic Romantic Dialogue

Often, what's left unsaid in a romantic scene is just as powerful as what is spoken. A look, a touch, or a simple phrase can carry a wealth of emotion. Subtlety can be far more effective and realistic.

Incorporate everyday language that reflects how people actually speak when they're in love. This doesn't mean the dialogue can't be beautiful or heartfelt, but it should feel grounded in reality and true to the character.

Ensure the dialogue fits the characters and their relationship's development. Two scientists might express their love through a shared discovery, while artists might reference a favorite piece of art, but both should feel true to who they are. My husband has a certain line from Chandler he quotes now and again.

Realistic dialogue often includes humor, flaws, and imperfections. People swallow at the wrong time, their voices get husky, they stumble over words. An emotional declaration is *emotional*. For everybody.

Reserve the most lyrical or romantic declarations for significant moments in the relationship. This buildup makes these moments feel earned and impactful.

And, by the way, read your romantic dialogue aloud. If that dialogue sounds like something out of a melodramatic play rather than a moment between two real people, you probably need to take it down a notch.

Creating authentic, resonant romantic dialogue is about balancing genuine emotion with realism. It's finding the extraordinary in the ordinary—how real people, with all their quirks and imperfections, express love and connection. This approach not only makes your romantic scenes more believable but also more impactful, allowing readers to see a bit of themselves in the characters' experiences.

CRAFTING DIALOGUE

Crafting dialogue that rings true, engages readers, and drives the story forward is a skill that can always be honed. Here are two creative writing exercises designed to help beginning authors improve and refine their dialogue writing skills.

EXERCISE 1: THE DIALOGUE SWAP

Objective: *To understand how dialogue reflects character personality and to practice creating distinct character voices.*

Step 1: Write a Short Dialogue

Create a brief exchange (3-5 exchanges) between two characters in a specific scenario. Keep it simple—a disagreement, a decision to be made, or a secret revealed.

Step 2: Character Swap

Rewrite the dialogue, but swap the characters' personalities. If the original had a cautious character and an impulsive character, switch their dialogue so the cautious character is now the impulsive one, and vice versa.

Step 3: Analyze and Reflect

Compare the two dialogues. How did the characters' voices change with their personalities? What words or rhythms did you use to convey their unique perspectives? Reflect on how altering a character's personality changes the dialogue's dynamics and implications.

This exercise helps you explore how deeply character personality influences dialogue. It sharpens your ability to differentiate characters' voices and makes you more adept at ensuring dialogue reflects character traits and relationships.

EXERCISE 2: REAL-LIFE EAVESDROPPING

Objective: To capture natural dialogue rhythms and nuances, improving realism in written dialogue.

Step 1: Eavesdrop on Real Conversations

Stay with me. You don't eavesdrop on people who you know. Spend some time in a public place—a café, a park, a mall—and listen to real conversations around you. Take notes on phrases, rhythms, and interactions that catch your attention. Pay attention to how people interrupt each other, use filler words, or change topics abruptly.

Step 2: Transcribe and Analyze

Without changing the content, transcribe a snippet of conversation as accurately as you can. Then, analyze it for patterns, natural speech rhythms, and how people actually convey information verbally.

Step 3: Incorporate into Your Work

Take a piece of dialogue from your current work-in-progress and revise it using insights gained from your real-life observations. Aim to inject more natural speech patterns, including pauses, interruptions, and nonverbal cues. Just don't get carried away with pauses, erms, ums, uhs, etc.

This exercise trains you to pay attention to how people speak in real life, which is invaluable for writing realistic dialogue. It highlights the difference between spoken and written language, helping you craft dialogue that sounds authentic while still serving your narrative needs.

Both exercises not only help in cleaning up and improving dialogue but also deepen your understanding of how dialogue functions as a tool for character development and story progression. By regularly practicing these exercises, beginning authors can enhance their ability to write dialogue that truly resonates with readers.

9

THEME, TONE, MOOD, AND ALL THAT JAZZ

THEME

THE DISCUSSION OF "THEME" IN THE CONTEXT OF THE COZY MYSTERY often refers to two different things.

The unique hook or concept of a cozy—for example, three former nuns now run Guiding Light Consultancy where they offer help and advice to those in need—is sometimes referred to as its "theme."

I'm not saying that's wrong, but in our discussion of theme, we're considering the underlying message, insight, or perspective about life and human nature that your cozy mystery novel conveys.

Theme is the central idea or concept that runs throughout a narrative, providing depth and meaning beyond the surface plot and character actions. The conscious and clever use of theme is one of those elements that sets your work apart from everyone else's.

Any given story will probably have more than one theme.

Themes can be explicit, directly stated, or explored through the narrative, or implicit, emerging subtly through characters' experiences, decisions, and changes.

Why do you need to think about theme?

Themes are essential because they invite readers to think deeply about the story, connecting the fictional world and its dilemmas to broader human experiences and societal issues. A well-crafted theme can resonate with readers, prompting reflection on their values, beliefs, and behaviors.

In mystery and crime fiction, including cozy mysteries, themes often revolve around justice, truth, the nature of good and evil, community, and the human capacity for change and redemption.

For example, a cozy mystery might explore themes of community bonds, the impact of secrets kept or revealed, or the importance of preserving history and tradition amidst change.

Why does that matter?

By weaving themes into the fabric of a story, writers not only entertain but also offer insights and commentary on life, enriching the readers' experience and elevating the narrative from mere entertainment to a work that can affect thought and feeling.

BUT WHY DOES THAT MATTER TO YOU?

The role and unique importance of theme in the gay cozy mystery genre blend traditional elements of cozy mysteries with themes relevant to LGBTQ+ experiences, offering both a comforting escape and a platform for exploring deeper issues. Here's how theme operates within this subgenre and why it holds unique importance:

Sense of Community and Belonging: This is one of the central themes often explored in gay cozy mysteries and is particularly poignant given the LGBTQ+ community's historical struggle for acceptance and inclusion. In these stories, the protagonist's involvement in solving the mystery often parallels their journey toward finding their place within a community, whether it's a small town, a specific social circle, or the larger LGBTQ+ community. The theme underscores the importance of acceptance, support, and the strength found in communal bonds.

Identity and Self-Discovery: Gay mysteries frequently delve into this theme, reflecting the personal journeys many LGBTQ+ individuals experience. While this cannot be the plot of a cozy mystery, these narratives can be explored through theme. The protagonist's process of coming to terms with their sexuality, navigating the challenges of coming out, or reconciling various aspects of their identity can be lightly, delicately explored. No, coming out can't be the main focus of your book. But the cozy mystery framework allows these themes to be explored in a context that is ultimately affirmative and supportive, offering a narrative space where identity is celebrated, and self-discovery leads to empowerment.

Resilience in the Face of Adversity: This theme is a hallmark of the cozy mystery. In the gay cozy mystery, we have characters who have very likely confronted societal prejudice, discrimination, or personal trials. Yet they face these new challenges—putting themselves potentially in the crosshairs of a ruthless killer—with determination, cleverness, and a sense of humor. The cozy mystery's typically optimistic resolution reinforces the theme of resilience, offering hope and affirmation to readers who may face similar challenges in their lives.

LGBTQ+ Relationships: While romance is a common theme in many cozy mysteries, gay cozy mysteries bring a unique perspective by exploring LGBTQ+ relationships within the framework of the genre. These stories offer diverse representations of love and partnership, addressing the nuances of LGBTQ+ relationships with sensitivity and depth. The theme of love, including its challenges and triumphs, adds a layer of emotional resonance to the mysteries, making them not just puzzles to be solved but stories of connection and affection.

Justice and Equality: These themes often underpin gay cozy mysteries, reflecting broader societal issues. So long as you know the difference between soapbox and suasion, the pursuit of justice in these stories needn't be limited to solving the central mystery; it is possible to encompass the characters' efforts to address inequality, combat prejudice, and advocate for LGBTQ+ rights.

Just don't forget that, first and foremost, your protagonist is there to solve an engrossing mystery. The cozy mystery format allows for a lighthearted yet impactful exploration of these themes, encouraging readers to consider issues of fairness and equity in their communities.

The unique importance of theme in gay cozy mysteries lies in the genre's ability to combine entertainment with meaningful exploration of LGBTQ+ experiences. These stories provide visibility and representation, offering LGBTQ+ readers narratives where they can see themselves and their experiences reflected with complexity and dignity. At the same time, they introduce broader audiences to LGBTQ+ perspectives, fostering empathy and understanding through engaging, accessible storytelling.

Because you're writing LGBTQ+ characters, theme takes on a more crucial role in your cozy mysteries. Most cozy mystery protagonists start out as outsiders. They've inherited a mansion or recently divorced and are starting over or are beginning adult life.

Your LGBTQ+ character will inevitably have even more of an outsider's perspective.

The balance of realism and cozy for LGBTQ+ characters resonates particularly in a time of political backlash and unrest.

In essence, the gay cozy mystery uses the comforting conventions of the cozy mystery genre—like the close-knit community, the absence of graphic violence, and the emphasis on puzzle-solving—to address themes that resonate deeply with LGBTQ+ readers and allies, making it a uniquely powerful vehicle for storytelling and representation.

MOOD, TONE, AND HUMOR

Mood, tone, and humor are closely related to a story's theme but are distinct elements that contribute to the overall experience and interpretation of the narrative.

Mood is the atmosphere of the story, or how it makes the reader feel. Like tone, mood can affect the reception of the theme but is not part of the theme. A dark, oppressive mood in a mystery novel might underscore themes of fear or isolation, while a light, whimsical mood could highlight themes of adventure or the joy of discovery.

Mood serves as the backdrop against which the story unfolds. It sets the emotional tone, influencing how readers feel as they navigate through the twists and turns of the plot, and it can change from scene to scene. In cozy mysteries, the mood is particularly important because it helps to create a contrast between the intrigue of the mystery and the comfort of the setting, making the genre uniquely appealing.

A well-crafted mood envelops readers, transporting them to the cozy world you've created. It's about more than just solving the mystery; it's about enjoying the journey there, complete with its quirks, charm, and warmth. When your sleuth climbs through the window of a spooky old mansion, we want to see the spiders (okay, maybe not), the spiderwebs, and smell the dust. We want to hear the creak of floorboards overhead in a house that should be empty...

The mood in a cozy mystery balances the tension of the crime with lighter, more comforting elements. This balance is key to maintaining reader engagement without veering into darker, more unsettling territory. Sure, you almost got yourself killed climbing into that spooky mansion at midnight, but here's your boyfriend, the handsome local doctor, to bandage your hand and bring you a nice hot cuppa—as well as a lecture about putting yourself in danger *again*.

The ideal mood for a cozy mystery blends warmth, curiosity, scary and startling moments, and a touch of humor. It's inviting and engaging, creating a safe space where the intrigue of the mystery adds excitement without causing too much distress.

Remember you can enhance mood by using the following tricks of the trade:

Detail-Oriented Descriptions: Use descriptions to paint a vivid picture of the setting and characters, highlighting elements that contribute to the cozy atmosphere—be it the quaintness of a village, the warmth of a local café, or the charm of a bookshop.

Incorporate the Senses and Engage Readers' Senses: Descriptions of sights, sounds, and smells evoke comfort and familiarity—or alarm. The aroma of freshly baked goods, the sound of laughter from a community event, or the visual of a well-loved bookstore on fire can all contribute to the mood.

Manage Pacing: Ensure the story unfolds at a pace that allows readers to savor the setting and characters without losing interest in the mystery. A leisurely pace, punctuated by moments of romance with periods of discovery or danger, maintains the cozy mood.

Use Light and Shadow: Literally and metaphorically, play with light and shadow to enhance the mood. Cozy mysteries often feature scenes set in comforting light (a crackling fireplace, a sunny garden) contrasted with the shadows where mysteries lurk (a dusty attic, an abandoned mansion), creating a balance between comfort and intrigue.

Tone refers to the author's attitude toward the subject matter or the audience. It's all about the authorial voice, conveyed through the choice of words, viewpoint, and style of writing. While tone can influence how themes are perceived (a cynical tone might color a theme of love with skepticism, for example), it's not part of the theme itself. Instead, the tone helps to shape the context in which themes are explored.

Author voice is one of those critical elements that really distinguishes one writer's work from another's. It's essentially the unique style or the particular way an author writes, which reflects their personality, attitude, and character. Think of it as the literary equivalent of your speaking voice—distinctly you, recognizable in a sea of voices, and carrying a particular tone, rhythm, and cadence that sets it apart.

Your author voice includes several components:

Attitude: This is the tone your writing conveys, which might range from humorous and cheery to serious and introspective. The tone sets the mood for your readers and can vary somewhat across different works, though a certain baseline—shaped by your unique perspective—remains constant. In the cozy mystery, you're using your inside voice AKA your light, humorous tone.

Word Choice and Diction: The words you choose and how you use them play a huge part in defining your voice. Whether your language is simple and direct, complex and flowery, or somewhere in between, your diction shapes how readers perceive your narrative and characters. When writing a cozy mystery, you might need to modify your tone a bit. You'll want to be more direct and plain spoken.

Pacing and Rhythm: The rhythm of your writing—how your sentences flow, the length and structure of your paragraphs, and the pacing of your narrative—also contribute to your voice. Some authors have a rapid, staccato rhythm that propels readers forward, while others may use longer, meandering sentences that invite contemplation.

Perspective and Point of View: How you choose to tell your story—the point of view you adopt, whether it's first person, third person, or even second person—can greatly affect the voice. The perspective you write from can influence how intimate or distant the narrative feels to the reader. In the cozy mystery, that will almost always be third person from the POV of your protagonist. Occasionally, it will be first person, but that's rare.

Characterization and Dialogue: The way you bring characters to life and how they interact through dialogue can also be a reflection of your voice. Characters often serve as vehicles for an author's voice, embodying its nuances in their speech and actions.

Developing your author voice is a natural process that evolves with time and experience. It's influenced by your personality, your life experiences, your reading preferences, and even your philosophical outlook. Your author voice is what makes your writing unmistakably yours. It's what readers come to recognize and love about your work, allowing them to pick up a new story of yours and immediately feel at home within its pages. Your author voice is also what will save you from AI.

Humor is a stylistic element that can be used to lighten the tone or mood, contrast with more serious elements, or highlight themes in a way that makes them more accessible or relatable. While not a theme in itself, humor can be a vehicle for exploring themes, especially in genres like cozy mysteries, where humor often plays off community quirks or character idiosyncrasies to delve into themes of belonging, identity, or the absurdity of certain social norms.

Incorporating humor into cozy mysteries is a fine art. It enriches the narrative, endearing characters to readers and balancing the tension inherent in mystery and crime. The key is to weave humor in such a way that it complements the suspense, rather than undermining it.

Cozy mysteries are rich with comedic possibilities:

Quirky Characters and Eccentricities: Create characters with unique quirks or humorous eccentricities that naturally lend themselves to humorous situations or comments. This can include the protagonist, side characters, or even suspects. Their peculiar habits or perspectives can offer comic relief without detracting from the plot's tension. Just don't be mean-spirited or cruel.

Witty Dialogue: Sharp, witty exchanges between characters are a prime vehicle for humor. Banter, playful teasing, or sarcastic remarks can lighten a scene and reveal characters' relationships and personalities. Well-timed humor in dialogue can also offer a breather during tense moments, maintaining the story's pace without diminishing suspense.

Situational Comedy: Placing characters in unusual or awkward situations where they must improvise or navigate unexpected challenges can add humor. These situations should feel organic to the plot and can serve as a means to advance the mystery or character development while providing entertainment.

Observational Humor: The protagonist's or narrator's observations about the peculiarities of small-town life, eccentric neighbors, or the absurdities encountered during the investigation can introduce humor. This perspective allows readers to laugh along with the characters at the quirks of human nature and society.

Humorous Subplots: Integrate subplots that are lighter in tone, perhaps involving a comedic sidekick, a pet with a knack for creating chaos, or a personal dilemma with humorous potential. These subplots can serve as comic relief, ensuring the overall tone stays upbeat amidst the mystery.

Playful Use of Genre Tropes: Cozy mysteries are known for certain tropes (e.g., the small-town setting, the gathering of suspects, the amateur sleuth). Playing with these tropes in a humorous way can delight readers familiar with the genre, adding a layer of meta-humor.

Balance Through Pacing: Distribute humorous elements evenly throughout the story, using them to break up tension or deepen character interactions. However, ensure that the buildup to the climax retains enough suspense. Humor should never overshadow the mystery; rather, it should enhance the reading experience.

Respectful Humor: Murder isn't actually funny. Ensure that the humor does not come at the expense of serious themes or disrespect the gravity of crime and its impact on victims. The balance lies in finding humor in the characters' journeys and interactions, not the crime itself.

Reactions to the Absurd: Characters' reactions to the absurdities of their situations or the idiosyncrasies of other characters can be a source of humor. This not only adds depth to the characters but also allows for humor that feels natural and unforced.

Incorporating humor into cozy mysteries is about enhancing the story's charm and making the characters more relatable. By striking the right balance, you create a captivating narrative where humor and suspense complement each other, making for a delightful and engaging read.

Tone, mood, and humor are essential to how a theme is presented and understood. They create the environment in which themes unfold and can emphasize or contrast themes, making them more impactful. For instance, a cozy mystery might have a light tone and a warm mood, with humor sprinkled throughout, all of which serve to enhance themes of community and resilience in the face of adversity.

These elements work together to ensure that the theme is not just communicated but felt and experienced in a way that resonates with readers.

EXERCISE:
TEMPERATURE GAUGE

The Temperature Gauge exercise is a method for cozy mystery authors to check the balance of theme with humor, mood, and tone within their manuscript. This tool will serve as a self-assessment guide to ensure that the essential elements of a cozy mystery are harmonized effectively. Here's how you can structure this gauge:

1. Setting the Baseline

Theme: Identify the core theme of your mystery (e.g., community, redemption, curiosity). Write a sentence that captures this theme.

Humor Level: Decide on the level of humor you aim to incorporate (on a scale of 1-10, where 1 is minimal humor and 10 is highly comedic).

Desired Mood: Describe the overall mood you want to evoke (e.g., warm and inviting, quirky and eccentric, breezy and hopeful).

Tone Consistency: Determine the tone you aim for (e.g., consistently light, varying degrees of light and serious).

2. Scene-by-Scene Assessment

For each chapter or key scene, ask yourself:

Theme: Does this scene align with my core theme? (Yes/No)

Humor Rating: On a scale of 1–10, how humorous is this scene? Does this level of humor fit the desired overall balance?

Mood Match: Does the mood of this scene contribute to the overall desired mood? (Yes/Almost/No)

Tone Check: Is the tone of this scene consistent with the overall tone of the book? (Consistent/Varies Appropriately/Inconsistent)

3. Overall Balance Check

After reviewing each scene, evaluate the overall manuscript:

Theme Representation: Are there parts of the manuscript where the theme feels lost or overshadowed?

Humor Consistency: Does the humor feel evenly distributed, or are there sections that feel too heavy or too light?

Mood Continuity: Is the desired mood maintained throughout, or are there jarring mood shifts?

Tone Alignment: Does the tone remain true to your vision, or does it fluctuate unexpectedly?

4. Adjustments and Revisions

Based on your assessments:

Theme Adjustments: Identify areas where the theme could be more effectively woven into the narrative.

Humor Enhancements/Reductions: Pinpoint scenes that could benefit from more humor or where humor needs to be toned down.

Mood Enhancements: Look for opportunities to reinforce the desired mood, especially in scenes that didn't fully match your mood goals.

Tone Corrections: Make note of where the tone needs to be adjusted for consistency or to better fit the scene's purpose.

5. Final Temperature Check

Once revisions are made, conduct a final temperature check:

- Did adjustments enhance the balance of theme, humor, mood, and tone?
- Is there a better sense of harmony between these elements now?

This "Temperature Gauge" is a dynamic tool, meant to be used iteratively throughout the writing and revision process. It encourages a holistic view of your manuscript, ensuring that each element contributes to the cozy mystery's overall effectiveness and enjoyment. By regularly checking the temperature, you can ensure that your story provides the warmth, intrigue, and engagement that fans of cozy mysteries love.

10

IS THAT ALL THERE IS?

A s you near the finish line, it's worth taking the time to double-check your manuscript to make sure you've hit all your marks. While you can certainly rely on your editor to pinpoint weaknesses and catch errors, it's going to make your life and your editor's life so much easier if you give your book one last read-thru for the following, all too common, issues.

Stereotyping Characters: Beginners in particular might lean on stereotypes, especially when crafting gay characters or relationships, missing the opportunity to create nuanced, multi-dimensional characters who reflect the diversity and complexity of real life.

Neglecting the Cozy Element: If you're new to the subgenre, there's a good chance you might focus too much on the mystery or the romance aspect and not enough on creating a warm, inviting setting that's integral to the cozy genre.

Underdeveloped Relationships: The heart of any story, especially in gay cozy mysteries, lies in the relationships—romantic, platonic, familial, or community. You never want to rush these relationships— remember, you're writing a series—or leave them underexplored, not giving the characters' connections enough depth or growth over time.

Balancing Romance and Mystery: Finding the right balance between developing a compelling mystery and exploring the romantic elements can be challenging. It's not always easy to integrate these aspects seamlessly, either overshadowing the mystery with the romance or vice versa.

Handling Conflict and Tension: It can be challenging to create legitimate reasons for conflict that are, at the same time, not so serious as to be beyond repair. Aim to create meaningful conflict and tension within these constraints. You don't want the story to feel too gentle or lacking in stakes.

Overcomplicating the Plot: With the excitement of weaving together mystery and romance, there's a temptation to overcomplicate the plot. You don't need a big, complicated plot. In fact, this can overwhelm readers and detract from the character-driven storytelling at the heart of cozy mysteries.

Inconsistent Tone: You're always trying for that sweet spot of balancing comedy, romance, and true mystery, without losing the cozy feel.

Overlooking Community Dynamics: Your little cozy community's reaction to and integration of LGBTQ+ relationships can add a rich layer to the narrative. Don't be afraid to fully leverage this and make the most of opportunities for conflict, support, and character development. At the same time, don't create a hostile and unwelcoming environment that is going to depress your readers.

Failing to Research: Authenticity is key, not just in representing LGBTQ+ relationships and experiences. If you've set your series in New England, read up on New England! If you've set your series on a dude ranch, you need to learn about how dude ranches operate. Lack of research can lead to inaccuracies or misrepresentations that make readers roll their eyes—or worse, offend and alienate.

Not Embracing Diversity: The LGBTQ+ community is incredibly diverse. One size does not fit all. And remember, your cozy mystery community must show diversity in other ways as well.

It bears repeating: No one is forcing you to write a gay cozy mystery.

In this brave new publishing world, you can write *anything* your heart desires. But if you've chosen, for whatever reasons, to write a gay cozy mystery, then, yes, you are constrained by the requirements of the genre.

I'm not sure why so many authors struggle with this. But there does seem to be a kind of Catch-22 for authors who resent the idea that they must follow certain commercial genre conventions yet set their sights on a particular commercial genre readership.

It's a complex issue and it touches on the delicate balance between creative integrity and commercial success. If you don't personally enjoy the conventions of the cozy mystery subgenre, then having to conform to those genre conventions is going to be onerous. But the reality is, you can't force readers to read what they don't want to read.

Do you want someone to force *you* to read what you don't like?

Inevitably, readers come to specific genres with clear expectations. For instance, the M/M romance genre typically promises stories that focus on romantic relationships between men, often with happy or hopeful endings. These conventions are not arbitrary but have evolved from reader preferences and market demand. When readers pick up a book in this genre, they're often looking for specific emotional experiences and themes.

Authors face a perennial dilemma: write what you love or write what sells.

Ideally, authors can do both, but it's not always straightforward, especially in niche or genre-specific markets like cozy mysteries.

We need to write stories that are authentic to our vision and interests. This authenticity resonates with readers and is often what makes a story stand out. However, if an author's interests significantly diverge from their target genre's conventions, it's going to be difficult. It really does help if you are honest with yourself about why you're writing.

There is no wrong reason to write. If you're just in it for the money, okay. If you're in it because you have a message you feel is important to share with the world, okay. If you're writing for both of those reasons, okay, but you're probably going to have to make some compromises along the way.

It will help a lot if you understand your audience and their expectations.

This doesn't mean you must sacrifice your unique voice or interests, but you're going to have to find a way to incorporate that personal touch within the framework that readers expect.

OR you're going to have to write something else.

And is that really so bad?

There's room for innovation within genre conventions. Authors can explore new themes, character dynamics, or plot structures while still delivering the key elements that define the genre. This approach allows for creative expression and can even expand the genre's boundaries.

But if your author interests don't align with the mainstream expectations of your targeted genre, it may be worth exploring (or creating) a niche that does align with your creative vision. While the audience might be smaller, it could also be more dedicated.

If commercial success in a specific genre is your aim, understanding and meeting reader expectations to some extent is necessary.

If creative expression without compromise is your priority, you may need to accept that your work might not reach as broad an audience.

It's unrealistic to expect readers to change their preferences to match an author's creative output, especially in genre fiction, where conventions and expectations are well-established.

You have to decide what's more important to you: commercial success or creative freedom. Many find a middle ground, infusing genre conventions with their unique voice and perspective, thus broadening their appeal without compromising their creativity.

Ultimately, writing and publishing are acts of communication between you and your readers. Finding the right balance between staying true to one's creative vision and engaging with the expectations of the genre is a personal journey and one that may evolve over time.

Writing LGBTQ+ characters into cozy mysteries, especially considering the genre's wide appeal and traditionally conservative readership, requires a thoughtful approach.

It's a balancing act of providing authentic representation while navigating potential political sensitivities and backlashes.

Here's some final words on how you can maintain this balance:

1. Integration Over Tokenism

Authentic Characters: Create LGBTQ+ characters with depth, avoiding stereotypes or reducing them to their sexual orientation or gender identity alone. Characters should be integral to the story, with their identities contributing to but not solely defining their roles.

Natural Inclusion: Integrate LGBTQ+ themes and characters into your story in a way that feels natural and reflective of real life. The focus on everyday aspects of the characters' lives can help normalize LGBTQ+ experiences for readers.

2. Focus on Universal Themes

Common Ground: Emphasize themes that resonate universally, such as love, friendship, justice, and community. Highlighting the shared human experience can bridge divides and appeal to a broad audience, regardless of their political or social views.

Subtlety and Nuance: Approach sensitive issues with subtlety and nuance, allowing readers to engage with the characters and their stories on a personal level, which can be more effective than confrontational or overtly political narratives.

3. Educate Through Storytelling

Gentle Education: Use your narrative to gently educate readers about LGBTQ+ experiences, challenges, and perspectives. A cozy mystery's comforting framework can be an excellent vehicle for introducing ideas and fostering empathy without seeming didactic or confrontational.

Complex Characters: Presenting LGBTQ+ characters as complex individuals facing universal dilemmas can help conservative readers see beyond labels, fostering a deeper understanding and empathy.

4. Community and Setting

Diverse Communities: Setting your story in a diverse community can help normalize the presence of LGBTQ+ characters and themes. A setting that reflects the real-world diversity of sexual orientations and gender identities can enrich the narrative and broaden its appeal.

Inclusive Atmosphere: Create an atmosphere of inclusivity and acceptance within your story's setting, which can serve as a subtle counterpoint to real-world divisiveness, offering readers a vision of community and acceptance.

5. Anticipate and Address Backlash

Preparedness: Be prepared for potential backlash or pushback.

Yes, unfortunately this is a possibility whether from LGBTQ+ writers who resent the idea of a heterosexual writer capitalizing on the experiences of a marginalized community or conservative readers hostile to the idea of gay people in their cozy villages and towns.

Having a thoughtful response—or choosing not to engage directly but instead letting your work speak for itself—can be strategies for dealing with negative feedback.

Support Systems: Engage with supportive communities, including LGBTQ+ readers and allies, who can offer encouragement and champion your work. Their support can counterbalance criticism and underscore the value of your inclusive storytelling.

6. Responsibility and Integrity

Writer's Integrity: Stay true to your vision and the integrity of your story. While it's important to consider your audience, compromising your values or the authenticity of your characters to avoid controversy can undermine the impact and authenticity of your work.

Positive Representation: Remember that positive and authentic representation has the power to change hearts and minds. Your work can contribute to a broader cultural acceptance and understanding, making the effort and balance worthwhile.

In times of political backlash and unrest, cozy mysteries with LGBTQ+ characters and themes have the unique opportunity to offer both escape and enlightenment, gently challenging prejudices and celebrating diversity within the comforting confines of the genre. This approach not only respects the genre's traditions but also broadens its scope and relevance in today's world.

WHAT'S NEXT OR WHAT THE HECK DO I DO NOW?

Congratulations! Finishing your first gay cozy mystery manuscript is a significant achievement. I'm not going to go into marketing plans or tell you how to self-publish or query an agent. There's already a wealth of material on all of that.

However, there are a few critical steps to take before sending it off to an agent or diving into self-publishing. These final considerations ensure your manuscript is polished, professional, and ready for the literary world:

1. Beta Readers

If you're still early in your career, beta readers can be a fantastic resource. Just make sure that you're gathering feedback from beta readers who enjoy cozy mysteries. An M/M reader who proudly avows she's only there for the smut is going to be worse than useless. But a cozy mystery reader, even if they don't typically read gay fiction, can offer invaluable insights into how your story resonates with your target audience, highlight confusing parts, and suggest improvements from a reader's perspective.

2: Professional Editing

Developmental Edit: Ensure the plot is coherent, the pacing is right, and the characters are well-developed. A developmental editor can help identify plot holes, inconsistencies, and areas where the narrative may lag.

Copy-editing and Proofreading: Attention to grammar, punctuation, and spelling is crucial. A clean, error-free manuscript makes a good impression on agents and readers alike.

3. Cover Design

For self-publishing authors, a professional and genre-appropriate cover is vital. The cover is often the first thing potential readers see, and it should convey the mood and theme of your book while fitting within cozy mystery genre expectations. It's worth paying for a great cover.

4. Blurb and Synopsis

Craft a compelling blurb and a concise synopsis. The blurb should intrigue without giving away the plot, while the synopsis (often required by agents) should summarize the story, including the resolution, in a clear and engaging way. Note: yes, you do "spoil" the ending when writing your synopsis.

5. Market Research

Agents: If seeking traditional publishing, research agents who specialize in cozy mysteries. Tailor your query letters to each agent, following their submission guidelines meticulously. Thoroughly vet any potential agent before you sign anything.

Self-Publishing Platforms: If self-publishing, research the best platforms for your book. Understand the differences in terms of royalties, distribution, and marketing support.

6. Formatting

Ensure your manuscript meets industry standards for formatting (font, margins, spacing) if sending to agents. For self-publishing, follow the specific formatting guidelines of your chosen platform, which may differ.

7. Online Presence and Marketing

Start building or enhancing your online presence. A strong author platform can be crucial for marketing your book, whether you're seeking traditional publication or self-publishing. Consider a website, social media profiles, and networking with other authors and readers in the cozy mystery genre.

8. Legal Considerations

Understand the rights you're selling or retaining, especially important for self-publishing authors. Familiarize yourself with copyright laws and consider consulting a professional for contracts or rights management if going the traditional publishing route.

9. Pricing Strategy (for Self-Publishing)

Research and set a competitive price for your book. Consider factors like the length of your book, the standard pricing in the cozy mystery genre, and whether you'll be offering promotions or discounts.

10. Advance Reviews

Before the official launch, try to get advance reviews from book bloggers, other authors, or professional review services that cater to your genre. If you're a new author, reviews are crucial for visibility and credibility.

Finishing the book is just the first step. There is still *so* much to do. But here, my writer friends, is where I leave you.

If, through the pages of this guide, I've successfully led you to craft a mystery that marries humor with intellect, heart with intrigue, all the while populating your story with a cast of characters as diverse as they are deeply human, then I consider my mission accomplished. But remember, this is merely the end of one chapter in your journey and the exciting start of another. Armed with these insights, your true adventure begins now—breathing life into your own gay cozy mystery that will captivate, entertain, and resonate with readers far and wide.

The pen is in your hand, the stage is set, and the world awaits the unique stories only you can tell.

ACKNOWLEDGEMENTS

I want to thank the following people for teaching me pretty much everything I know about writing cozy mysteries: my first agent, Jacky Sach, Simon and Schuster editor Christina Boys, Simon and Schuster senior editor Micki Nuding, and Penguin Group editor Sandra Harding.

I'd also like to thank editor Jennifer Jacobson and Debbie McGowan at InRoad Publishing for helping me turn the idea for this book into a reality.

And of course, thank you to my partner in crime, Kevin.

ABOUT THE AUTHOR

Author of 100+ titles of Gay Mystery and M/M Romance, Josh Lanyon has built her literary legacy on twisty mystery, kickass adventure, and unapologetic man-on-man romance.

Her work has been translated into twelve languages. The FBI thriller *Fair Game* was the first Male/Male title to be published by Italy's Harlequin Mondadori and *Stranger on the Shore* (Harper Collins Italia) was the first M/M title to be published in print. In 2016 *Fatal Shadows* placed #5 in Japan's annual Boy Love novel list (the first and only title by a foreign author to place on the list). The Adrien English series was awarded the All-Time Favorite Couple by the Goodreads M/M Romance Group. In 2019, *Fatal Shadows* became the first LGBTQ mobile game created by *Moments: Choose Your Story*.

She's an EPIC Award winner, a four-time Lambda Literary Award finalist (twice for Gay Mystery), an Edgar nominee, and the first ever recipient of the Goodreads All Time Favorite M/M Author award.

Josh is married and lives in Southern California with her irascible husband, two adorable dogs, a small garden, and an ever-expanding library of vintage mystery destined to eventually crush them all beneath its weight.

Find other Josh Lanyon titles at www.joshlanyon.com

Follow Josh on:

X: twitter.com/JoshLanyon
Facebook: facebook.com/pages/Josh-Lanyon-Fan-Page/107401402656849
Goodreads: goodreads.com/group/show/34844-q-a-with-josh-lanyon
Instagram: instagram.com/josh__lanyon/
Tumblr: tumblr.com/blog/josh-lanyon

For extras and exclusives, join Josh on Patreon.
https://www.patreon.com/joshlanyon

NOVELLAS

THE DANGEROUS GROUND SERIES

Dangerous Ground
Old Poison
Blood Heat
Dead Run
Kick Start
Blind Side

OTHER NOVELLAS

Cards on the Table
The Dark Farewell
The Dark Horse
The Darkling Thrush
The Dickens with Love
I Spy Something Bloody
I Spy Something Wicked
I Spy Something Christmas
In a Dark Wood
The Parting Glass
Snowball in Hell
Mummy Dearest
Don't Look Back
A Ghost of a Chance
Lovers and Other Strangers
Out of the Blue
A Vintage Affair
Lone Star (in *Men Under the Mistletoe*)
Green Glass Beads (in *Irregulars*)
Blood Red Butterfly
Everything I Know
Baby, It's Cold (in *Comfort and Joy*)
A Case of Christmas
Murder Between the Pages
Slay Ride

Stranger in the House
The Lemon Drop Kid

SHORT STORIES

A Limited Engagement
The French Have a Word for It
In Sunshine or In Shadow
Until We Meet Once More
Icecapade (in *His for the Holidays*)
Perfect Day
Heart Trouble
Other People's Weddings (Petit Mort)
Slings and Arrows (Petit Mort)
Sort of Stranger Than Fiction (Petit Mort)
Critic's Choice (Petit Mort)
Just Desserts (Petit Mort)
In Plain Sight
Wedding Favors
Wizard's Moon
Fade to Black
Night Watch
Plenty of Fish
Halloween is Murder
The Boy Next Door
Requiem for Mr. Busybody

COLLECTIONS

Short Stories (Vol. 1)
Sweet Spot (the Petit Morts)
Merry Christmas, Darling (Holiday Codas)
Christmas Waltz (Holiday Codas 2)
I Spy...Three Novellas
Dangerous Ground The Complete Series

Dark Horse, White Knight (Two Novellas)

The Adrien English Mysteries Box Set

The Adrien English Mysteries Box Set 2

Male/Male Mystery & Suspense Box Set

Partners in Crime (Three Classic Gay Mystery Novels)

All's Fair Complete Collection

Shadows Left Behind

As Diana Killian

THE POETIC DEATH SERIES
High Rhymes and Misdemeanors
Verse of the Vampyre
Sonnet of the Sphinx
Docketful of Poesy

THE MANTRA FOR MURDER SERIES
Corpse Pose
Dial Om for Murder
Murder on the Eightfold Path
Death in a Difficult Position

www.ingramcontent.com/pod-product-compliance
Lightning Source LLC
Chambersburg PA
CBHW070642100726
47907CB00007B/2079